UNSPOKEN DEVOTION

DOLCE OBSURITÀ #1

UNSPOKEN DEVOTION

CHELSEA BURTON DUNN

4 Horsemen
Publications, Inc.

DEDICATION

If you are related to me, I suggest you either put this book down or agree that we never discuss it.

For all those who love a little danger with their romance, this one is for you.

TRIGGER WARNINGS:

Mentions of sex trafficking
Graphic death
Graphic violence
Torture
Mentions/threats of rape
Instances of misogyny
Graphic sex

ITALIAN WORDS/PHRASES:

Cazzo!: Fuck!

Cretino: Idiot

Vaffanculo a chi t'è morto. Mangia merde e morte!: Eat shit and die (basically)

Cosa ti hano fatto, piccola mia?: What have they done to you, my little one?

Figlio di puttana!: Son of a bitch

Amici: Friend

CONTENTS

PROLOGUE
CARMEN

EIGHT YEARS OLD

"Carmen, wake up," my papa's voice said in my ear, pulling me from the dream I was having about playing on the beach of the lake house with my brothers.

"Mm?" I mumbled, turning over and opening my eyes slowly in my dim bedroom to see my papa's smiling face. He was the most handsome man I knew, with his green eyes shining down at me.

"Want to go on another adventure with your papa?" he asked quietly. I nodded my head, already awake with the prospect of undivided attention from him and the snack we always had before we snuck back into our house in the wee hours of the morning before Mama, Adrian, or Benny woke up.

Quickly slipping my shoes on, my papa took my hand, guiding me to the car where we stole off into the night.

The drives were always long to me, but papa always chuckled when I complained and said it was only fifteen or thirty minutes. We went to a different place each time, and I hoped this would never end because I loved our special Carmen and Papa time.

"Can we get ice cream this time?" I asked, the heat of the summer, even at night was oppressive and the car's air conditioning was not quite cool enough yet as he got onto the highway.

"I'm not sure there are places open right now," he said, glancing at the back seat toward me. "But we'll try."

My papa loved me. He loved my brothers and my mama. It struck me, as I watched his profile from my seat, that the Lupos didn't have that. Our next-door neighbors were my parents' best friends and their boys played with my brothers. But Leo told me sometimes his dad was mean to them. My papa wasn't mean to us.

The tall highway light gave way to darkness. I sang quietly to myself as he drove until I saw the roller coasters lit up and coming nearer to us, my papa getting into the right lane to take the exit.

"Are you taking me to Worlds of Fun?" I asked, staring eagerly at the tall rides of the amusement park I could see out the car window. He laughed, glancing at me through the rearview mirror, those green eyes crinkled in the corners with actual happiness.

"No, my *Carmenetta.* But maybe we can go there later this summer and take the boys," he said. When he said "the boys" he meant *all* the boys and I stuck my tongue out in disgust at the prospect of having to be the only girl, as usual, with all the stinky boys around. It was worse now that Adrian was thirteen, because he *actually* smelled bad.

Papa laughed at the look on my face but didn't say anything more as we went through strange streets with big trucks passing us, until he finally came to what looked like a big parking lot with lots of little garages all lined up. He went up to one, the numbers listed on it were "913."

"That's my birthday!" I said, grinning from the back seat while he turned around to look at me.

"You're right!"

"Are we gonna go in?"

"Yes," he said, his voice a little more serious this time.

The last few times Papa took me on these trips he brought me to places that were sort of like this. It wasn't bad, he just put my hand on something or shined a light in my eyes and then we went to get our treat.

We got out, Papa holding out his hand for me to take after he unlocked the padlock on the garage door and pushed it up.

The whole thing was full to the brim! The other two had a few things in there, but nothing like this. He led us through the maze of piles, bringing me to the back of the room like the other two.

"This time might hurt just a tiny bit," he said, his eyes mournful as he kept my hand in his grip. "I promise it will only hurt for a moment and then you'll feel better."

"I don't want to, Papa," I whispered, a shake in my voice.

"Just this one more thing," he said, touching my cheek gently with his calloused hands. I nodded. He pricked my finger, putting it against the same weird box that was in the other garage places.

I tried not to cry, but my finger was still bleeding as we went back to the car. Tears fell down my cheeks against my will. Papa closed the garage, locking it just as I was climbing into the back seat, and the headlights shined, blinding me.

There was the sound of a car door slamming and the clacking of heels on the pavement.

"What are you doing here?" Papa asked, and I tried to see who he was talking to, but all I could see was a shadowy version of a woman with the lights of her car behind her.

"What are you hiding? What does Morelli not want to come out?"

I didn't know that voice. I didn't know this woman, but Papa did. Somehow that made me feel uneasy, uncomfortable.

"You don't know what you're talking about. I'm here with my daughter!" he said, his voice rising like it did when he was angry.

"You know a secret can only stay that way so long, Bernardo," the woman said, her voice sounding scary, like she meant for something bad to happen, before she got back in her car and drove away.

"Who was that?" I asked when he got back in the car, but he didn't answer me.

We didn't get ice cream that night and Papa lied. I still felt the prick on my finger even a week later when Mama told us he was dead.

CHAPTER 1

LEO

"**A**nything good in those emails? You're always so eager to get to them," John said from the couch of the safe house we were in. We had been out on a mission for months tracking down a shipment. Mercenaries had been tasked with bringing the merchandise bought to a place known as the Island. Not the most ingenious name, but what criminals lacked in creativity, they tended to make up for in secrecy and cruelty. The merchandise in question was women and girls that had been stolen, packaged, and shipped to where they would be broken down and taught to be proper sex slaves for the rich and powerful men of the world.

This wasn't the first mission like this that my team had been tasked with. In fact, these specific types of missions were usually what we were sent on. The four of us were a well-oiled machine, tasked not only to hunt down, but to take down pieces of these operations in the hope that they would be weakened and networks would crumble. But something about this mission was making us nervous. Something was different about it and none of us could quite put our finger on what.

We had been compromised. The youngest in our group, Logan, had been spotted by the group we had been tracking twice, spooking them, and gaining him a tail for thirty-six hours. So, we retreated to a safe house in Messina, Sicily, as soon as he lost them. The safe house didn't put us too far from where we believed they were taking the stolen women, while the techs back home took our intel and used it to go through satellite data. Once we had a location, we'd be able to hopefully bring that operation down and get more information about the main investors.

But while I was eager to continue the mission and hopefully save as many of those women as possible, I was secretly glad for the opportunity to check my personal emails. The safe house provided us with cover, so I could reach back home.

"Sad because you don't get any emails, John?" I teased, as they finally popped up.

Two emails were from my mom telling me little details about her best friend Maria and her kids who I had grown up with, and of course, my brothers. Mom didn't say much about my brothers—other than her disdain that neither of them had secured a wife—since they both worked for my father. To keep her safe, she wasn't allowed details of what they did. Though she was smart enough that even what she *did* know wasn't mentioned. I may have had access to my personal emails, but I was still an agent of the government, and what my father did was far from legal.

One was an email from my best friend, Benny, who was Maria's middle child. He told me all about his exploits in the main city where he had been mostly living since finishing his physical therapy residency and landing a position at a prestigious practice. I missed him dearly, another brother on top of the two I already had, but he was far more fun to get into mischief with.

And then there were the emails from Carmen. She was Benny's little sister, only two years younger than us, but she and I had our own weird little connection, being the youngest kids in our respective families. I counted six emails this time. It had been about two months since I could check them, so it wasn't an outrageous number. There had been some stretches where I opened them to find she had emailed me every day for a week.

Not that I minded. I loved every little word in those emails. I could imagine her typing them, fingers flying over the keyboard or her phone, brow scrunched in concentration over her striking green eyes.

"Never any pictures. What a waste," John grumbled from over my shoulder. "She does have a thing for you though, doesn't she?"

"She's my best friend's sister, asshole," I said, shoving him away from me while he laughed.

"Yep! Your best friend is probably completely fine with you emailing her so much while you're away," he teased.

"Leave him alone. I think it's sweet," Kia said from where she sat lazily on an armchair, a smile on her face as she looked at me. So far she had been the only person I could confide in minimally about this without judgment.

I nodded at Kia and shook my head at John, turning back to the laptop and diving into the last two months of her life. While I had been torturing men for information and breaking into buildings to pull their security footage, she had been … going on dates.

My lip involuntarily pulled into a snarl, hand not scrolling on the mouse pad, but clenching into a fist as I continued to read. Her best friends and mom had decided she needed to get out more, so she was pushed into going on various dates.

I hated it.

I hated everything about it.

Carmen shouldn't have been holed up, not living her life. I didn't want her sitting around waiting. That's exactly why I didn't say anything about how I felt for her or make any promises before I left. The type of work I was doing came with the very real possibility that I came home in a body bag. She had already lost enough; she didn't need to add losing me on top of that... if she even felt the same way.

But as I read closer, I realized with pleasure, that she had hated every second of these dates. There were a few dates it seemed, where looking back, amusing moments happened, but otherwise, she was under-whelmed and unimpressed.

```
...Rory says I have unrealistic stan-
dards because I'm always com-
paring men to a fantasy, but a girl
should have standards, right Leo?
Unfortunately for me, my fantasy is
about someone I can't have. Anyway,
I think they'll finally drop it for a
little while since I'm applying to
that pastry chef program, so we can
both rest easy that the bad dates
will be on hiatus.

I hope you get a chance to read
these soon.
```

Please be safe. Come home to us.

I miss you, Leo.

Carmen

That was the first time she had said, "I miss you," instead of, "We miss you." My heart seemed to stutter for a moment before galloping quickly against my ribs. My fingers hovered over the keyboard. So many things I wanted to say, and yet it felt so cold being typed on the screen. I wanted to talk to her, to look at her face when I said everything that I felt burning within me.

But before I had a chance, the satellite phone rang, jarring my team into a more alert state. John answered, listening intently for a stretch while we all waited with bated breath.

"They confirmed the location," he said after hanging up. "Lupo, I need the computer." I nodded, closing out Carmen's email and logging out for the more secured network. He pulled up the coordinates, and we spent the next few hours plotting our plan of attack.

We had taken a boat, loaded only with the weapons that had been stashed in the safe house and what we had left from before, and headed to the Island. Kia was on the scope as soon as we got within range to see if the intel we had was accurate.

"Looks like we have a clear path if you go straight. We can get in," she said confidently.

Logan steered us through the open and unguarded water until he shut off the engine and we swam the rest of the way to shore. Shucking our wet clothes and replacing them quickly with dry ones, we silently made our way up the rocky beach, guns drawn.

I spotted two guards before they saw us, shooting them with the silencer so there was only a muffled sound before they dropped to the ground. Kia collected their walkies and guns, and we continued closer.

The building didn't seem like much, a sprawling one-level island home, but the sick feeling that was growing in my gut told me there was so much more hidden below. We found an exterior wall to crouch beside with mild cover provided by the large leaves of a tropical plant of some kind. John peered into the window, signaling that there were four guards visible on that floor. Logan and John could handle that while Kia and I headed to the back entrance, where surveillance footage showed a garage entrance. Conspicuously, they had regular monthly deliveries by vans whose sole task was to be packed with merchandise at the private dock—only in the cover of night—and then driven to this very garage and pulling right up to the house, obscuring the contents from view while being unloaded.

We moved like ghosts, Kia and I, rounding the corner to see two guards posted there. Without hesitation, we went for them before they could even notice we were there. Almost in synchronization, we pulled knives from our vests and came behind them silently. A soft, but surprised groan came from the man I held as the blade from my knife pushed through the back of his neck, severing his spinal cord. Kia's dropped to the ground a moment after mine, blood quickly pooling around them.

I took a moment to also take out the cameras that surveilled the entrance. We had about two minutes on average before whoever was watching the cameras alerted the others to this location and what they just witnessed happen, but two minutes was plenty of time to get in.

I didn't hesitate, darting to the door of the garage and pulling open the pocket on my vest that held my smaller tools. The keypad that kept this door closed wasn't very elaborate. I would have expected more from an operation like this, but apparently, they were a bit too comfortable having their private island. Less than thirty seconds later, we had gained entry into the space. Kia stood with her gun drawn and ready to defend us once the door opened as I slipped my tools back into my vest, but it was shockingly quiet and empty when the door opened.

I glanced at her with concern. This was unusual behavior. Guards should have been posted inside and out. Even if we were on a remote island, all entrances should have been manned. It didn't change our mission, however strange this was. We had to get in, and we had succeeded.

I had barely made two strides when I saw a familiar symbol. The O'Shea Clan's insignia was branded on a crate just inside the garage. Irish mob. Sex traffickers often delved into other forms of depravity, but something about that insignia brought a chill to my spine. I knew my father and the Big Boss had been trying to move past a truce to an alliance with the Irish back in the United States. If U.S. Mafia relations were solid, then the European branches may have better interactions, and that would help the global black market a little bit.

I was sick at seeing it. Sick at having such a reminder of the two halves of my life. Sick that in this moment, they seemed to be threading together.

I glanced at Kia, giving her the hand signal for us to move forward, taking out cameras as we saw them and heading through the garage to the first door we saw there. Just as I began to deactivate the second keypad, the sounds of open gunfire split through the air.

"We've been spotted," came Logan's gruff voice over our comms.

"Shit!" Kia whispered, gripping her gun to cover me as the lock finally disengaged, and I gripped the handle to pull open the door.

The gunfire was mostly coming from outside the garage, meaning Logan and John were drawing away the guards, giving us the opportunity to push through and finish the mission.

I ripped open the door, stepping into the hallway with Kia right at my back. Our guns were drawn, but no one was in this part of the house to stop us. The eerie feeling that something was very wrong here seemed to settle further in my gut. I had enough experience from both sides of my life to know this was unusual, and though John and Logan continued to pull attention their way, that should have never taken every man in this house from their stations.

Based on the crude layout we had of the house, we knew the basement entrance couldn't be far from the garage where they unloaded the girls. Three doors in this hallway were left wide open, presumably the other guards running out to help with the other half of our team, but one was left closed. Another keypad sat, baring us from entry, but we didn't have time anymore. I shot out the door handle, kicking the remnants away to reveal a set of metal stairs that lead to the basement. Immediately a bullet whizzed by my head, embedding in the wall behind me, and I glanced down to see three men covering behind various pieces of furniture below.

Without a second thought, I lunged down the stairs, firing at the first body who made a move and hitting him in the forehead, nearly taking the top of his head off. Kia, on my heels, hit another in the shoulder, while the third tried to come close enough to get point blank. I twisted the gun from his hands, reaching one hand out to grip his throat while the other pressed his own weapon to his temple.

"Where are the girls?" I demanded.

"I'm dead either way," he said, his Italian accent thick, voice shaking.

"We can get you immunity if you talk," Kia said after she landed a blow to the guy who she had shot, knocking him out cold.

"It doesn't matter. This batch was ruined anyway," he whispered, tears springing to his eyes. But he wasn't crying for the girls who had been stolen, beaten, drugged, and probably raped. No, he was crying for himself. His own pitiful existence, and it disgusted me.

"*Cretino,*" I growled. "*Vaffanculo a chi t'è morto. Mangia merde e morte!*" I hissed, unable to hold back my rage. I squeezed tightly to his throat before throwing him back against the column he had been hiding behind previously, shoving his gun in his surprised, gaping mouth, before pulling the trigger. The blood of that filth hitting my face was oddly satisfying.

"Get as many out as you can!" John yelled from the comms, jarring me from the red I was seeing and bringing me back to the mission at hand.

"I'll take left," Kia said once she saw I was back to myself, letting her eyes drift from me to the line of doors down here. This space we were in was large, a whole pretend house set up down in the basement, complete with a kitchen. It was a bit sterile, only the basic necessities and lacking decor of any kind, as if the girls were made to play pretend here, ensuring they behaved appropriately when they were sold off to the highest bidder. Farther, past this mockery of a living space, was a hallway with a series of doors, but at the end was a large set of double doors.

We each kicked in the first door on our side at the same time, guns pointed and ready for more men to come from the shadows.

"Clear!" Kia called, but my room was far from empty.

Three girls were huddled in the corner. They all looked to be between the ages of sixteen and eighteen. They were clean, dressed in thin white dresses that looked more like a slip than an actual piece of clothing, and they wore collars around their necks.

"We're here to help you," I said quietly, hoping one of them spoke English.

"There is no help for us," one girl said. She was a little taller than the other two, but not by much. Her accent told me she was from Southern France, maybe the Basque region. Her eyes were shockingly green, and despite her words, there was still a bit of strength in her eyes. She reminded me just a little of Carmen, and my heart squeezed slightly at the thought of Carmen ever having to be put in a situation like this. Just for a moment, I allowed myself to solidify the burning in my heart that Carmen's emails about going on dates with other men had ignited. I would somehow get home to her and make sure no one else ever touched her.

Gunfire and shouting seemed to come back into the house, my eyes darting back to the hall where Kia was already moving down her side, carting out some of the other girls she found along the way and telling them to stay close. Seeing that, the three girls before me appeared to be inspired to move, joining the other freed girls, and we made it down the hall with quick precision.

"What's behind here?" I asked the green-eyed girl once we got to the double doors.

"The new ones. They're still breaking them."

My lip curled into a snarl as I looked at Kia and saw similar anger and disgust on her face. But we didn't get a chance to go through, as the sound of feet on the metal stairs told us we had company.

Time seemed to slow as I stepped away from the girls for Kia to cover them, knowing our only path for escape was on the stairs that were now blocked by whoever was descending them. John was being pulled down the stairs by two men, blood splattered all over him. They may have gotten ahold of him, but he had taken out a fair number of their forces first.

"Leonardo Lupo, I wasn't expecting to see you here," came a voice I recognized and was not at all happy about. My eyes landed on the figure moving down the stairs behind John. Tailored suit, dirty-blond hair, bright blue eyes glimmering with a mixture of sick satisfaction and simmering rage.

Freddy O'Shea, a mob prince. He was the son of the O'Shea Clan of the American-Irish mob Boss. Next In line to take his father's seat, he oozed smugness like any crowned prince would.

"Funny to meet here like this. When I heard you'd joined the Marines, I was astonished. After all, your brothers have followed in your father's footsteps. But you decided to be a hero instead of following the darkness that runs through your veins. I suppose you got promoted," he said, stopping at the end of the stairs while his eyes moved over my tactical gear that was not standard issue for the Marines. "Funny that even when you try to escape the life, you still end up here," he said with a humorless chuckle, tightening his grip on John, who winced slightly.

"And here you are," I said back coldly. Kia and John both looked at me in confusion. No one knew my father was a Caporegime for the Italian Mafia in the States. Had they known, I wouldn't have gotten as far as I had in the short six years since I decided to join the military. My life was tilting on its axis, and I knew there would be some long explanations to my team in the future if we made it out of this mess.

"You're not getting away with our merchandise," Freddy said, a smirk on his face as he crossed his arms confidently, despite mine and Kia's guns trained on him and his men.

"You aren't leaving this island," I countered. He laughed. The sound echoed around the fairly sterile space and made my stomach clench.

"Neither are you," he said finally, his voice cold. Whatever humor was in his face before melted away as one of the men holding John, a great brute of a man with a deep scar running over his cheek, punched the back of John's head with such force, I could hear the crack of his skull.

And then there was an explosion.

CHAPTER 2
CARMEN

TWO MONTHS LATER

I heard the buzzer going off behind me in the kitchen just before the bell chimed, indicating a new customer had just stepped into the coffee shop. It had been a busy morning, but that was to be expected when the suburb was getting flooded with out-of-town friends and family the week of Independence Day. It helped that there was more than one lake nearby, and though it wasn't nearly as big as the city twenty minutes away, it boasted a fair number of bars and restaurants for visitors to have fun at before they all made their way to the boats and lakeside beaches.

"I'll be right with you!" I hollered without looking at the new customer, before dashing back toward the ovens, snatching out the cinnamon rolls before they were ruined, and turning back to the main counter. I normally wouldn't have made another batch in the middle of such a crazy day by myself, but originally, I *wasn't* by myself, and I couldn't let them go to waste.

This amount of business wouldn't have been such a problem if Ingrid had been there with me, but her daughter had gotten sick at summer camp, and there was no one available to sit with her until afternoon closing. Nora was only five, so she couldn't be left home alone either. Katy, our high school part-timer, had taken this week off because her family was visiting relatives in Florida, so it was just me, manning it all on my own for the next—I checked the watch on the wall—two hours. *Great.*

Not that I hadn't handled something like this before. Ingrid and I had been the only two consistent workers at the coffee shop other than the owner, Liliana, since I moved back home after college. It was easy to slip into the routine of working there, since I had worked there every summer through high school and college. Liliana Lupo graciously gave me a full-time job when my mom got sick. Although it probably helped that Liliana was basically another mother to me. The reason she wasn't here herself was because she was with my mom, getting scans done to confirm Mama was still in remission. She beat the cancer two years ago, but she still had to get scans every six months to make sure it hadn't come back.

I would have gone, but Liliana had been with Mama for the last two scans, and being a very superstitious Italian woman, she was insistent when she said to me, "I'm going. We don't change anything about the routine, Carmen. You know that! *It* will come back if we change anything now!" I rolled my eyes at her, but internally I agreed. You don't mess with tradition or routines, lest you want to bring bad luck down on your family. That was just the way I was raised.

I took a moment to tighten my ponytail, which was barely holding back my unruly, dark curls, before finally rounding the little wall that separated the kitchen from the front counter. As I did so, I finally took in the new customer who had made their way up from the front door. It felt like the wind had been knocked out of me.

Standing on the other side of the counter was my childhood next-door neighbor, Liliana's youngest son, and my brother Benny's best friend.

Leo.

He looked a little different than the last time I had seen him: his face was more weathered and a deep tan adorned his skin, which only seemed to accentuate his dark hair and the sharpness of his features. The military uniform that seemed to be sewn on his strong form also didn't fall short of being awe-inspiring. There was definitely something about a man in uniform. But the expression on his face was nothing short of the same old Leo I had known most of my life. Mischievous hazel eyes sparkled as a smirk played at the corner of his mouth.

I wasn't expecting to see him until much later this evening. We were having dinner together, both our families, to welcome him home. And I was a nervous wreck about it.

"Same loud mouth that you had before. I'm glad some things never change," he said, his voice just as deep as it had been when it finally dropped in high school, and hearing it again seemed to hit me straight in my center, causing heat to cascade through my body.

"What do you want, Leo?" I asked, crossing my arms over my chest.

I'm sure I looked like a frazzled mess. My cheeks were probably flushed with the exertion of doing everything by myself and running myself ragged. It was probably for the best, since he wouldn't be able to tell my cheeks were heating up just at the sight and sound of him.

"A coffee, of course. It doesn't feel like I've actually come home without having a cup from Mom's shop," he said, letting his white teeth show with a playful grin.

"And to annoy me?"

"What makes you think I came here just to see you?" he asked, though his eyes burned with something I had only seen a few times before.

"Right. Coffee," I grumbled.

"It's almost like you forgot I was coming home," he said, leaning against the counter so our faces were level.

"How could I forget, Leo? Our families have been talking about it nonstop since we heard."

We hadn't heard from him in months, then two months ago we got notice he was being honorably discharged. The elation of him coming home was something I could still feel vibrating in my bones, and even though he was right there in front of me, it almost didn't seem real. Part of me wished it wasn't.

"I missed your emails," he said as I turned away from him to start the process of getting his favorite coffee made. His voice was quieter that time, but I didn't show how it affected me.

I thought I had prepared myself for him being around again. For so long, the only Lupos I ever saw were Liliana, Enzo, and, very rarely, Sal, Leo's brothers. And though I didn't see my brother Benny often since he moved back and forth between here and the main city for work, he had been talking and texting nonstop about Leo's return. Having his best friend gone for essentially the last six years had been hard on him. Leo was moving back with his mom until he figured out what he was going to do post-military.

He was moving right back next door to me.

My back was still turned. Though tensed with his words, I went about getting the espresso grounds ready to make the red-eye he always ordered.

"I didn't say what I wanted!" he said a little louder, since I had moved down to the machine, tamping down the grounds a bit more aggressively than I normally would have.

"I'm getting your red eye. The same damn thing you've ordered for the last eight years," I hissed back, shooting him a look since he started farther leaning over the counter to watch me. The amusement didn't falter from his face.

"You remember what I like?"

"How could I forget? You made *me* make it for you almost every day all summer, every summer when I started working here."

"And don't forget weekends," he said with a chuckle. My scowl faltered slightly, a little twitch of my own smile making its way to my lips.

"There she is," he said quietly again, so only I could hear. The sound flooded me with feelings I shouldn't have been having, heat creeping up my cheeks at his attention.

Most of the people in the shop had moved on, and the only few left were engrossed in their own activities. Mary was reading the worn romance novel I think I'd seen her reading no fewer than five times, and Evan was on his laptop, noise-canceling headphones firmly in place.

"Where I always will be," I grumbled.

He and our combined brothers could come and go as they pleased. Everyone had left at some point for something a bit more grand than the suburb of Lee's Summit and the larger Kansas City that it was attached to, everyone but me. They all came back; that was proven time and time again, also being the last place to return to, but it still chafed to know they could all go again, and I'd be left waiting for them.

Waiting for him.

Waiting for something I would never get.

"Why are you so mad, Little Song?" he asked as I turned my back to him once more to pour the drip coffee into a paper travel cup while the espresso dribbled into the little shot glasses.

I cringed at the question and at the use of the familial nickname I'd had since I was little. My name technically meant song, poetry, and truth, and my love of singing at the top of my lungs for most of my childhood definitely lent itself to having the nickname stick.

But why was I *really* mad? Other than the fact that instead of catching up during this little lull in business and icing the cinnamon rolls sitting in the back, I was making his coffee—which was always free of charge, of course—was his presence here now, a month since I had last heard from him.

Perhaps emailing your brother's best friend regularly while he's deployed was not such a normal thing for everyone else, but our families had grown up together. I missed him. I was proud of him. I worried about him. So, of course, I had kept my promise and emailed him regularly. Weekly, and sometimes daily, depending on what was going on. I couldn't tell him everything that went on in our families, not with the delicate nature of his position, and our unfortunate position with whom his father was, but I didn't want him to feel like he was missing out on anything while he was away.

It was all fine. Perhaps I shared too much with him, or confessed how much "we" missed him at family dinners and outings. But I made a critical error the last time we communicated.

He had just gotten back to base from his last deployment. He had texted Liliana and Benny, letting them know, and then he texted me. That wasn't so unusual. The few times he had come back to the States before being redeployed, we'd usually have a few short text conversations, but in the past, I had been busy with school or taking care of Mama. This time had been … different.

I had been out with my two best friends, twin sisters Rory and Daph, so perhaps I had a few drinks in me and let my inhibitions down just enough that my logical mind took a back seat to the feelings I had kept locked securely within me, and maybe only whispered in the ears of my two best friends.

[Leo: I'm back in the States. Won't be long until I get to come home.]

[Me: When?]

[Leo: Not too long. A month maybe? They're giving me time to pack my stuff to ship home first.]

[Me: Oh yeah, you have a whole apartment, don't you?]

[Leo: It's not much. I never stayed here long enough.]

I tried to imagine that. I looked around my room. It had been mine since I was a child, but after coming back from college I had made it less a teenager's room and had gotten rid of a lot of my old stuff. It was all still the same four walls though. I couldn't really imagine being in his place where there wasn't much that you even cared to pack.

[Me: I think it would take me a lot longer than a month to pack just my bedroom.]

[Leo: The Barbies alone would be a whole week.]

I laughed quietly, shaking my head.

[Me: 😳 You know I don't have those anymore. I think it was you who took me to donate them when I was 16, Leo.]

[Leo: 😁]

[Me: So, show me what you have to pack.]

I was curious, of course, about the place he had called home for all these years, even if it was only for a brief period of time, but more than that, I wanted to keep our little communication going. It felt so good to text him and have him text me back right away.

A few minutes later, I got a picture in place of a message. In it were two boxes, still not completely full, a huge military duffle that looked like it was open and ready to be filled, and the suitcase he had taken with him when he left six years ago. But the picture was positioned in front of a large mirror, presumably on the door to his closet, and I got a good look at him, as well as the few things he was planning to bring home.

He looked different, but not in a bad way. He was in a white undershirt with gray sweatpants. The muscles of his arms looked large, flexing involuntarily in the photo as he raised the phone to capture the few items he was bringing home. The undershirt hugged his cut torso, the white fabric clinging to his tanned skin. He had tattoos now, black ink that snaked up his arms and I could also see the hint of through his shirt on his chest.

I felt the heat soar through my body at the image, no longer caring whatsoever about what he was bringing home with him.

[Leo: It's not much.]

[Me: Good, then you'll have plenty of time for me to text you and bother you all the time instead of just sending you all those emails. 😉]

[Leo: You're never a bother.]

[Me: You said differently once upon a time.]

[Leo: Once upon a time I was stupid & young. That me had no idea how much I'd look forward to an email from you. Or a text.]

I chewed on my lip for a minute, letting the knowledge that he looked forward to my emails while he had been away sink in with glee. I had worried that I annoyed him, but my anxiousness during the stretches between was always answered by a reply from him. It may have been weeks or months later, but he always let me know he was okay eventually, encouraging me to keep them coming.

[Me: I'm so glad you're back in the States. I always feel like a ball of nerves when I'm waiting for you to respond to my emails.]

[Leo: You are?]

[Me: I thought that was sort of obvious with how I say "be safe" at the end of every email...]

[Leo: Sometimes your emails were the only thing that kept me going.]

My heart fluttered in my chest. The combination of instant gratification of having him text me back so quickly, and what he was saying to me, was doing wonders for my ego.

But before I could think of something else to say in response, the three little dots popped up, indicating he was typing something else.

[Leo: Do you miss me, Little Song?]

I could almost see his playful smirk through the screen, but when I thought of it this time, instead of letting my irritation at the nickname take over any other feelings, the wine from the night with the girls let the other feelings I usually pushed away flood to the front.

Did I miss him?

So much. Painfully, if I was being honest with myself. The boy I had crushed on for most of my life, while simultaneously being my brother's coconspirator to torment me, was so very far away, and I had wanted him here. I wanted him safe in our little slice of the suburbs, making me crazy, not almost dying.

[Me: What if I said I did miss you?]

[Leo: I'd tell you I miss you too. That I can't wait to see you again.]

My heart hammered harder in my chest. But before I could say anything in response, he sent another.

[Leo: I think I'm looking forward to seeing you again the most.]

What did that mean? I chewed my lip, trying to rationalize it with my not fully coherent brain, but the warmth that was spreading through me quickly took precedence over any sort of logical thinking.

[Me: Oh, too bad I didn't send more interesting material then.]

[Leo: More interesting?]

[Me: Maybe I should have sent pictures, just in case you'd forgotten what I look like.]

[Leo: I could never forget what you look like.]

I smirked, somehow feeling so confident with the way this exchange was going, loving the surge of flirtatiousness bubbling through me, along with my liquid courage. And before he could say anything more or I could think better of it, I reached my hand up, snapping a selfie that consisted of me laying across my bed, dark curly hair splayed over the pillow, with nothing but my lacy bra on, bottom lip caught between my teeth as I looked into the camera.

My finger hit the send button, and immediately my heart went from pounding with eager anticipation to fear.

What did I just do?

The dots returned, coming and disappearing several times over the course of several minutes before a text finally came through, my face now hidden in my pillow. I cringed at the sound of the incoming text chime, but looked at it anyway.

[Leo: Carmen... I don't want to do this through text.]

Oh god… what have I done?

[Me: That was a mistake.]

My text went out quick. So quick. Too quick.

[Leo: I'd rather talk to you.]

[Me: Just delete it.]

[Leo: Can I call you?]

I'd rather die than have to feel more embarrassed than I do now.

[Me: Delete that. Forget this. I was out with the twins earlier.]

My phone vibrated with the telltale buzz of an incoming phone call. Leo's name popped up on my screen. Without another moment to spare, I shut my phone off and threw it on my bedside table, the offensive thing somehow still taunting me from where it sat black and silent.

The next morning, I turned my phone back on, seeing that I had only one message back from him.

[Leo: I deleted the photo. I'll see you when I come home. We can talk then.]

That was the last thing he said to me. The last time we spoke, and it was over a month ago. I had allowed myself to wallow in self-pity about it for a few weeks, mourning our previous friendship, while also hating that if there had ever been a chance with him, it was now certainly dashed. But I finally shook myself off, steeling myself in the knowledge that I would have to just be brave and strong to face him. He wasn't going anywhere. He was going to be part of my life forever, so I'd just have to push past this horrible embarrassment … somehow.

Now he was here. He was standing on the other side of the coffee counter. His face was just as nice as it always had been, angular and stunning with those dark Italian features, his eyes twinkling, his lips saying that stupid nickname. He was still dressed in his uniform, filling it out nicely with what I could only imagine were thick ropes of hard muscle, tattoos I had never seen in person, hidden from sight, making him even more mouthwatering than he had been when he left. And I was still making him his free coffee like I had been since I was a teenager.

So why was I so mad, he had asked?

"It's been a bad day," I lied. It had been busy—overwhelming—but nothing about this day could be bad, because Leo was home, safe and whole, even if I had been an idiot.

I turned back in time to see his brows crinkled in concern, eyes scrutinizing every little shift in my body. I poured the espresso shot into his cup, setting it in front of him on the counter and trying to paste on a smile that was in no way genuine.

"Red eye. Your favorite. Now if you don't mind, I have some cinnamon rolls to ice," I said, so desperate to get away from this situation.

"I think our moms are making dinner together tonight," he said, snapping a lid over the top of his cup.

"They always do on Wednesdays, Sundays—"

"Holidays, and birthdays," he finished with a little smile. "But this isn't one of those," he pointed out, being that it was a Monday and the holiday that had brought in all the business that day wasn't happening for three more days.

"Well, you're home. So that may as well be a holiday," I said, immediately regretting the fact that I didn't include "for your mom" in that sentence. His hazel eyes glinted a little at that, clearly having noticed my omission.

"See you at dinner, Little Song," he said, that smirk back on his face, before he turned around and strode right back out of the shop.

CHAPTER 3

CARMEN

The rest of the day moved quickly. 4 p.m. came around and I was in the process of closing everything up when Liliana called.

"It was smooth as a whistle," she said as a greeting, the sound of her voice slightly muffled by the Bluetooth connection in her car. She had the unfortunate habit of mixing sayings up, but it was something that we all found endearing. Sometimes I wondered if it was on purpose.

"As usual," I said, grinning as I tucked the phone between my ear and my shoulder.

"If it works, don't mess with it," she said seriously, only making my smile widen. "How did it go at the shop today? Was it crowded with all the incoming visitors?"

"I was basically slammed all day," I confirmed, knowing she'd be pleased. We were open only briefly in the morning tomorrow, then closing the shop for the rest of the week since most people would be heading to lake houses.

"You? Wasn't Ingrid supposed to be there?"

"Nora got sick," I said as I flipped the switches on the display cases full of sweet treats to turn off the light, glancing around at the front to be sure I didn't miss something.

"Oh no! I wish we would have been home," my mom said. "I would have watched Nora."

"Or I could have come in," Liliana added.

"I managed," I told them as I did a similar sweep of the kitchen.

"Are you still closing up? We can come by and help if you need us," Liliana said, her concern so evident in her tone. I loved that woman, almost as much as I loved my own mother. Thank goodness they were best friends. It meant I didn't have to choose between them pretty much ever.

"I'm done. It died off at about 3:30, and I made good use of the time. Need me to bring anything home with me for dinner?"

It wasn't all the time, but, for special occasions, we would bring a dessert back from the shop to share. Tonight's dinner would be no exception, even if I was hating myself for being so stupid with that text to Leo.

"Is there any tiramisu left? You know it's Leonardo's favorite," my mom said. My eyes darted to the tiramisu I had made that morning. I had claimed to the customers all day we were out, even though it sat within the refrigerator in the kitchen, beautiful flower patterns of cocoa on top of the creamy top layer. Of course, I knew it was his favorite. That's why, despite the pit of embarrassment in my stomach, I had come in extra early when no one else had been there to make one to perfection for him.

"Looks like we still have a whole one," I murmured, delicately pulling it from the case before slipping my bag over my shoulder and heading out the back door.

"Oh, what good luck. Bring that over this evening. I can't wait!" Liliana said brightly.

"I'll see you at home, honey. Love you!" my mom said.

"Love you!" Liliana called.

"I love you too!" I said with a chuckle, before the call ended and I turned to lock up.

But as I turned back to the alley behind the shop, I grew alert of my surroundings. The past month hadn't been a disaster, simply because of that idiotic text, I also made another mistake that involved a date gone horribly wrong.

Jeremy Wallingford, a boy who had been in the graduating class between me and Benny and Leo, had been so insistent on asking me out over the years, that in my haste to get over Leo before he got back in town and spare myself the embarrassment of being hopelessly in love with him, I agreed to go on one date with Jeremy.

The date was awful. He was just as boring and misogynistic as I remembered, if not more so than he had been, because, despite his decent looks, he seemed to be rejected rather often, which clearly took its toll on his perspective on women.

All this to say, although I thanked him and told him I didn't want another date, he took that as a challenge instead of a kind way of turning him down. Over the past few weeks, there had been numerous times where he approached me as I was leaving work, following me to my car and trying his hardest to touch me. And I knew for a fact that he had come by my house more than once. One time, I saw his car leaving through the partially opened curtains in my bedroom after taking a shower.

It was after that that I finally broke down and told my brothers what was going on, and while I still saw him, and he still texted me incessantly, I felt a little safer now that they were in my corner.

Thankfully, as I unlocked my car, there was no sign of Jeremy anywhere, but I still relocked the doors quickly once I got inside and turned the key in the ignition.

I made it home before Mom did, which was just as well, because it gave me an opportunity to shower. I stopped even trying to shower in the morning. If I worked, I always ended up smelling like a strange combination of coffee, sweat, and baked goods by the end of my shift, and depending on the day, I often went to the gym afterward.

As the warm water rushed over my skin, I thought about Leo. In these private moments, I sometimes allowed myself the fantasy that he could ever remotely feel the same way about me as I did about him. It was a long shot. He probably just saw me as a little kid, his best friend's sister, who had been annoying, dependent, and someone to torture during our childhood. I was off limits in reality, but in my fantasy, there was nothing to stop us.

He would step into the shower behind me, his body heat would press against my back, softly pulling my heavy, damp curls over one shoulder to give him access to my neck. His lips would trail over my skin, hands wrapping around to touch the flesh of my stomach and cup a breast in one hand.

Just the thought of his hands and lips on me had me trembling. My body flushed with heat. My hand traveled down to where I wanted him to touch me most, where I had imagined him touching me for years, and I knew it was going to be a long dinner.

CHAPTER 4

LEO

The red eye tasted good, familiar and rich, as I left the cafe, but it sat nearly untouched on the kitchen table at my mother's house where I had come directly after stopping at the cafe. Everyone had been too busy to pick me up from the airport. Well, I suppose that hadn't been true. I didn't ask *everyone* who would have been willing. My brothers both were on errands from our father, and Benny was still in the bigger city, having to work one last shift at the physical therapy office before he had the rest of the week off for the holiday. My oldest brother Sal had said Dad could have "arranged" a ride, but I didn't want even that small of a favor from him.

I had gotten a taxi, since I wasn't a fan of ride-share services, and had them drop me right at home to leave my bags, but as soon as I had entered the empty house, I felt restless. True, this had been my home my whole life, but after years of being away, it felt strange to be back in such a familiar place. My job in the military had me moving all the time. I'd barely get comfortable before I was packing up again.

After a month of debriefing the two of us who survived the last mission as well as time in the hospital, the government decided to honorably discharge us. I was feeling an odd mixture of emotions; frustrated that we had failed our mission, sorrow for Logan and John, who we lost, happy to be able to come home, and horrified that I now was free. Free for my father to try to take me under his wing, as he had for my two older brothers.

This strange sense of safety and comfort that being home provided seemed false. Like I'd snap back to reality and have to go once again. There was only one thing, one person who had felt like a safe place, a comfort, all throughout my time away. Which was why I had immediately set back out. Not even bothering to change from the uniform I had worn the whole journey home, I made my way to the coffee shop, which was not far from our house. I had walked this path so many times through my life, I didn't even have to think about each turn.

I told myself the whole way there I was just wanting that familiarity without the strangeness of my empty home, but the truth was that I wanted to see her. I wanted to lay my eyes on Carmen, to take in all her little movements and facial expressions I had missed.

I knew she would be working. It was a Monday, after all. She always worked Mondays. It had been regularly mentioned in her emails to me overseas. Usually, the things she mentioned were just normal and mundane. Sometimes she'd share what was bothering her at any particular moment. Often, she would tell me her newest pastry creation, which sounded mouthwatering. But my mind flashed back to those last few emails, where she mentioned the dates she had been forced to go on by her mom and best friends. The idea of her dating anyone was enough to make me want to kill someone with my bare hands. And I could. I knew many ways to kill a man and most of them could be done without anyone suspecting foul play.

But none of those men lasted, or at least she had never mentioned someone more than once.

I had asked her to email me, after all. It was the day before I was set to leave when I did so. We had a dinner together, one of the few times everyone in both of our families made the effort to come home. Benny came back from college, Adrian, Benny and Carmen's oldest brother, flew in from the base he was stationed at, and even my father had made an appearance, which he didn't often make time to do. Mom's house seemed so crowded and familiar, but for some reason, the girl about to go off to college who sat beside me all night was all I could think about.

I would be gone. What would she do while I was away? Who would she call when her brothers were busy and she needed help? Who would she trust to tell her dreams to? Who would she confide her insecurities to?

Sure, she had Rory and Daph. Her two best friends, but…

Would she flirt with someone else and blush as she looked up at them with those green eyes? That coy smile playing on her plush lips?

The table started stirring, my dad moving to smoke a cigarette out the back door, our moms cleaning up the kitchen, while our combined brothers moved to find something to watch on television.

"I'm going to use the restroom," she had said quietly, only me paying her any attention.

I watched her move past the first-floor bathroom, up the stairs to the second bathroom in the hall, and I couldn't help but follow her. No one seemed to notice as

I slipped up the stairs a few steps behind her, catching the door before she could close it and making her breath hitch in her throat as I pushed my way in, letting the door snap closed behind me as I crowded the room with my frame.

"What are you doing in here, Leo?" she asked, staring up at me with those green eyes that held such a depth of sadness. Was she sad that I was leaving?

"Carmen, I don't want you to-to..."

To what?

I don't want you to be sad?

Don't forget about me?

Don't fall in love while I'm away?

"You shouldn't be in here. I'm coming back down. I just needed a minute," she said, turning away from me.

"Will you email me?" I had blurted, when the words I really wanted to say were so much more, and quite frankly too scary to say out loud. This was my best friend's little sister. The girl next door I had seen growing up beside me, taking just as good as she gave with all the boys in her life keeping her on her toes.

"What?" she asked, her face incredulous as she turned back around to see if I was serious or not.

"Email me when I'm gone?"

Her face transformed. That confusion and sadness leaving, just a little, to make room for a little happiness and humor.

"You going to miss me, Leo? You'll get plenty of emails from Liliana and at least Benito, if no one else," she said, her tone teasing.

"What if I said I am?" I asked, stepping a bit closer to her in the small space. That humor faltered, a light blush coming across her pale olive cheeks as she looked up at me. I wanted to own that blush, that look on her face. I wanted it to be for me and me alone.

There was heat, tension between us, and knowing I was leaving tomorrow and might not be home for a long while made me unable to stop, as my hand moved up to touch that pink on her cheek and brush down to her chin. Her lips parted, eyes on fire as she looked up at me, and that zing of spark traveled up my arm from my fingertips at just that light touch.

I wanted to kiss her. I wanted to pull her to me and feel her. I wanted to make her mine, even if I knew there were so many things that could go wrong if I did so. Somehow, in this little bathroom, the fear of all that could go wrong ceased to exist. My hand at her chin tilted her head up a little farther, while my head turned down, our breath mingling for a moment as our noses touched, and I was about to cross a line I had never thought I would.

"Leo! The TV's got nothing! We're going to pick a movie! Get your ass down here!" Benny called from the bottom of the stairs, ripping us from the little bubble we had been in.

Carmen had stepped back immediately, my hands already missing the way her skin felt. I wanted to go back to how we had just been. I wanted to pull her close and press her small body against mine, to feel her lips, which I could only imagine were as soft as they looked, pressed against mine, but the moment was lost. Her arms came around her middle, shoulders hunching as if to protect herself.

"Be right down!" I called over my shoulder.

"You should insist on Total Recall. You know how much Benny and Enzo hate that one," Carmen said with a little smirk, though her voice seemed a little breathless and there was still a blush on her cheeks. I couldn't help the smile that pulled on my lips at her suggestion. She knew me so well. But the strange tug at

my heart, at the way she was folding into herself, made it only half-hearted.

"You'll email me?" I asked this time.

"I promise," she whispered, our eyes locking once more, before I nodded, turning the doorknob in the bathroom and leaving the room to grab Total Recall *from my bedroom.*

I had been certain that was all there was. That even though the thought killed me, we would change over the time I was away. That moment in the bathroom and the slightly lingering hug she gave me just before her family left to go to their house at the end of that night, would be the only true moment we had, and it was squandered.

Now, here I sat six years later, a changed man in many ways, but the girl next door still nagging at my brain, tugging at my heart.

My phone rang, and I saw Benny's name pop up on the screen.

"Hey," I said after swiping to answer.

"I got off work early. My last patient went back to the hospital, so I'm on my way home. You want to me to come grab you and we can get a beer before our moms go all mother hen?"

The idea was far better than sitting at the kitchen table reminiscing about almost kissing his sister.

"That sounds perfect."

His car pulled up twenty minutes later, which had given me time to change out of my uniform into regular clothes. I was sitting on the front porch steps, and jumped up, eager to see him, when I saw an unfamiliar car pulling into the driveway next door.

"Leo!" Benny said with a broad smile as I hopped in the passenger seat. "Man, it's so good to have you home."

"I missed you too," I said with an equally large grin, clapping his shoulder, before my eyes went back to the strange car that pulled in right where Carmen usually parked. "Who's that?" I asked as he started pulling out of the driveway. He paused at the end, eyes darting over to the sedan that was idling there. His hands tightened on the wheel for a moment, before he returned his gaze to the road, completing the reversal and heading down the street.

"Some guy that keeps bothering Carmen. They went on a date a month ago and she turned him down, but he still won't leave her alone. Adrian is about one step away from beating him to a pulp," Benny said, stopping at a stop sign and pulling out his phone. "Just going to text Adrian now. He can swing by the house before Car gets home."

My fists clenched against my leg, eyes trained on the side mirror where I could still sort of make out the man getting out of his car and wandering up to the LaMartina house.

"What is he even doing there?"

"Probably seeing if she's home or leaving her something. He keeps thinking if he just bribes her with enough crap, she'll say yes. Really makes me wish one of us still lived at home with Mom and Sis just in case he gets too out of hand."

I had never been happier to be home than I was at that moment. Perhaps the idea of sleeping in my childhood bedroom wasn't particularly appealing, but the fact that I was just a few steps from Carmen's house in case this asshole showed up made me giddier than I had felt in some time.

We made it to the bar, which sat directly beside the gym where Adrian and my brother Sal worked most of the time. The bar, like quite a few of the establishments in this area, was owned by my dad, Salvatore Lupo Sr. We sat at the bar quietly for a few minutes, beers in hand, just listening to the quiet murmurs of the few early afternoon patrons sitting around.

"So discharged, huh? What are you going to do now that you're home?" Benny asked.

The question was loaded. From almost anyone else that would have been pushy, but Benny had been my best friend for our whole lives. We had been texting about it off and on since I had made it back to the States. I was pretty good on funds, if not great, but I would, at some point soon, need to get a job and figure out what I wanted to do with my life. No one really prepares you for how strange life is when you're discharged from the military.

"I know Adrian has connections with private security. I thought maybe I'd look into that, but right now I guess I'll just try to get used to living the civvy life," I said, taking another pull from the beer in front of me.

"You know Sal is going to ask you. Your dad has been pressing him and Adrian since we got word you were coming home for good," Benny murmured, his forehead wrinkling as his brows pressed closer together with concern.

We were all mad when Salvatore Sr. managed to sink his claws into Adrain LaMartina, the oldest of the LaMartina kids after his discharge from the Marines. He had avoided it as long as he could, but when he decided to leave the private security life, hating all the travel, he had decided to settle for a personal trainer job at the gym, which gave my father the opportunity he needed to make Adrain an offer he couldn't refuse. It was a gift that only men in the Mafia seemed to possess, wrangling people into their clutches against their will. None of us had ever been able to get it out of Adrian what my father had offered him, or held over him, but I imagined it was something huge.

"It's not going to happen," I muttered, my voice bitter. Adrian had been someone I had looked up to. He was younger than my oldest brother, Sal, by a year, but the two of them had always seemed like the protective duo of older brothers, banding together to help the rest of us. Adrian was the one who had gone against the grain first, joining the Marines right out of high school and making something of himself that didn't involve the Mafia, but he still ended up there anyway.

As if sensing the tone had gotten too dark, Benny took a swig of his beer before turning back to me. "Carmen will be happy you're back."

I tried not to outwardly stiffen.

"Probably not. She's gotten some reprieve from having all of us boys messing with her for so long. She's probably dreading dinner tonight," I said, trying to keep myself playful.

"I don't know, Leo. She's always had a soft spot for you," Benny said, grinning behind his bottle. Benny had loved teasing Carmen that she had a crush on me for years. At the time I had always assumed it was just normal, older brother taunting, using it to rile her up, but now I almost wished it had been true.

"Well, if it isn't Leonardo Lupo, the infamous military man," came a loud voice from behind us, thankfully disrupting the course of conversation away from Carmen. I turned to see Adrian, who waltzed through the room, straight to the bar where we were perched. He looked almost just like Benny. Black curls and wide-set eyes like his other siblings, but where Benny was clean cut for his physical therapist job, Adrian was not. His tattoos covered his arms and up his neck, and he was sporting athletic shorts and a black shirt. I stood, setting my beer down to give him a clap on the back.

"Infamous is a bit of a stretch. You did it first," I said when we parted, grinning.

"You did it better," he said, squeezing my shoulder.

"Did you check the house?" Benny asked when Adrian went to sit beside me on my other side.

"He was gone, but he left another letter," Adrian said, tossing the envelope in front of me toward Benny. "Carmen" was written in a messy scrawl on the top of it. It was thick, like there were multiple pages stuffed within it.

"Who is this guy?" I asked, gesturing to the envelope which I was itching to rip open to read, before I burned it to ash.

"Jeremy Wallingford. He went to high school with us. A year under us, I think. He came into the shop a bunch over the last year, and Carmen finally agreed to go on a date with him a month ago. Mostly out of pity, I think, but she seemed pretty down at the time too. I think something else happened that she didn't tell me about before she agreed," Benny said, reaching over to take the envelope, tearing it open quickly, and pulling the pages of notebook paper filled with that same messy handwriting from the envelope.

Immediately I thought about what happened a month ago. A little over a month ago, I had finished debriefing and texted her that I was coming home. A little over a month ago was the last time we had spoken before today, and she had sent me that picture.

Just thinking about that picture, which would forever be burned in my mind, as well as saved carefully in my phone, despite her request that I delete it, made my heart rate speed up, and my cock grow half hard in my pants. Thank goodness we were at the bar and my tenting pants were easily hidden.

But the timing was too perfect. She was sad about what? That she had sent the picture? That she was embarrassed?

I had tried to call her right after. I couldn't say what I wanted to through text and she had turned her phone off or declined my repeated calls. Each time her voice came on indicating it had gone to her voicemail, I had waited, listening to the sound of the message, before hanging up. I couldn't say those words to her without knowing her immediate response.

But what if she was sad about something else? *Someone* else?

"Anyway, she wasn't interested. Thanked him for the nice evening and all the attention and then told him it wasn't going to work out. He didn't seem to like that answer," Adrian said, flagging down the bartender to bring him a beer too. "Did he forget who we are? There were rumors in high school when you went there, weren't there?"

"There were rumors, but the LaMartinas were not quite as scary as the Lupos," Benny said, knocking into my elbow with his.

Yeah, word tended to get around that my father was in the Mafia pretty well, though he was around so infrequently and nothing big ever happened in Lee's Summit, that people tended to think it was only that, a rumor.

"I wish I had caught him while he was there. Why didn't you get out, Benito?" Adrian asked, leaning over to glare past me at my friend.

"I didn't want to get our boy here mixed up in it if it came to blows. But Wallingford doesn't seem to be getting the hint, so I'm sure there will be another opportunity," Benny said with a scowl.

"If Carmen doesn't take care of it herself," Adrian said with a bit of pride in his voice.

Growing up with two older brothers and essentially three additional brothers next door made a girl tough. She tussled with us just as much as we did with each other. She may have looked like a meek little Italian girl, but she could pack a punch just as good as one of us if she had enough anger behind it. Almost all of us had been on the receiving end of her fist at one time or another.

"It's the only reason I've held off as long as I have, honestly," Benny continued. "If I didn't know she could take care of herself, I would have left him bloody in a ditch weeks ago."

"This conversation seems to be headed in an interesting direction," Enzo said, stepping out from the kitchen doors behind the bar. I glanced up at my older brother, a grin breaking through as I stood to awkwardly hug him over the bar ledge. "Sorry I couldn't pick you up earlier. I had to time something just right."

Enzo was into computers. On paper, he was the head of technology and cyber security for our father's various companies, but off the record, he handled ensuring illegal money transfers, and all the Mafia's dealings on the dark web. He was insanely good at what he did, but it didn't mean any of us liked who and what he was doing it for. The only benefit seemed to be that our dad, and subsequently the big boss, were intrinsically dependent on him, and if there was a move he thought was too risky or would cause too much damage to innocent people, he often would tell them it just simply wasn't possible, and they tended to believe him.

"I didn't mind the taxi. But it was weird coming home to an empty house," I said once I sat back down on my stool.

"Well, it won't be empty tonight. Ma's making lasagna for the occasion. She hasn't made it since you were home two years ago."

The grumble of anticipation went through all four of us at the thought of her lasagna. I had seen the jars of her sauce sitting out on the counter when I came home earlier and wondered what magnificent pasta dish would be on the menu tonight.

Lasagna never disappointed.

CHAPTER 5
CARMEN

I came back down from my shower, just in time to see Mom pulling out all the ingredients for the salad we were bringing with us to dinner tonight. Liliana had probably started on the lasagna immediately when she got home, so it had plenty of time to cook in the oven before the boys all got there. The last time we had all been together like this was for seeing Leo off six years ago. Every time Leo had been back in town, someone else had been away. I hadn't been able to come back from college because my car wasn't starting or I had a big test to study for, Adrian was deployed as well, Benny was obligated to stay through his clinical rotation, and even Sal and Enzo had missed a time or two, off doing business for their dad.

But this stretch had been the longest. Two whole years since he had been home, and since then… well, things were different. The last month had been the longest that we hadn't communicated, or at least the longest *I* hadn't communicated with him, and seeing him this afternoon in the shop, looking like he did, like some gorgeous, muscled version of himself, was enough to have me trying not to hyperventilate. How was I going to get through this dinner if I couldn't even think about him without losing it?

There was no way I was going to be able to pull off pretending to be normal. Not now that I had sent him that picture. Not when I had been so, so close to giving in and telling him I had been crushing on him for the past decade.

"Oh good! *Carmenetta,* my love. Can you start cutting the onion for me?" my mama asked when she turned from the refrigerator and saw me entering the kitchen.

"Of course, Ma," I said, pulling out the tools I'd need before finding the red onions hiding in the pantry where they always were.

"You're not wearing that to dinner, are you?" she asked after several minutes of comfortable silence, while I moved on to the bell peppers she had washed and set beside my cutting board.

"What's wrong with this?" I asked, though I knew exactly what she was referring to. I had just thrown on a ratty college sweatshirt over my black leggings after my shower. I had planned on switching into something a bit nicer as the time got closer to our 6 p.m. dinner.

"Carmen," she said, her tone admonishing. "It's all of us together after so long. Can't it just be nice? I know all of you are going to be dressed down the rest of the week with the festivities. Can't we have one nice dinner together?"

I laughed as I chopped the peppers, shaking my head at her.

"I was going to put the green shirt on over the leggings, unless you think that's still too casual. I wasn't aware Liliana's house has become such an upscale establishment."

"The green one? That's a little sheer?"

"It's not *that* sheer. If she doesn't turn every light on in the house, I'm sure it will be fine," I protested.

The sheerness of the shirt was barely noticeable, or at least I hadn't thought so. Usually, I wore it with a blazer for interviews, not that I had gone on any in quite some time. The color really brought out my eyes, making them look much more striking, but that wasn't why I chose that shirt. It was nice, but not overly so, when paired with the high-waisted leggings I was currently wearing.

"Are you excited to see Leo again? I know it's been so strange around here with Benito gone and Leo off overseas. The three of you did so much together when you were growing up."

Other than Rory and Daph, my time had mostly been spent with my brother closest in age and his best friend. In fact, there were plenty of times growing up when it had just been me and Leo, when Benny had a game or a date, Leo would always be there to make sure I had a ride home from school or we would just sit in companionable silence doing our homework until my mom came home from work. He was always there to be an ear for me, to help me when I wasn't sure about something, and *I* had messed that all up.

"He came by the shop earlier. Got his usual," I said without thinking.

"Did he?" she asked, her tone somehow seemed like she knew more than she was letting on.

"What, Ma?"

"He came there right after he got home from the airport to get a coffee?"

"I'm sure he was tired," I said, trying to convince myself just as much as her. Why had he come straight to the shop? Did he think his mom would be there? It couldn't have been to see me.

"Of course. The long journey he had to get home," she said, though she chuckled lightly under her breath.

My stupid heart kept doing this thing where it began beating too hard against my chest. I was finally applying my lipstick after spending a ridiculous amount of time scrutinizing my make-up selection. We were about to go. The tiramisu and salad were sitting on the counter, ready to go out the back door and across our joined yards to the Lupo's kitchen. Mama had already gotten herself all dressed, and she was just doing a final sweep of the kitchen to make sure it was spotless before we went over, while I was trying not to panic up in my room.

How was I going to be normal? How could I possibly act correctly around any of them, after I sent that stupid half-naked picture of myself to Leo?

"Carmen!" my mom yelled from the bottom of the stairs.

"I know! I'm coming!" I yelled back, taking one last look at my appearance, before heading down the stairs to where she waited with the salad bowl already in her arms.

"You look very nice, sweetheart," she said approvingly as she went up on her toes to kiss my cheek. She was a few inches shorter than me, which wasn't much, considering I was a mere five foot six. The boys all seemed to tower over me as a kid, and that hadn't really changed since.

"Thanks, Ma," I said before I carefully grabbed the cake from the counter and we both stepped outside to head to Lupos'.

When we entered, the house was already loud. Leo and Benny were sitting on the sofa laughing, while Adrian, Sal, and Enzo were reenacting some bizarre incident they had witnessed at Breakers a few months back. I recognized the story from when they had reenacted it to me the following day. Some hick had decided to make a fool of himself on the billiards table and threw a fit about it when he lost, blaming everyone except himself and the three pitchers of beer he had consumed over the course of his time there.

"Maria!" Liliana said, coming to take the salad from my mom's hands and hugging her as if they hadn't just seen each other a few hours ago.

"What can I do to help?" my mom asked, taking the tiramisu from me and pushing me by the small of my back out of the kitchen to where the boys all sat. It had been that way since we were children, the moms in the kitchen, ushering the rest of us out to play together until it was ready. Although, now everything was a bit different because we weren't children anymore.

"Carmen!" Enzo said, jumping up from where he was crouched on the ground, pretending to try to fend off Adrian and Sal's relentless attacks, to come give me a squeeze. He was always the goofier of the five boys, and even though I saw him arguably more than even my own brothers, I laughed and hugged him back with gusto.

The six of us really were like siblings. There was no doubt in my mind that any one of the men in this room would defend me, and I would do the same for them.

"Hey, Enzo," I said.

"You sure look pretty tonight. Got all dressed up for Leo's big return?" Adrian teased as Enzo pulled away.

"If you think this is dressed up, none of you have seen me at my best," I said, flipping my curls over my shoulder, surprising myself with the quick, effortless quip. They all laughed.

"Your best is when you're angry and pummeling someone, Carmen. And we've all seen that," Sal said with a grin.

"Scarier now that she's been training at the gym," Adrian pointed out.

It had been Leo's suggestion a couple of years ago when I had been unable to find an appropriate outlet for my anger. Mom was finally through her cancer, but my life was still on hold. I had no plans for my future, no prospects. My life had become mundane, day in and day out, the same old thing, living in the same house, the same room I had since I was a child.

Leo had suggested I hone my fighting skills, something I hadn't worked on since the start of college, that way I could at least take out my anger on a punching bag or a sparring partner, and not explode on someone who didn't deserve it.

And then the *incident* happened. I hadn't ever told anyone what happened, quite frankly never thought I would, but between Leo's encouragement and my various needs for an outlet, it was the one point of focus I had, training my body into a fighting machine.

I hadn't stopped since.

Leo looked up at me, a little knowing smile on his lips, and I had to tear my gaze away from him before my face gave away what it did to me.

"Beer or wine?" Enzo asked, glancing at the kitchen as if wondering if he should dare intrude on our mothers' domain.

"Wine goes better with lasagna," I said, raising an eyebrow as if he should have known better. And he probably should have. He, Adrian, and Sal had family dinners with me and our moms the most often.

"Wine it is!" he said, bounding off to the kitchen and dodging swatting towels and coarse words from the moms as he tried to fill a glass with red wine for me. I moved to sit, but Adrian and Sal had already taken the two armchairs, leaving only one spot left on the couch for me to sit on, right beside Leo. It would have been too obvious if I opted for the floor since we had all battled over seats our whole lives for me to give up a spot so easily, so I moved to settle in next to him, being sure to lean heavily on the armrest. His body heat seemed to radiate into me, even though I was nearly half a foot away. I fought my body's urge to lean into him, to take on his masculine scent that seemed to permeate the air around me.

Enzo came back with my glass and the whole bottle.

"Ma told me to just take it in here, so I don't get in their way again before the table is set," he said sheepishly as I took the glass from him.

"Fine with me. After the day I had, I might just need the whole thing," I said, sipping the wine gratefully.

"What happened?" Adrian asked, taking a swallow of his own beer while Enzo settled himself in front of the fireplace.

"Nora got sick at summer camp, so Ingrid had to leave. I was alone at the shop during the extremely long rush, and it was crazy. Sold out of nearly every pastry," I said, settling into the couch a bit more.

"I hope Nora's okay," Enzo said sweetly. Everyone could tell Enzo had a thing for Ingrid. It was why he so often ended up at the shop. She didn't seem to mind the attention, but every time I tried to bring it up to her that he was flirting, she would change the subject, saying no one would be interested in a mom body who worked at a coffee shop while she transcribed medical records on the side.

"I texted Ingrid earlier. She said Nora was feeling better. I guess they put cheese on Nora's snack, even though they know she's lactose intolerant," Liliana said as she made her way into the dining room with the pan of lasagna cupped carefully between her oven mitts.

"Go wash your hands and top off your drinks," my mom said, coming up behind Liliana with the salad and a basket of bread.

We all moved at once, the boys splitting between the two bathrooms, waiting in line to wash their hands, while I took the wine bottle and my glass to sit by my spot on the table, before heading to the kitchen with the moms.

"Usual spots?" I asked them as they got their own glasses and a second bottle of wine to take to the table. I asked, even though I had already set my glass beside the spot I had at the table for nearly my whole life. The table was large and round. Liliana said that long tables were for when Salvatore was the boss, but here in their actual home, no one was the boss. They were just family.

"Of course," Mama said as she made her way to her usual place.

Liliana and Mom would always sit beside one another to chat. I usually sat beside Mama, while Enzo sat on Liliana's other side. Benny and Leo would usually select a spot next to one another, while Adrian and Sal did the same. If Salvatore ever joined us, he seemed to sit in the spot between the two sets of friends, but somehow Leo had always ended up beside me, meaning I was either the object of his and Benny's torment growing up, or a coconspirator in their games as I got older.

My stomach clenched a little as I walked over with clean hands, pulling out my chair and settling in beside Mom. We always waited until everyone was seated before filling our plates, it was tradition, so I just listened to the moms chat, taking perhaps a few more sips of wine than I normally would have before the meal began, as the boys all trailed in from washing their hands and grabbing new beers from the fridge.

Everyone settled and last to make it to his place at the table was Leo, who slipped into the chair beside me, like he always had, setting his fresh cold beer next to his plate.

"Salvatore, since you still have yet to get married or give me grandchildren, you can say grace tonight," Liliana said, her eyes narrowed toward her oldest son across the table as she reached out her hands to Mama and Enzo to clasp. Sal sighed heavily, not even bothering to argue as he reached out his own hands to take Benny's and Adrian's beside him. Mama took mine, and I hesitantly reached out my other hand to find Leo's already outstretched and waiting for it.

Immediately, electricity seemed to shoot up from where our skin connected. I tried to control my breathing, but I could feel the heat building over my skin. His hand was rough, far more calloused than it had been the last time I had touched it, but somehow that texture wasn't a deterrent. Instead of the prayer Sal was saying, I was paying attention to the warmth of Leo's fingers wrapped around mine, and the way that heat seemed to radiate from the rest of his body, encasing me in its glow.

"Amen," everyone said, and I murmured it at the end, letting my fingers slip away from Mom's and Leo's at the same time, and keeping my eyes firmly on the lasagna that Sal had begun cutting into pieces for everyone.

"So why doesn't everyone go around and tell Leo what's happened since he's been gone? I tried to keep him updated through email, but you all know how hard that can be," Liliana said as she handed Sal her plate for a slice to be placed on.

"Ma, I don't think that's necessary. I feel pretty well informed," Leo said as he put salad into his bowl, and then passed it to me.

"You may have caught up with your brothers over a beer before dinner," she started, shooting all the boys a sideways glare before continuing. "But you didn't catch up with Carmen."

"He came by the shop earlier," my mom said as she got her plate back from Sal. I paused in filling my salad bowl, cringing internally at my mother calling out my slip-up from earlier to the whole group.

"You went to the shop?" Benny asked Leo, pausing as he lifted his beer to his lips. I felt Leo stiffen beside me at the question, ignoring Benny's eyes as he passed Sal his plate for lasagna.

"I didn't get to sleep on the plane much," Leo said with a shrug, after a brief, but loaded pause.

"Well, she was probably not able to chat much, with how busy the shop was, right Carmen? Tell Leo what you've been up to," Liliana said, not looking at any of us as she filled her fork with her first mouthful.

"There's not much to say," I muttered.

"Does he know you're going to be taking those pastry chef classes soon?" Liliana pressed.

"Soon" was a bit of a stretch, since the classes didn't start until September. The program was three days a week for eighteen months straight, with only a few short breaks in that timeframe. When it had become clear that I wasn't going to be doing anything else with myself, I thought about how much I enjoyed making the baked goods for the coffee shop and thought maybe learning some additional skills would help.

And of course, Leo knew. It had been something I mentioned in my emails countless times while I tried to decide if it was the right decision. It was his encouragement that had actually been the thing to tip me over the edge and go ahead and apply. My acceptance in the program came right when he returned to the States, and I never got a chance to tell him before I ruined everything.

But now came the bigger issue. Was he going to tell them he knew I had been applying? No one else knew that I had emailed him as often as I did while he was gone. Everyone had emailed him occasionally, but even Liliana kept them to every few months, while I had sent him countless emails during his time away.

The moment seemed to stretch forever while I waited to see if he would reveal that fact to them.

"She always was good at baking," he said.

That simple sentence kept our secret while opening the table for more discussion. The tension in my body seemed to deflate slightly.

"True," Sal said with a mouth full of pasta.

"Do you remember that awful pie that the Masons brought over the day before Thanksgiving that one year?" Enzo asked, his face brightening at the memory.

"Oh Enzo! It would have been fine if you boys had just left it alone until the next day!" Mama admonished, shooting him a look while he grinned sheepishly.

"It looked like it had gotten run over before they brought it over," Adrian said. "You think they dropped it and didn't want to admit it?" he mused, rubbing his bearded chin as he considered it.

"Carmen truly saved that Thanksgiving," Benny said, making them all nod in agreement.

"She's the only reason all of you weren't horribly punished for what you did to that pie," Liliana reminded, pointing her fork at each of them.

It was one of many years that Rory and Daph came to our Thanksgiving. Their dad, Paul, was a police officer and often had to work on major holidays, and since their late mom's family lived out of state, there were many holidays they spent with us. The day before said Thanksgiving, they brought the pie that they insisted would be their contribution. It was a burned, smashed thing that did, in fact, look as if it took a tumble in the driveway.

Benny had found it in the fridge, rummaging for a snack while Mama and I had been prepping for our portions of the dinner and took it upon himself to call all the other boys over to the house to scrutinize it. They, as boys tended to do, ended up tasting it, only to find a crucial ingredient had been left out. Sugar. The pie was disgusting and looked terrible.

"I think I held my breath for that entire phone call," my mom said with a shake of her head.

"We all did," Leo agreed, turning to look down at me with a little smile on his face.

"I'll never forget it," Benny said dreamily. "'Rory, I'm so sorry. Somehow, one of the casserole dishes got placed directly on top of your pie in the fridge. We had to throw it out when the sauce spilled all over it.'" His high-pitched, slightly nasally imitation of my voice had me throwing a hard piece of bread at his face, which smacked him right in the nose, leaving a trail of garlicky oil running down his face as he laughed.

"I would have been devastated if I had been those girls. I'm sure they worked so hard to make it," Liliana scolded as the boys all laughed.

"They didn't seem too distraught," I said, remembering the relief in Rory's voice when I told her the lie. She knew how bad that pie was, but they didn't have any way to make something to replace it, and they had already promised they were bringing dessert.

"Then Little Song got right to work, baking pies for the rest of the night," Adrian said, grinning at me from the other side of the table.

"And Leo," Mama said, giving him a warm, approving smile. It looked like he could have blushed, but instead, he nodded at her, smiling down at me.

"It was supposed to be *all* of you helping her," Liliana said harshly. "Leo was just the only one that stayed. My good boy," she said affectionately, turning her gaze back to him.

"I helped for a little while!" Benny whined.

Once the boys had been discovered defacing the pie in our joined backyards and I made the phone call getting them off the hook for the dessert destruction, our moms had insisted they all help me make the replacement dessert. For about thirty minutes, they all unhappily listened to my commands and helped me get the pie crusts made, but one by one, each of them had dropped out, wandering away to find something more entertaining to do. All of them, except Leo, who stayed with me until the bitter end at the wee hour of three in the morning when the last pie finally was ready to come out of the oven.

I was exhausted the next day, but it had been worth it, for many reasons. Mostly because I had spent so many uninterrupted hours with him and when he finally left to head back to his house, he gave me the tightest hug, apologizing for all of them and hoping I wasn't too mad that I had to stay up so late.

Leo's leg pressed against mine under the table, bringing me back from the memory. My body seemed to pulse with the touch, and I couldn't help but press back gently.

"Those pies were magnificent," Sal mused, leaning back, having finished his massive slice of lasagna already.

The lasagna pan was basically scraped clean, and we sat around the table, chatting for a while, letting our dinners digest.

"You boys clear the table, and Carmen can bring out dessert," Liliana said, instructing us as she had our whole lives. We moved with practiced ease, the boys taking the dishes to the sink and getting them soaking, while I pulled the tiramisu from the refrigerator.

"What'd you make, Sis?" Benny asked, coming up beside me as I started opening the box.

"Just go over there and wait with everyone else," I said, pushing his face away while he laughed, turning to head back to the table.

I left the kitchen last, pulling the tiramisu carefully from the box and bringing it out. The delicate floral designs were still beautiful despite the trip home, and it looked mouthwatering as I placed it in the center of the round table for everyone to enjoy.

"Tiramisu!" Enzo said, rubbing his hands together with delight.

"How'd you know it was Leo's favorite?" Sal teased, but his eyes didn't stray from the cake.

"It almost looks too pretty to cut into," my mom said from beside me. Perhaps it was the wine getting to her, but it seemed like her eyes were filling with tears just looking at it.

I turned to Leo, expecting him to be staring at the cake along with everyone else, but his face was turned to me, eyes taking me in like the others were taking in the cake.

"It's beautiful, thank you," Leo said quietly, still only looking at me. I couldn't hide the blush that crept to my cheeks.

Leo did the honors, cutting slices for everyone and passing them around. Instead of more praise, the groans of approval did that job, letting me know how much everyone was enjoying it.

"I told you she had a soft spot for you. She never makes *me* anything this good," Benny said to Leo through a mouthful of creamy cake.

"Ask and you shall receive, Benito," I said with a tease.

"Can I be your taste tester when you start school?" he asked, his voice eager.

"If you ever come home from the city, maybe we'll save some for you," Mom said with narrowed eyes. He gave her a sheepish look and ducked his head back into his dessert.

"It's delicious, as usual," Leo said so quietly it was almost as if he was only talking to me. I looked over, my face heating again as his hazel eyes locked with my green ones, and for one split second, it was like the rest of the world fell away and it was just the two of us. It may have been all the wine I had consumed with dinner going to my head, but I could have sworn the look on his face was just as heated as I felt under its attention.

CHAPTER 6

LEO

We all leaned back once our pieces were demolished, stuffed full of good food and drink. It felt right having us all together. The weird feeling from earlier today in the empty house seemed more distant now that I was surrounded by everyone I held dear. The conversation was pleasant and easy, our mothers joining forces to tease and scold as they always had, but now it was getting late.

"It's past my bedtime," my mom announced, pushing her chair back from the table.

"My pillow is calling me too," Maria said, following in her friend's footsteps.

"We'll clean up the kitchen, Ma. Don't worry," Sal said, being the first to kiss our mother on the cheek before she headed up the stairs and Adrian escorted Maria back through the yard to her house.

The rest of us got to work, Benny and Enzo taking to the dishes, while Carmen and I cleared the table.

"Are we heading back to Breakers after this?" Benny asked, though he betrayed himself with a yawn as Adrian stepped back through the back door.

"I can't. I've got one more program to run tonight before I can call myself truly on vacation," Enzo said, tossing a dirty towel on the counter aggressively.

"We all know you'd get one beer in and be asleep on the bar, Benny," Sal said, watching him try to recover from the yawn that made his eyes water. "Leo? Too tired from the trip?"

I was tired, but not nearly as to the bone exhausted as I had felt so many times overseas. I had lied before when I said I hadn't slept on the plane. Learning to force yourself to sleep in strange situations was a given if you were put through what I had been for the last few years.

I shrugged, glancing at Carmen as she pulled the tablecloth away and began folding it. She was probably tired from the day she had, waking up early to open the shop and then working it all by herself. The idea of going to the bar without her seemed almost painful. Now that I had her right here with me again, I didn't want to leave her side.

"Car?" Sal asked, bringing over a wet washcloth to wipe down the table for us, while she turned to head toward the laundry room off the kitchen.

"Not me. If I show up at the gym tomorrow hungover, Ash will kill me," she said with a little shake of her head.

"Good point. Ash would, in fact, kill her if she was hung over," Adrian said as he walked back through the back door. "No mercy."

Irrational anger filled me, a white-hot flash of jealousy coursing through my veins at the idea that this *Ash* was going to have any say in Carmen staying out.

"Ash?" I asked the room at large when she disappeared into the laundry room. I was somehow managing to keep the jealousy neatly tucked away from view, even if my hands had curled into fists. First this Jeremy asshole and now some guy named Ash at the gym?

"Ash is one of our employees at the gym. Runs classes and has been giving Carmen private training," Adrian offered, which did nothing to quell the fire burning its way through me. I was imagining some hulk of a man, probably covered in tattoos and rippling muscles, hovering, maybe even pressing against her as she went through exercises.

"Okay, boys. You got the rest of this, or do I need to supervise your dishwashing skills?" Carmen asked, emerging from the laundry room with hands on her hips. The light from the kitchen hit the shirt she wore just right, the sheer fabric showing off the skin of her torso that wasn't covered with the high-waisted leggings she wore or the black bra. My eyes couldn't stop taking in the sight of her curves, or the way her hands fit against the dip of her waist above her hips. She seemed leaner than the last time I saw her, I realized, and my eyes feasted on the small sight, wanting to take in more of her form, perhaps without the shirt there to obstruct anything.

"Go on to bed, Sis. We got this," Adrian said, moving to give her a kiss on the head. His voice seemed to snap me out of the little fantasy that had started in my mind, which was for the best since it might not have gone over well if I had taken the few steps between us and pulled her against me like I wanted to.

"Night!" she called, giving a visual sweep of all of us, lingering on me for a moment, a light tinge of pink adorning her cheeks before she headed out the back door herself to go home.

"'Night!" the rest of them said back to her in unison.

Benny went back to his mom's house to sleep, which should have been a comfort to me since that meant Carmen and Maria had someone there in case Wallingford decided to do something, but it wasn't. Carmen was probably in her bed fast asleep, but as I paced my room uneasily, I couldn't hold off from the urge to text her. When I felt like this before, I would write out an email to her, even if I couldn't send it right away. Just the idea of talking to her would usually put me at ease.

[Me: I wish we could have talked alone for even just a minute today.]

I wasn't expecting a text back. It was well past midnight, and when she had left to go to bed, it had only been about 11 p.m. But a moment later, when I had finally settled myself in bed, feeling like I could stop pacing now that I had sent her that text, my phone buzzed with an incoming message.

[Carmen: I don't work tomorrow. We can talk before everyone heads to the lake house.]

My heart stuttered in my chest.

[Me: I thought you were sleeping so you'd be ready to train with Ash in the morning.]

Even texting the name of this person left a bitter taste in my mouth.

[Carmen: Couldn't sleep.]

[Me: Why?]

[Carmen: Can't seem to shut my brain off. Why are you still awake? Benny got home an hour ago.]

[Me: Same. Thinking about too much.]

I took a breath, glancing at the window I knew faced hers. Benny's room was the set of windows closer toward the front of the house, the room next to hers.

[Me: Won't Ash be mad if you're too tired?]

My jealousy was stupid and childish, but for some reason, I couldn't help myself. Jeremy was one thing. She had turned him down and he wouldn't leave it alone, but someone else? Her trainer? Someone she not only worked out with on a regular basis, but trusted?

[Carmen: Leonardo Lupo... why do you keep bringing up Ash? Are you jealous?]

For some reason that question made me jump right back out of bed, heading to my window to look out across the separation between our childhood houses to hers. We used to wave at each other as if saying goodnight.

[Me: I'm just curious.]

I looked at the window, seeing the curtains move a little.

[Carmen: Ashley is my trainer, and as hot as she is, since all she does is work out and train properly to fight, she's not really my type.]

I had to stifle the laugh that wanted to burst from me as I read her response. Of course, Ash was a girl.

[Me: Well, I feel foolish.]

[Carmen: So, you were jealous?]

The curtains parted in her window, her face peeking out from between them. I knew she could see me, my curtains were fully drawn back, and I was standing in the window looking over the short distance like I had so many times before.

[Me: Would you like it if I was?]

She turned her gaze down to read the message I sent, the phone illuminating her face so I could clearly see when she sucked that thick bottom lip between her teeth, contemplating her answer. She looked up at me for a moment, her eyes taking me in. I was only in a pair of sweatpants, so my chest was on full display.

[Carmen: Goodnight, Leo]

She sent the text, but stayed in the window, moving to kneel on her bed to close the curtains again, but in doing so, gave me a full view of her. She was only in a cropped tank top and little shorts that left nothing to the imagination. Her body, even from this distance, was somehow better than it had been when I last saw her sporting a bikini at the age of eighteen. She had filled out over the last six years, her waist small, but flaring out into lusciously wide hips, her breasts barely contained in that little crop top.

Without thinking, I called her. I had wanted to call her so many times, especially after that photo she sent me, but her rejection of my call that night had kept me from trying again.

She stopped, looking startled as she glanced down at her phone and then back up at me, before answering it, pressing the phone to her ear. She didn't say anything at first, her soft breathing the only sound coming through.

"I've been jealous a lot today," I told her, watching her chest rise and fall a little faster.

"Why's that?" she whispered.

"Because I don't want you to be with someone who won't be good to you."

"Is there someone who would be good to me, Leo?" The way my name came from her lips, whispered, but no less filled with feeling made me hungry to hear it more.

"Why did you send me that picture, Carmen?" I countered, my eyes raking over her body. She was too far away. I wanted to feel the way she would tremble with anticipation of my touch; I wanted to feel the way her breath would fan across my skin as she said my name.

A shivery sigh seemed to burst from her, her lids dropping a little as she stared over at me. I was getting hard at just this, not even really talking about anything sexual. Just looking at her, and the tension between us mounting higher and higher.

"I sent you that picture because I wanted you to see it. See me," she said, her voice breathy and hushed, but her hand splayed over her stomach, like she needed it there to help her breathe.

A groan tore from my throat, my other hand clenching at my side with the need to touch myself, but I wouldn't. Not unless she did.

"I didn't delete it," I admitted, watching her eyes flare a little.

"Why not?"

"Because I want to look at you. I wish you'd sent me one sooner, so I would have had your face to look at every day I was gone. So I didn't have to feel the hollowness that came when I thought I couldn't remember each detail of your features." Her nostrils flared; I could see the hand slip a little lower on her stomach. "If you had sent me that picture sooner, I could have better imagined the things I wanted to do with you every night I went to sleep. You're so beautiful, Carmen."

Her breath hitched, eyes wide, and her lips parted as if she were going to say something, but then she whipped her head away from the window, body turning more toward her bedroom door.

Someone else was awake. I glanced over at Benny's window and its curtains were closed, the lights still out, but that didn't mean much.

"I'm fine, Ma," she suddenly said, her voice louder than it had been when we had been talking. Relief flooded me. "Just Rory… Yes, I'll go to bed soon." She sighed heavily, her free hand flailing in the air with annoyance, which made me chuckle. "Goodnight, Mama."

When she turned back, much of the heat in her face was gone, but not completely.

"I need to get my own place," she whispered with her annoyance. I chuckled again.

"Mm… I agree," I said, my voice still dark with desire, but then a yawn betrayed me. She smiled, momentarily blinding me.

"I think I know a boy who needs to go to bed too," she whispered.

"I wish I could just come cuddle in your bed," I said, truthfully. She blinked rapidly. That chest heaving again as if my words made it hard for her to breathe.

"Go to sleep, Leonardo Lupo, before we both say more things that we'll wish we hadn't in the morning," she said it with playfulness, but her words felt like a sock in the gut. Nothing I had said to her would I ever come to regret. "For real this time. Goodnight." She hung up the phone before I could respond, but she lingered in the window for a moment, looking at me with an expression I couldn't read, before finally backing up on her bed and laying down, her bare legs still in view.

CHAPTER 7

CARMEN

Somehow, I eventually fell asleep. My heart had been pounding in my chest at the insanity of that conversation. Had he said he wanted me? He didn't say it outright, no, but he had implied it. Right?

When I did sleep the dreams were vivid. The renewed image of Leo, his tanned skin, and more muscular body had done nothing to tone down the intensity. I woke sweating, flushed, with panties ridiculously wet.

I should have been more tired, but I woke to my 6 a.m. alarm, quickly slipping into my gym clothes, before heading downstairs to fill up my water bottle. Mama was at the kitchen counter, mug in her hand, with her most recent book purchase in front of her.

"It's a bit early still for the gym," she said as I twisted the lid back on the bottle.

"I was going to run there. I feel like I need to blow off some steam." She looked up at me from the top of her glasses, those eyes far more knowing than they should have been.

"Couldn't have anything to do with staying up on the phone past midnight, could it?" she asked, her tone that familiar disapproval I had heard many times over the years.

"You know I'm an adult, right Ma? I have a college degree and everything."

"Rory needs to stop keeping you up late with her nonsense."

"Don't blame Rory, please," I said as I pulled my house key from the link, slipping it into my zippered pocket on the side of my workout leggings with my phone.

"So, you weren't talking to her last night?" she asked, her curiosity piqued.

"I'll be back in a few hours," I said, instead of answering.

"Was it a man?" she pestered, fully putting her book down to give me her undivided attention.

"Bye, Ma!" I said loudly, slipping out the back door quickly and moving around the house to the front. Normally I would stretch a little before a run, but I had to get out of sight before she followed me to the front yard and started to make a scene.

While my mother didn't often approve of my dating choices, she, like Liliana, was getting to a point where she wanted grandchildren. It was like some biological flip was switched when the first of us turned thirty. Adrian's birthday two years ago made her crazy with the need to see her legacy, and she didn't care which one of us fulfilled that first. Never mind that any woman Adrian decided to marry would be trapped in the same life she had been as a Mafia wife.

I heard the back door open and started to jog away before she could make it within earshot of me. I didn't always run to the gym, but when I did, it usually made for a great workout. I usually used the time to center my thoughts and keep myself from getting too over-whelmed with whatever I was feeling. But currently, my feelings were far too much for me to get into any sort of normal headspace.

To say nothing else about what occurred last night in the space between our bedroom windows, Leo and I changed something about our relationship. I thought I had ruined everything with that picture, but that con-versation, while we stared at each other behind panes of glass in our darkened bedrooms, that was somehow a lot more.

I made it to the gym, noticing a strange car with an Illinois license plate parked on the furthest edge of the parking lot. There were a lot of people from out of town here this week, so I wasn't terribly surprised, but it was odd that the person in the car just seemed to sit there, watching me as I crossed the lot to go into the gym. Travis, one of the Mafia members who was usually on security detail, nodded to me as I entered.

"Morning sunshine," Ash said, stepping out from around the front counter with a smirk. Her hair was a shock of blue this month. Last month it was purple. The blue matched her eyes impeccably and gave her an almost haunting look to go with her tan skin that was covered in intricate black ink almost everywhere you could see. "Didn't stay up too late last night, did you?"

I narrowed my eyes at her. Other than Rory and Daph, Ash was perhaps the only other person who was somewhat privy to my feelings about Leo. Part of that was because of the frustration I let out during my training with her.

"Does it matter?" I asked as I followed her back to the weighted bags. I tossed my phone and house key on the bench, following her along as she started the stretches that we normally did.

"I don't know. Leo being home seems to have everyone out of sorts," she said, glancing at the back office. I wasn't sure if Adrian had gone out last night, but six in the morning wasn't an unusual time for him to already be at the gym. "You can get deeper in that stretch," she snapped when her eyes moved back to me. I grunted and complied, bending lower so my hands touched the mat, legs separated and straight.

"At least you don't have to be surrounded by all of them for the next week, like I do. You just get an extended weekend," I grumbled, coming out of the stretch and moving into arm stretches.

"Being alone isn't all it's cracked up to be," Ash said quietly, grabbing the tape and handing me a roll.

I looked at the way her face seemed to contract as she said it, having forgotten she was on her own. I was so used to having essentially two families, it was hard for me to imagine having no one, like Ash. My heart twinged a little, regret for my complaints about them to her immediately making me wish I could take back what I said.

"You're welcome to come to the lake house. We have space, and we're not leaving until tomorrow afternoon, so you can follow us down," I offered. And it was true, she would be welcomed there with open arms. She shrugged, glancing over to the office where my brother emerged.

"I'll think about it," she said quietly, tearing off the tape from her left wrist so she could do her right. Her demeanor immediately changed with Adrian's presence, clearly shutting down any possibility for me to continue pushing her to join us.

"When do you head over to the shop?" Adrian asked me, having spotted us and walking over.

"Thought I'd get thirty minutes in and then I'd head over," I said as I finished my second hand and flexed my fingers.

"Leo's almost here and he said he wanted to go help Liliana close down for the week, so we'll just do a quick run and then he'll take you over," Adrian said, glancing up as the door opened.

"I was going to jog there as a cool down," I countered, stepping closer to the bag. "He can just come once you are finished."

"Carmen…" Adrian said, his tone annoyed, but I just started swinging, faster than Ash was expecting, so she scrambled to grab hold of the bag and keep it steady for me as I let loose.

"Clearly she's got something to work through here, so unless you want those fists aimed at you, keep moving," Ash said to Adrian as Leo entered the gym. I could only see him in my periphery as he came over to where Adrian stood, but I could feel his eyes on me, feel his presence in the space.

"Let's go, treadmills are on the far wall," Adrian said, patting Leo on the shoulder and tilting his head in the direction of the treadmills. Leo didn't respond, so I imagined he nodded, but I could feel his continued gaze making my core clench a little more, before it was finally gone, having walked away with Adrian.

Once they were a safe distance away, Ash let a grin stretch over her face.

"Someone kept you up last night, and I think I know who," she singsonged quietly.

"Shut up," I huffed out, raining a series of quick jabs into the bag, then landing a powerful roundhouse kick.

She did just that.

"Your form still gets sloppy at the end," Ash said as we sat, pulling the tape off our knuckles. "I want more than thirty minutes tomorrow. You can make time."

"No work tomorrow, so I have until the afternoon," I said, redoing my ponytail, since my mess of curls was trying to escape.

"Good, we're going in the ring then," she said, gesturing to the practice ring that stood a bit away from the hanging bags.

"You and me?" I asked with a smirk. Ash was a fighter. Prior to working at the gym for my brother and Sal, she had almost gone pro in women's MMA. I didn't know the story of why she stopped, especially since the few videos I had seen of her in the ring were amazing, but I certainly knew better than to ask her.

"You're just as good as I am. You just need more practice with an opponent, not just a bag."

"See you tomorrow then," I said with a smile, grabbing my things and stuffing them into my pocket.

As I walked by the front counter again, my eyes drifted to the treadmills on the other side of the gym. There they were, Adrian and Leo, running side by side and chatting as if was completely normal to be able to hold a conversation while running so fast. They were probably discussing private security work, given that's what Adrian had first jumped into when he was discharged, but of course that was before Salvatore got his claws in him.

Leo's shirt had been shed, and I got a much better idea of the tattoos I had seen adorning his torso and arms the night before. What looked like vines seemed to travel up his arms, spilling over onto his chest, though now I saw that it wasn't vines at all, but lines of sheet music.

Leo wasn't a musician of any kind. In fact, I was fairly certain he couldn't hold a tune to save his life, so whatever that song was that he had beautifully wrapped around his arm and over his heart had to be meaningful. I desperately wanted to take a closer look.

I shook myself, realizing I had been standing there staring for at least thirty seconds, before quickly heading out the door, starting my jog over to the shop that was only really the length of the parking lot away.

As I got to the back entrance, my phone buzzed in my pocket, and I pulled it out to look at it.

[Leo: You snuck out.]

I grinned.

[Me: Places to be.]

[Leo: You know I'm heading right over there. You should have just waited.]

[Me: I'm not the one wasting time. I'm already at the shop.]

I stuffed the phone back in my pocket before he could say anything in response, but as my hand grasped the handle of the back door to open it, hands descended on my shoulders, turning me around. Jeremy stood before me, his dirty-blond hair a bit disheveled, blue eyes shifting from a menacing glare to wide and innocent, as if I wouldn't notice the malice that had been there moments before.

"Did you get my letter?" Jeremy asked, his voice coming out rushed and frustrated.

"What letter?" I snapped, shoving him roughly away from me so his hands fell away, but there was no relief with him so close to me.

"I left it yesterday, on your porch," he insisted, stepping forward again.

"I didn't see a letter. But I've been clear, Jeremy. I'm not interested in being with you. Please just stop," I said, glancing down the alley and hoping someone, anyone, would be coming down it soon.

"Carmen, you know we have this chemistry. You can't deny it," he said, his hand reaching out to touch my hip. I tried to back away but just ended up with my back pressed to the door, the pressure in his fingers only getting tighter. "And if you keep this up, I'll assume you want me to chase you harder. Maybe need a strong man to make you understand? Hm?" His other hand came up to touch the column of my throat, caressing it, while the fingers at my hip pressed into my skin roughly. "Do you need to be tied down? Do I need to start dominating you before you understand you and I are supposed to be together?"

Bile rose in my throat, one hand curling into a fist as the other gripped the door handle.

"Jeremy, if you don't take your hands off me, you'll regret it," I hissed.

"Oh, Carmen. I'll have you no matter what. My brother is going to make sure you're nice and available to me. I was just hoping you'd choose me first," Jeremy said, his face twisting with a sick grin.

I wasn't sure what he meant by that comment about his brother. I didn't even know he had one, but it didn't matter when he essentially said he planned on raping me if I didn't give myself over to him. I was preparing to hit him, my fingers curling into fists, muscles bunching in preparation for the strike I was planning on taking, when the rumble of an engine came close to the mouth of the alley, and the weasel moved a step back, his hand thankfully dropping away.

Without a second to lose, I twisted the knob, backing into the shop and slamming the door. I braced myself against it, looking through the peephole and watching as Jeremy looked torn for a second, fuming at the now closed door, as well as glancing down the alley at whoever parked there. Apparently, the fact that there was a door between us, and the alley was no longer empty, was enough to deter him for now, since he let out an irritated grunt and turned, heading back to wherever he parked his car.

Once he was out of sight, I turned around and headed toward the kitchen. I wasn't dressed for helping guests and I knew Liliana was out at the front handling that business, so I went to work moving things for longer-term storage. The back door opened after about ten minutes and Leo stood by the door, the muscles in his shoulders tense as he took a few deep breaths.

When he turned to see me holding the box of whole coffee beans I was moving to the freezer, he seemed to almost ripple, a fresh wave of tension filling his form as his burning eyes looked me over.

"Your brothers told me what happened," he said, his voice holding a bit of a growl. Ah, so he must have seen some of the interaction between me and Jeremy.

"I see," I murmured, watching him with interest.

I had seen Leo mad before. There were plenty of times growing up that I bore witness to that, but it was somehow different in this moment. I could see him holding himself back, but also the difference in him, his physique, the beast behind his eyes that could only come from having seen and done things that normal people could only imagine. He was deadly now, and something about my interaction with Jeremy had awak-ened his desire to kill. If only he knew the nature of the conversation, I bet Jeremy wouldn't be able to stand right now.

"Did he talk to you?" he demanded, taking a step forward.

"He did," I said stiffly, walking away toward the freezer. I didn't hear his footsteps, but I felt it when he moved behind me, following me into the freezer.

"Did he touch you?" His voice was rough, like he was holding himself back by the skin of his teeth.

"He tried. I'm fine, Leo. If he tries something again, he'll get a broken nose out of it," I told him, turning around once I set the box down and finding us almost chest to chest. "It's not your concern. If I really wanted to, I'd get Adrian to take care of him. Just leave it alone."

"Not my concern?" he asked, narrowing his eyes. "Maybe I wasn't clear last night, but I don't want you with anyone who doesn't deserve you, Carmen. *He* is definitely on the list of undeserving." Suddenly, despite how close we were and how much my body was burning for him to touch me with those hands, the idea that *anyone,* that any *man,* felt that they had a say in who I should or shouldn't be with ignited rage within me.

"And who then, Leonardo *Salvatore* Lupo, is on that list, hm?" I asked, poking a finger on his chest. "You and my brothers want to give me a list with who I'm *allowed* to date?"

His eyes flashed with something other than fury, pupils dilating and nostrils flaring. The cold air of the freezer at my back and the ridiculous heat coming from him at my front, coupled with that gleam in his eye, made my whole body explode with desire. Deep-seated and primal.

"Carmen *Valeria* LaMartina, don't test me," he growled, stepping closer so our chests really did touch.

"You can make demands, but I can't get an answer to my question?" I asked, but the strength of my tone was faltering now.

"Do you really want me to answer that question, Little Song?" he asked, his voice husky as his head dipped lower, our breath visibly mingling in the cold freezer air.

The moment seemed to last forever. We looked into each other's eyes, the desire for one another palpable in the air. My chest was pressed firmly against his, and he could certainly feel my hardened nipples against his abs. His hands came up, fingers lightly tracing down my arm, making me tremble at the contact. His head dipped lower, as my chin tilted up, our lips only a breath apart now. It would take nothing to close the distance between us.

"Carmen? Don't forget to put the dough for the sweet rolls in the freezer," Liliana called from the front of the kitchen. Suddenly the ice-cold air felt like it. We both became aware of where we were and that we weren't truly alone, stepping away from one another.

"I won't! Leo's here to help me," I called back, watching the little smirk form on his face.

"Oh, good!" she said, before the sound of her pushing back through the door to the front of the shop.

We stood there, several steps apart for a beat before I moved to walk past him. He grabbed my wrist as I passed, pulling me back to his chest and dipping his head so his mouth was to my ear.

"You think about that question and let me know," he whispered, making my whole body tremble.

Thankfully, Ingrid came in as I pulled myself away from him again, little Nora in tow, and we all worked diligently for the next several hours to get the shop set for the long closure. Liliana had Leo head home to get the meat she was making for dinner marinating and the salad made at about eleven, Ingrid left with Nora shortly after for lunch, leaving me and Liliana to finish closing.

The air seemed to grow lighter when Leo was finally gone. I could feel his eyes on me all day, not that my eyes strayed far, what with the way his shirt and joggers hugged his muscles. Despite the tension, we managed to converse with everyone easily, if not falling back into the old teasing that we used to do when we were teenagers. But now that the tension was gone, I felt like I could fully breathe again, going about the close-up with practiced ease.

"I'm so glad Leo's home. Aren't you, Carmen?" Liliana asked as she finished reconciling the register. I paused my mopping of the floor to glance over at her. Her eyes were on me, a little gleam in them.

"Of course," I murmured, continuing to mop and keeping my head firmly aimed at the tiles beneath my feet, though her chuckle was not lost on me.

CHAPTER 8

CARMEN

Liliana gave me a ride home. It was a little after one and Benny was sitting on the couch watching some action movie when I walked in.

"Hey, Sis," he said as I passed, heading to grab some water from the kitchen.

"Benny. I see you're making yourself at home," I said as I reentered the living room, pointedly staring at his socked feet on the coffee table.

"This *is* my home, Carmen," he grumbled, though he slid his feet off the table immediately, patting the cushion beside him. I joined him, sitting in silence for a minute and watching the characters on the screen somehow emerge from a car crash with minimal damage and start running after the bad guys.

"So unrealistic. That guy, the one who was in the passenger seat? He would have at the very least dislocated his shoulder or gotten a concussion. No way he'd be *running* after that," Benny said, scoffing. I smiled.

"You would know, wouldn't you?"

"It's either old people, workmen's comp, or personal injury cases that I see, so yeah. I would probably be someone who would know," he said, nudging my arm with his elbow playfully. The silence resumed as more action followed, the main characters coming out of a shootout with whoever was after them equally unrealistic.

"Leo came to the shop yesterday, huh?" Benny asked, after both of us groaned when the lead didn't reload a gun that should have been empty twice over. Clearly, Benny had been thinking about that little slip of Mom's since it was revealed at dinner. I glanced at him, his face was still turned to the screen, the features similar to mine, but much more angular and masculine. His eyes were green too, but darker, whereas Adrian's eyes were blue.

"He did," I said slowly.

"Is there…" He trailed off like he was unsure what or how to ask the question on the tip of his tongue. "I know he cares about you. More than a friend. I used to tease you about having a crush on him, but I stopped when I realized I was kind of teasing him too."

I sat still as a statue, not sure how to respond to this. Benny was a big reason why I didn't think anything could happen between me and Leo. The kind of friendship they had shouldn't be squandered over my stupid feelings.

"We've talked some over the years," I admitted, keeping my eyes on the television without really seeing it.

"I figured."

We sat in silence for a few moments, me not completely sure what Benny meant by anything he was saying. He didn't seem angry or even upset, but there was something still hanging in the air there.

"I'm not mad at either of you. I just want you to be happy, Sis," he finally said, making me turn to look over at him.

"Benny, I don't even know if there's something there for you to be mad about. We haven't even kissed," I said, my voice an awkward chuckle. But he was looking at me with such an expression of sadness.

"I'm sorry you had to give everything up. I don't want you to have to do that again." I knew both of my brothers felt bad I took on the brunt of Mom's care when she got sick, giving up my job and moving back in with her. They didn't always bring it up, knowing the reminder of my setback was painful for me, but they tried to tell me how sorry they were for it often enough that I knew it wasn't just words.

"Me either, but it was worth it," I whispered, scooting closer to let him envelop me in his strong embrace. He smelled like him and home, and I breathed it in happily.

Our two families ate dinner separately, of which I was thankful. Not that I didn't want to see Leo, I definitely did, but it was more that with Benny's little confession to knowing *something* was going on between us, and the odd comments and looks both the moms had given me the last few days was enough to make me a strange ball of nerves.

It also didn't help that there was a promise in Leo's voice when he whispered in my ear earlier this morning. A promise that I wanted him to keep.

I was finishing up a post-dinner shower, having put mine off to sit and watch the end of the movie with Benny, then helping mom with dinner, when several texts came through on my phone charging at my bedside table.

[Enzo: Drinks at Breakers!]

[Benny: Yes!]

[Leo: I don't know if I can keep up with you guys anymore.]

[Sal: Oh, you're coming, Leo. We didn't get our welcome home drink fest last night.]

[Adrian: Free drinks for the newly free man.]

[Leo: Let me change.]

[Benny: Carmen?]

[Enzo: Carmen you have to come.]

I stared at the thread. I had no real reason not to go. I planned on going to train with Ash the next day, but it didn't have to be too early. I could manage to have a few drinks with the boys and still make it home in time to get enough sleep.

[Adrian: Ash won't give you any shit. I'll make sure of it.]

[Sal: You know he can't promise that, but we want you to come anyway. It's not right if it's not all 6 of us.]

I laughed at that. Ash *would* give me shit no matter what, but it felt so good to be included. It wasn't just the boys; I was one of them too.

[Carmen: Just showered. Give me 15 to get ready.]

I hastily got myself together, throwing on minimal makeup, happy I didn't wash my hair, so all I had to do was throw a little extra hairspray in there and select an outfit. I stood at my closet in my bra and panties, contemplating, when another text came through.

[Leo: You didn't close your curtains.]

My head immediately snapped up to look at the window where he stood. He was dressed, but even from this distance, his eyes burned with hunger. At first, I felt shocked, but who could blame me? The last six years, he wasn't home, and I didn't have to worry about anyone seeing me naked as I moved around my room. But then the hunger in his eyes seemed to ignite my own. A strange rush of confidence came over me as I stood there in nothing but the black lace bra I had been wearing when I snapped that picture, and the matching set of boy short panties that left little to the imagination.

I crawled up on my bed, smirking a little and taking my time to close the curtains. A little shiver of delight ran through me in the way I saw his chest heave at the sight.

[Me: See you in a few minutes.]

And then I knew exactly what I was going to wear.

Breakers was full. So full we had to squeeze through the crowd of unruly people single file, before getting to the bar. Enzo snagged us all fresh beers, and we made our way to the only table that was left in the corner of the room. It was a tiny high top, all the stools had been dragged away by other patrons, so we were left standing by it, huddled around so we could hear each other over the loud music.

I didn't usually go to Breakers. Rory, Daph, and I chose to go out to a bar and restaurant that had better food, and very rarely we'd indulge ourselves at a dance club. Breakers was more of a sports bar, with a billiards table and darts, while most of the walls were lined with sports and celebrity memorabilia and huge flatscreen televisions to show off all the various games that the patrons could possibly want to watch.

I sipped my beer, wedged near the corner between Benny and Leo. It wasn't on purpose, but the way Leo's shoulder was propped behind me made it incredibly easy for him to wrap his arm around my waist without seeming to be anything more than saving space for the others. The skintight jeans and my silky tank top gave him access to the skin on my side easily, but he hadn't taken advantage of that fact just yet.

"Anything crazy you boys are thinking up for the Fourth?" I asked, yelling over the music.

"Only the best fireworks show you've ever witnessed," Enzo boasted, giving Benny a high five. Somehow the two of them had become the pyromaniacs of our group, always coming up with crazy displays and dangerous schemes to delight and sometimes horrify us. One year Benny lost his eyebrows for several months, but he claimed the whole time it was worth it.

"Have you already gotten them?" Sal asked, a knowing smile on his face. Benny had been in the city, and Enzo had been so busy with whatever newest thing his father had been having him work on, that neither of them had started gathering the supplies, never mind planned a display.

"We always come through. We know what we're doing," Benny insisted.

"Of course you do," I teased, feeling a squeeze on my waist from Leo's hand as he chuckled into the mouth of his beer bottle.

"So, you're a lightweight now, huh, little brother?" Sal teased, referencing the text thread from earlier in the evening.

"Didn't have so many chances to get drunk overseas," Leo said with a shrug. "Though give me a few days and I'm sure I can drink you under the table, old man."

We all laughed at that. Though Sal gave a playfully sour face, he was the oldest of all of us, having turned thirty just a few months previously. Adrian wasn't far behind, only a year younger.

"Still haven't found that old lady that Ma keeps yelling at you about," Enzo said with a chuckle.

"Just you all wait. I turned thirty and suddenly I was being hounded," Sal grumbled, sighing at his empty beer.

"I'm already getting it too, Sal. Don't you worry," I said, tilting my own almost empty drink toward him before downing the rest.

"Ma's already on you to have kids?" Adrian asked, horrified.

"She's on me to find a *man.* I assume her reasoning is the grandchildren. She keeps telling me she had you when she was twenty-two, so clearly there was something horribly wrong that I have yet to find 'the one,'" I said, feeling that hand tighten a bit more on my waist.

"If that's not a sick double standard, I don't know what is," Benny grumbled, glaring at his empty beer. I grinned at my brother's assessment, knocking my glass into his, which was also empty.

"We need more beer!" Enzo announced, now that those of us who had any left were down to dregs.

"And maybe a shot," Adrian said with a slightly pained look on his face. Apparently, the fact that his little sister was being pressured to find a man, when he didn't even like the idea of her dating, was enough to have him needing something a little stronger.

"Come on, we'll get beers and shots," Sal said, putting an arm over Adrian's shoulder and pulling him toward the bar.

My phone buzzed in my pocket, which happened to be right next to where Leo's hand was resting. I went to pull it out, but his hand slipped from my waist, fingers curling around mine for a brief moment before resuming their place on my hip, but this time the tip of his fingers seemed to press a little deeper, slipping under my shirt and into the top of my jeans, but just the tiniest amount.

I was glad the bar was so dark, otherwise Benny and Enzo, who were discussing the bizarre sports poster behind Enzo's head, might have been able to see the way my cheeks flushed a bit and my eyes darkened.

Grabbing the phone, I pulled it out. It was a text from Rory.

[Rory: I know you're all busy with Leo being home. But stalker was sighted at the wine dive. I think he's looking for you.]

"Stalker" had to be in reference to Jeremy. Rory had asked me to come out with her and Daph shortly after the boys decided we needed to go out together. I would have invited the twins to come along, but we had never done anything like this, just the six of us. Without Leo? Sure. While he was gone, we got drinks together, but one of us was always missing when he came home. I didn't want to squander the opportunity, even if I felt guilty for leaving the two of them out.

[Daph: And he's got some other dude with him. Hot, but I wouldn't associate with anyone who hangs with that creep.]

[Me: Ugh! Why won't he just stop? We're at Breakers, so just let me know if they leave. You two are the best.]

[Rory: Oh, we know, girl.]

[Daph: I can't wait to find out if your dashing soldier makes a move on you finally. Maybe with a few drinks in both of you, one of you will just go for it.]

[Me: My brothers are here.]

Both of them sent me a series of laughing emojis.

"Jesus, those drinks are taking long enough. I'm going to pee, and I bet they still won't be back yet," Benny said, moving Enzo with a playful shove, so he could get out of the corner of the table with me and Leo.

"Enzo!" came Sal's voice over the crowd. He flagged him over, presumably to help with all the drinks. Six beers and six shots were too much for so few hands. Enzo moved through without hesitation to the bar, leaving me and Leo wedged in our corner alone.

"That's why you went on so many dates?" Leo asked after a moment, having ducked his head down to talk directly in my ear. The combination of his deep voice, his hot breath fanning over my ear and neck, and the way his hand at my waist started moving, gently caressing my skin just under the waistband, had my blood pumping, heat pooling.

"Yes," I breathed, sure he could only hear me barely over the sounds around us. I wanted to pull him closer, to press myself to him, to feel more than just the side of his body. I wanted him to completely encase me in that blissful heat that was coming off of him. Almost as if he could read my mind, the leg that was positioned slightly behind me moved closer, letting the full length of his side and leg press into my back and ass.

"But no more dates since Wallingford, huh?"

"I didn't want to go on them anyway," I murmured, wishing so desperately I had a beer to take a drink of, anything to keep me from reaching my hand down to pull him closer. To feel if the proximity was doing to him what it was doing to me.

He grunted, pulling his hand from my waist, but not pulling away from my body as the others returned. Apparently, they caught Benny on his way out of the bathroom, since he also had a handful of drinks. Setting them on the table, they dispersed them, all of us happily taking a drink from our fresh beers.

"This is the first time we're all together getting drinks legally as adults," Adrian said, making us all laugh. "Hopefully it's the first of many," he said, raising his whiskey shot and prompting us all to do the same.

"Salute!" we all said in unison, downing our whiskey and slamming our upturned glasses on the table.

"Weird to think the last time we went out together was when Carmen was still in college," Benny said, with a bemused look on his face. "Poor Car couldn't come home because she had some big exam to cram for or something, isn't that right?"

That was about four years ago. All the boys made it home to see Leo, but something happened to me that week that had me reeling and in a dark place. I couldn't face any of them, let alone Leo, and had pretended I had a test I needed to cram for instead.

"She missed a good time," Enzo said with a wiggle of his eyebrows. "We took Leo to a strip club."

White hot jealousy suddenly licked through my body. I knew he hadn't been celibate during the last six years, but somehow the fact that he went to a strip club, watching naked women prance around on stage, really felt like a sock to the gut.

"He did not like it, did you, Leo?" Benny asked, making them all laugh. I wasn't sure if that was a joke or not, but I chugged the beer in front of me, not really caring how it looked to the rest of them. The only one who seemed to notice was Leo, whose hand found my waist once more, fingers gripping a little harder than they had been as his side pressed more firmly against me.

"We have to do this more often, now that you're home. Feels right having us all together," Sal said, bringing seriousness back to the conversation.

"As long as you're not dragging us to strip clubs, yes," Leo said from behind me. Somehow that made me feel marginally better, but my mind was now going down a strange path, seeing all the years that Leo had been gone and all the potential women he had in his life over that time. Was there a fellow soldier he had feelings for? Or some girl from one of the countries he had visited that he still thought about?

"I've got to use the restroom," I said, pushing Leo away from me enough to squeeze through.

I moved through the crowd, finding myself in the line to the ladies' room. I could have made my way to the back where the employee bathroom was. I wasn't an employee, obviously, but my association with the Lupos came with some perks that I only used in desperate situations. There was only one woman ahead of me, so it wouldn't be a terribly long wait before I could have a moment to myself and push these raging feelings back down where they belonged.

The woman ahead of me slipped in the door once the person who had been occupying it came out. As I was about to take a step closer, it snapped closed again, and I felt a hand wrap around my arm above my elbow, steering me away from the line, toward the back. I looked up to see Leo, face unreadable, but grip so firm on me I didn't even try fighting it. I didn't really want to fight it.

We got to the deserted employee hallway, the two bathrooms sitting opposite each other and empty. He pulled me in front of him, looking down at me, still holding onto my arm, when he started backing me into the bathroom, closing the door with his foot once we were both inside.

"What are you doing?" I breathed as I backed into the sink. He stalked forward, his hand going to my throat and tilting my chin up toward his face.

"Are you jealous?" he asked, his voice amused but still rumbling.

"Are you?" I countered, watching his hazel eyes flash.

"Yes," he said without hesitation, his other hand moving to touch my hip, the one that Jeremy had grasped earlier today. His eyes flashed down to the

spot where Jeremy had left little bruises from his fingers gripping me hard. "He did touch you today. Didn't he?"

"It was nothing," I whispered as his fingers ghosted over the marks he could see now that we were so close and in the bright fluorescent light of the bathroom.

"Nothing?" he asked, his eyes flashing back to mine, pushing me more into the counter as his hand slipped under my shirt, large fingers fanning out over my stomach like I had imagined so many times in my fantasies.

"Leo," I let out in a whimper.

That was apparently all it took for the thin shred of control he had to snap. His mouth descended on mine, lips moving ravenously. I could taste him and the booze on his lips and it just made me more hungry for him. My fingers moved to the nape of his neck, lacing through his hair to pull him closer, his body responding immediately, pressing himself against me and pinning me to the sink.

I wasn't sure if this was him letting himself go because of the booze coursing through us, the obvious attraction to each other finally being released, or if the way he was kissing me meant more, but either way, I couldn't stop once I'd started. My hips pulsed forward, feeling the growing hardness, and a moan escaped my throat as his tongue pressed into my mouth.

Our mouths moved fluidly. The only pauses were to take in a breath or nip at each other's lips. His hands were gripping my thighs, his body pressed between them, like he was made to be there.

But a brisk knock on the door brought us back to our senses. He pulled away from me, chest heaving as he looked at me with burning eyes.

"I'll just be another minute," I said quietly as another knock sounded.

"Carmen…" He looked like he wanted to say something, but his eyes darted around the dingy bathroom and fell back on me. "Later," he said, before turning and leaving the bathroom. No other knock sounded, so I presumed he got whoever it was to leave me alone.

I tried to cool myself down, peeing, as I had intended to do, and staring at myself in the mirror for a long moment while I tried to make sense of what had just happened.

Did we just kiss?

It had to be the booze. He wouldn't have done that if he was used to drinking. And if that's what the consequence was, I wasn't sure if I could handle the heartbreak of his regrets later. There wouldn't be a later. I needed to get home.

I made my way out to the crowd once again, pushing back to our table, where the men were preparing for another round.

"I'm going to head home. I wanted to spar with Ash tomorrow," I said loudly in Adrian's ear.

"You sure? She won't mind you missing if you stay out with us," he said, looping his arm over my shoulder and squeezing me into him. I was sure I smelled like Leo, but I hoped he wouldn't notice.

"I'm sure," I said, keeping my eyes firmly away from Leo's gaze.

"I'm walking you to your car at least," Adrian said, taking a swig of his beer, before pulling us away from the table, leading me out of the throng of people and the table of men who hollered their goodbyes and good nights to me as we pushed through the crowd to the front door.

CHAPTER 9

LEO

I watched Carmen leave with Adrian, every part of me wanting to go with her, to be the one to walk her to her car, or maybe go home with her, so we could talk and maybe more, but I couldn't. What had I been thinking taking her into that bathroom? Carmen wasn't some fling. She wasn't sating a bodily function. She was the reason I felt this way in the first place. The air I wanted to breathe. Our first kiss was in the disgusting bathroom at a bar the Mafia owned. And I hated myself for it.

"You two have been looking rather cozy tonight," Sal murmured when Carmen was finally out the door and out of my line of sight.

"I don't know what you mean," I said, taking another sip of my beer.

"You were practically on top of her back in your corner there. You sure there's not something going on there?" Sal continued, a grin spreading over his face as he watched me squirm uncomfortably, glancing over to Benny, who seemed enthralled by a FMMA highlights reel playing on one of the televisions over the bar.

I shook my head at Sal, giving him a warning glare, before Adrian made his way back to the table, settling in between Sal and Enzo once more and taking up his beer.

"I feel bad for whoever ends up with my sister. She's so damn stubborn," he grumbled.

"Didn't like you walking her to the car?" Benny asked with a grin, seeming to snap out of his trance at Adrian's reappearance.

"No, she was pretty insistent I was being ridiculous, but I didn't leave until she was pulling away." I grinned at that. Sounded about right. Feisty might as well have been her middle name, although with a middle name like Valeria, which meant "vigorous and strong" I suppose it was close enough.

We settled into a comfortable silence for a moment, letting the sounds of the bar around us take over. It wasn't bad without Carmen, just didn't feel quite right. Kind of like the night a few years ago that they mentioned before, when we went to the strip club. Nothing felt right that trip home. Carmen's bedroom was dark and desolate at night and she couldn't come home for even one night because of her classes. I didn't remember what held me back, why I didn't just go to her myself. Twenty minutes and I could have been on her campus, seeing her pretty face, all flustered and irritated that I went out of my way for her.

I would remedy that. There was no such thing as going out of my way, or any task that was too inconvenient or burdensome when it came to her.

"I don't know if Mom told you, but the lake house is ready and we're all going to head up there tomorrow," Sal said loudly, as a chorus of happy yells took over the bar in response to whatever game was playing on one of the screens that had most of their focus.

Mom hadn't mentioned it, but I assumed that's what we'd be doing. We went every year for the Fourth growing up, often spending weeks of our summer playing in the lake and getting into trouble, unless it was bad weather or Dad was entertaining "guests" there.

The house was huge, so it wasn't a surprise that he liked to bring potential partners there. It was far more secluded than our house, and it was decorated far more lavishly to show off the wealth that the Mafia had to offer.

"Dad said he'd be coming for the Fourth this time," Enzo chimed in, looking as unhappy about that as I felt.

I didn't want to see our father. I had managed to avoid him on most of my trips home, and even though I knew being back meant I'd have to deal with him eventually, I had hoped he would stay away for the Fourth as he usually did.

"I guess I should have some idea of what I'll be doing for a job before he starts thinking he can use me," I said bitterly, glancing at Adrian, who gave me a pitying look. He knew intimately the situation I was in, having just been in the same situation himself not long ago.

We were silent for a bit, letting the sounds of the bar take over while we all felt the pit in our stomachs that Salvatore Lupo brought out in all of us, when Adrian stiffened across from me, straightening himself and glaring across the room. The rest of us turned, eyes easily finding what had made Adrian go on full alert.

Jeremy Wallingford was in Breakers and right beside him was Freddy O'Shea. The Irish mob had dwindled out of the Kansas City area, never really making a true resurgence for almost a century. They had much more influence in other larger cities, like Boston and Chicago, but from what Sal had told me, they were making moves to have a bigger foothold here once again, which made the big boss, and subsequently all his underlings anxious.

Freddy O'Shea was well known as the son of the Irish Boss in Chicago. He had been at my last mission, one that failed miserably. Not only did I lose friends and teammates, but all those girls he was planning on trafficking … we lost all of them too.

I had seen my fair share of death and loss over the last six years, enough that even though it had only been a few months since it happened, I could compartmentalize the pain of losing John and Logan away. Somehow, seeing O'Shea here, on my home turf, had the anger surging to the surface. My stomach balled into a knot, nausea and rage filling me as I looked at his smug face.

Why was he here, in Lee's Summit of all places? Why was he so close to my home?

"What is *he* doing here?" Sal said, his voice barely above a growl.

"And why is Wallingford talking to him?" Benny asked, his fist clenched like he was holding himself back from starting a fight. I glanced to O'Shea's left, where Wallingford stood, looking smug as he glanced at the crowd. My immediate reaction was wanting to cave his face in with my fist. I'm sure the crunch of the bones in his face would be extremely satisfying, especially since I got a little glimpse of the light bruises he had left on Carmen earlier that day.

"I have to text Dad," Sal grumbled, taking out his phone and shooting a quick text to our father, who would undoubtedly have something to say about a rival being in the same suburb where his family was stowed safely.

Lee's Summit had become a safe zone, a place the other gangs and mobs didn't dare trespass, which was why our father had chosen to keep us here, instead of with him in the city. It meant less protection detail for us as we grew up, and more opportunities for him to spread his wealth and make sure his more illegal businesses remained appearing clean.

O'Shea seemed to sense our eyes on him and he smirked, tilting his head up as a greeting, but continuing to chat with Jeremy, who I was quickly learning to despise. It wasn't just that he was stalking Carmen; now he was in league with an enemy, someone dangerous who could create havoc on our little slice of peace.

Before any of us could move, the two of them began making their way over to our corner. Jeremy seemed to have a strange sense of calm about him, which he certainly shouldn't have had when approaching Carmen's brothers. Not if he knew what was good for him, at least.

"Ah, the Lupo and LaMartina boys. You all have quite the reputation and here you are, out together. How fun," Freddy said when they finally made it through the thick crowd of people to our table in the corner.

My eyes glanced around at the people in the room, immediately taking notice of six guards positioned at various points of the bar, all keeping an eye on their boss, making sure he was safe. I could have easily still killed this fucker if I wanted to, but it would put the whole bar in chaos, potentially killing innocent people.

"What are you doing here, O'Shea?" Sal asked, eyes narrowed.

"Oh, just chatting with my friend here," he said, looping an arm over Jeremy's shoulder. "He had some *very* interesting things to say about what's been going on in this little suburb."

We all stayed still and quiet, bodies tense and on alert.

"How interesting that your father seems to own so much property around here. He's got businesses out the ass so far away from Kansas City, where I was certain he was permanently located. Even that cute little coffee shop down the street is his, isn't it?" he continued when none of us said anything.

My gaze went to Jeremy, who I now recognized a bit better from the past. He had been on the football team, classically handsome, but nothing to write home about, and he gave off an arrogant air. But the mention of Mom's coffee shop made my spine rigid. The connections were too apparent. Jeremy, Carmen's stalker, was with him, and he mentioned where she worked. Had he seen something in our few interactions and knew she would be a good way to get back at me?

"Lee's Summit is off limits to you," Adrian said with a glower that could have burned a hole through someone if he stared long enough.

"We'll see," O'Shea said with a smirk. "I have some business here, myself. So I'd say it's not off-limits to *me*, at least not right now. Come on Jeremy, we've taken up enough of their time tonight, don't you think? And especially now that the most interesting member of their group has headed home." My body tensed visibly at the overt mention of Carmen. There was no one else he could have been mistakenly talking about.

And with that, they turned and left the bar, the security coming behind them, slithering through the crowd like ghosts.

"I'm going to tail them," Sal said, glancing at Adrian, who nodded, the two of them slipping out of the crowd as well. Enzo had his phone out, immediately tracking O'Shea's movements through our little suburb and putting together how long he had been here and perhaps why, while Benny and I stared.

"Let's head home," Benny murmured, finishing off his beer. Those words were exactly what I wanted to hear, since there was no way in hell I wanted to be farther than one house away from Carmen when I knew something was in the works and she was somehow a target. It was just too coincidental that O'Shea seemed to mention her with Wallingford with him. And if there was anything I learned from being the son of a man in the Mafia, there were no true coincidences.

Benny parked in the driveway, and I headed back over to my house, crossing through the front yard as I had so many times before to go to my front door. My mom was probably long in bed, seeing as how it was now past midnight and my brothers each had their own places to stay, though I imagined Sal and Adrian would be long from calling it a night, and Enzo probably headed back up to the offices at Breakers to work on tracing O'Shea's movements.

Carmen's light was off, but I could see a faint glow in the room, like she was on her phone.

[Me: Not asleep yet?]

There was nothing for a moment as I stripped out of my shirt and jeans, pulled on some sweatpants, and sat at the end of my bed. Perhaps she was asleep, and I was just hoping she'd be awake. I wasn't sure why I couldn't just leave her alone for the night. Perhaps it was the fact that there was now a very real threat hovering in the air, the exact nature of which we had no way of knowing. Or maybe it was that I just simply longed for her. If I had done what my heart wanted me to, I wouldn't have been in that bar at all during the confrontation with O'Shea, I would have been back here with her.

[Carmen: Daph called. But your text rescued me, so thank you.]

[Me: Rescued you? From your best friend?]

I grinned. Rory and Daph had a tendency to take over a conversation and let it go on forever. Carmen had always had a hard time getting off the phone with them when we were growing up.

[Carmen: You know what I mean.]

[Me: I'm sorry about earlier.]

Sorry our first kiss was in that filthy place. Sorry I hadn't done it sooner. Sorry for so, so many reasons. But she didn't seem to take it that way.

[Carmen: You don't have to worry. I know it was just the booze, Leo. You don't have to apologize.]

[Me: Oh, I'm not sorry I kissed you, Little Song. I'm just sorry it happened in the shithole my father owns. Next time will be better.]

The little dots indicating she was typing came and disappeared several times. It seemed like she had been talking to Rory and Daph, probably about the kiss, and managed to convince herself it was just what she said before, the booze. But now she was struggling a little with the idea that I wanted to do that again, perhaps in a better setting. I grinned.

[Carmen: Goodnight, Leo.]

[Me: Goodnight.]

But there was nothing particularly good about the night with her a whole house away and me hard in my childhood bed just thinking about the way her body felt against mine, the scent of her as her legs spread a little, the taste of her on my tongue. I glanced out the window, imagining her in her room. Maybe she spread her legs, thinking of our kiss, thinking of the way I pressed against her. She no doubt could feel how hard she made me almost immediately.

I pushed my sweats down, letting my cock spring free, precum already beading at the top, just from thinking about kissing and rubbing against her in that bathroom. I squeezed the head of my cock, gathering it in my palm, before I began stroking long and slow. As I had so many times over these years, I jerked myself to the thought of Carmen LaMartina, only this time I could still taste her mouth against mine, and the scent of her hair still lingered against my neck and shoulder.

CHAPTER 10
CARMEN

I decided to run to the gym again. I slept wonderfully last night, but only after getting myself off to the thought of how things could have gone in that bathroom. And from the sound of Leo's text message last night, he was planning on doing it again. Just the thought made me so wet that all I had to do was barely touch my clit and I was biting my tongue to keep myself from crying out and waking my mother or alerting my brother who came home not long before.

Mom and Benny were still asleep when I came down, stashing my phone and key in my pocket like usual and heading out of the house and down the familiar path to the gym. I slowed at a red light, lightly jogging in place as I waited for it to change when I noticed a strange car. I had caught of glimpse of it in my periphery a few blocks back, but didn't think much of it. The streets were all pretty bare because of the holiday and the early hour, but there was always someone up, getting into things, even this early. I happened to be one of those people on a regular basis.

But the way it crawled to a stop beside me made me feel uneasy. I risked a glance at the front seat. There were two men in the car. One was blatantly staring at me, his blond hair shaggy in his brutish face. There was a scar that ran down the length of his cheek, and his eyes were menacing as he took me in. The other was more decent looking, sitting in the passenger seat and clearly looking at me every moment or so, but his expression was more of mild interest than whatever hateful expression his car-mate was giving me.

The light turned green, and I sprinted across the street, picking up my pace. I knew the gym wasn't too far. Maybe just a block or two, but I wasn't in a car, and if those guys were still behind me, still following when I turned at the next light to go through the parking lot of the gym and Breakers' bar, I would know this wasn't a coincidence.

Sure enough, I made my turn, not letting up on my pace as I raced through the lot, barely making it to the doors of the gym before the car screeched to a stop in front of it. The man driving pulled a gun, aiming it at me as I tore the door open, barely making out when the other man began shouting "Not here!" to his friend. I was halfway inside and ducking behind the check-in desk where Ash had watched the whole thing play out. Travis, who usually stood guard, immediately raced out the door after him, gun drawn from his waistband as he followed on foot.

"What the fuck was that?" she asked, her phone already out and taking a video of the car as it peeled out of the parking lot and back onto the street once again, Travis racing like his life depended on it all the way to the intersection, before slowing and turning around to come back.

"I have … no idea…" I panted, gasping for breath after having run for my life. My adrenaline was through the roof, my body buzzing, but I couldn't seem to get myself up from the crouched position I was in on the floor.

"Adrian!" Ash screamed from where she was, half staring out the large glass windows of the gym as Travis came back in, and now mildly hunched with her hand on my head, murmuring for me to breathe through my nose.

"What?" he snapped back from somewhere in the gym. Luckily, it seemed to be dead in there at the moment, so the only people in there were either people who worked for the gym or other Mafia members.

"Someone just pulled a gun on Carmen as she ran up," Ash said, her voice laced with anger. I wasn't sure how much Ash knew about what my brother and Sal did here, but it was enough, clearly, since she seemed livid and was taking it out on him. Adrian's nostrils flared, his jaw clenching as he looked down at where I was crouched and took me in. "What the fuck did you get her mixed up in?"

"*Everything* I do is to keep her and my mother safe, Ash," Adrian snapped, glaring at her in a way that was almost daring her to say another word. She kept her lips in a tight line, glaring right back, before she resumed the way she had been brushing my hair back from my forehead.

Adrian's eyes turned back down to look at me once Ash had dropped hers, taking me in.

"With me," he said in a low, cold voice that I had never had directed at me before. When I didn't make a move to come with him, he took my upper arm in his large grip, pulling me up to my feet, and balancing me with his hands on my shoulders. "Can you walk?"

"Yes," I said shakily.

"With me. Now." He turned on his heel, walking back toward the offices. I followed, my feet tripping a little as I moved, the adrenaline making my legs want to run instead of walk. Everyone had stopped and followed us with their eyes as we moved. This was definitely Mafia business, and I was now, unfortunately, in the midst of it.

Once we entered the back office, he slammed the door closed, pulling out his phone and placing a call.

"They tried to get Carmen. I'm putting you on speaker so she can tell you what happened," he said, before setting his phone down on the desk and hitting the button to turn the call to speakerphone.

"Carmen?" came Sal's voice. I didn't realize until I heard it that I was expecting to hear his dad, Salvatore, and a shock of relief flowed through me at the familiar and friendly voice of Sal.

"Yeah?"

"Tell us what happened," Adrian said, beginning to pace the room.

"I decided to take a run to the gym this morning instead of drive. Noticed the car partway through. They pulled up beside me at a light, stared at me. I felt uncomfortable. I hadn't seen either of them around here before. I see most people at the shop…" I knew that wasn't pertinent to the story, but I just couldn't seem to stop myself now that I was talking. But as I said that, I realized I *had* seen that car before. The previous day, I had noticed the car in the parking lot of the gym as I came in. "I—I actually did see that car yesterday morning parked in the lot," I said, glancing up to see Adrian punch his fist against the wall, the sound of plaster cracking as dust rained down making me jump with my already frayed nerves.

"Keep going," Sal encouraged over the phone.

"I decided I would know if they were following once I hit the lot, and then I booked it. They sped through, but I made it to the doors first. The one driving pulled a gun, but the other one stopped him from firing before I got inside."

"What did they look like?" Sal asked.

"The driver was bulky, scar on his cheek, blond. Scary. The other one was smaller, but still bigger than me, light brown or dirty-blond hair. He wore a nice suit. Who wears a suit at this hour the day before a holiday?" I thought about Salvatore and immediately knew. Why hadn't I figured it out before?

"That was O'Shea," Sal said, and Adrian nodded in confirmation, flexing his plaster dust-covered fist repeatedly like he was considering adding another hole to his office wall.

"Why would he be going after Carmen?" Adrian asked, looking at me now with a strange mixture of worry and anger.

"Why was he with Wallingford last night?" Sal inquired. That seemed to snap me out of the haze I had been falling into now that the adrenaline was starting to wear off.

"Wallingford?" I asked, looking up at my brother's face. "*Jeremy* Wallingford?"

Adrian sighed, his fists going to rest on the front of his desk, flanking the phone he had set there.

"Last night at the Breakers we saw Freddy O'Shea with Jeremy. O'Shea said some threatening things," Adrian said quietly, though it was more dangerous sounding than any time he had ever yelled at me when I was younger.

"Why would the Irish mob be talking to Jeremy?" I asked the room at large or maybe the universe, since it didn't make any sense.

"Enzo is looking into it, but his actions this morning make things a bit different," Sal said. His words were heavy, like they held additional meaning that I wasn't privy to. This was only confirmed when Adrian nodded his head solemnly.

"I'll see if Leo and Benny can stick with her until we head to the lake house," Adrian said, standing back up straight.

"And I'll get some additional security detail. Doesn't seem like Lee's Summit is protected space anymore," Sal murmured with sadness before the line went dead.

The room was quiet for a long few minutes, my mind swirling as I took in all the information I just learned. For some reason, I was being targeted. It could only be because of our connection to the Mafia, a connection that should have died when my father did years ago, but instead, we were all trapped here, still just enough in it that my mother couldn't leave, and Adrian was pulled in when he tried his hardest to escape.

"Why me?" I asked, looking up at Adrian.

"I don't know, Carmen, but we'll find out," he said back, but the thickness in his voice told me that something about what he said wasn't the complete truth.

I wasn't sure what I was expecting when I arrived back home, but it certainly wasn't the scene that was before us. Leo was pacing angrily from where he stood in the living room, my mother was gone, presumably over at Liliana's house to get the list of things that needed to

be taken to the lake house, and Benny was snapping at someone on the phone. Sal, maybe?

"Well, fucking find out!" Benny yelled into the phone.

"I can't stay. I have to do some things. You're armed?" Adrian asked, making Leo's head snap up.

"Of course, I'm fucking armed," Leo practically growled.

"I'm just trying to make sure she's safe before I leave," Adrian said, his voice barely restrained.

"I've got her," Leo said back, his face so much more serious than I had ever seen it. Adrian stared into his eyes for a long moment, studying his expression, and apparently coming out satisfied, when he nodded once, turning his attention to our brother who had finally tossed his phone on the couch when he was fed up with whatever the person on the other end was saying.

"Enzo hasn't found anything yet?" Adrian asked.

"Still tracking his movements, but I want to know *why*."

Adrian nodded, closing his eyes and smoothing his beard as he let out a breath. He was trying to soothe himself and keep from exploding. I saw this fairly often. There was a reason he ran the gym; he needed the outlet just as much as I did.

"Benny, stay with Ma and Liliana. Take your gun. Pack up, head to the lake house. We'll meet you there later," Adrian instructed. "Don't be surprised if you see Travis and Paolo. Sal is sending them to keep watch."

Without another word, Adrian turned, marching out of the house and down the front steps to his car.

I watched him go, pausing for a moment before turning to see Benny pulling his phone from the couch once more and stuffing it into his pocket.

"The moms will want to go to the grocery store," Benny said with a grumble, but this time it wasn't just annoyance over the errand as it would normally be. It was clearly anxiety about being out in public with them. "Just head to the lake house as soon as you're ready," Benny said, taking a moment to come over and kiss my still-sweaty forehead. "We won't let anything happen to you, Car," he whispered against my forehead, before patting his low back to make sure his gun was stowed there and clapping Leo on the shoulder, then heading out the back door to get the moms moving.

Leo and I stood there for a moment, looking at each other. Leo was still radiating rage, and I felt exhausted from the slingshot emotions of the last hour.

"I'm just going to take a shower and put the last few things in my bag, and we can go," I said, turning to the stairs and moving like a zombie to wash this morning away.

CHAPTER 11

CARMEN

Once I was clean, I pulled on some leggings and a cropped tank top, throwing the last few necessities into the bags I had already packed for our stay at the lake house, before heading down the stairs. Leo was still brooding and pacing the living room as I came down. He didn't say anything as I grabbed my keys and purse, making my way to the front door so we could leave. The ride was short, only about ten minutes, but it seemed to drag on for far longer since the cab of the car was silent as a tomb. Leo spent the whole time looking around, eyeing each vehicle that got close to us with suspicion. He was still so angry, and while I appreciated the seriousness, I hated that his anger somehow seemed aimed at me as well.

"Spit it out," I said finally, breaking the silence as I drove down the last stretch of road until we entered the lake. The roads here were narrower and winding.

"Excuse me?" he asked, finally turning his gaze back to me.

"Whatever it is that has you pissed and brooding over there, spit it out," I repeated.

"I don't know if you recall, but you almost got attacked this morning. I think that's a pretty good reason to be pissed off," he snapped.

"There's something else. I can tell," I grumbled, glancing at him and then back to the road. It was enough to catch the subtle raise of his brow and flex of his jaw.

"That's all there is," he said stiffly.

"No, it isn't," I hissed, taking the winding lake roads a bit more quickly than I would normally, but his denial was just fueling a fire within me. Anger from this morning was finally pushing through the fear and shock of what had happened. Anger that he could possibly be mad at *me* for this at all.

"Don't push it. Not right now," he said, clearly clenching his teeth as he spoke. I skidded to a stop in the driveway of the lake house, not bothering if it was straight or not. No other cars were there, so we were the first to arrive and probably would be for a few hours. Our neighbors on this strip were quite a way away, giving the house plenty of privacy.

"Oh, I'm going to push it, Leo, because whatever the hell is holding you back from saying it, is exactly why I said goodnight last night. But fine," I said, throwing my hands in the air and wrenching the car door open. "Let's not talk!" I screeched before slamming the car door.

I stalked up to the house, rifling through the keys in my hand until I found the right one, but I didn't have a moment to put the key in the lock before strong hands were grasping my shoulders, spinning me around. Leo was mere inches from me, caging me in between his arms, his hands on either side of my head.

"Why did you go out with that piece of shit?" he asked, his voice low and quiet, for my ears only.

"Who?"

"Wallingford," he bit out, making me press a little farther into the door.

"I told you; my mom wants me to find the one," I lied.

"Anyone with a brain could have told you *he* wasn't the one. Your brothers said you were sad. Why were you sad, Carmen?"

"It doesn't matter," I breathed, trying to avoid his eyes. He was so close. So very close, his breath washing over my face, his mildly spicy and undeniably manly scent enveloping me. The memory of his mouth on mine the night before seemed to ignite me, and I could feel the heat and wetness pooling simply from his proximity. One hand reached to touch my chin, cupping it and tilting my head up so I couldn't look away from him.

"It matters to me," he said firmly.

"It was the picture," I finally breathed out, watching as his pupils seemed to dilate as I said it. "I ruined every-thing by sending you that stupid picture," I whispered. Like I had slapped him, he pulled back, not completely, but enough that he could more fully study my face.

"So, you went on a date with him, to what? Make me mad?"

"To get over the feelings I shouldn't have for my brother's best friend. Who, by the way, doesn't feel the same," I said back, my voice a little louder with my defensiveness before I could think better of it. For some reason it seemed like when he was this close, I couldn't hide anything I was feeling, or shut off my body's reac-tion to him.

It was like my words flipped a switch within him. His hazel eyes burned and the muscles in his arms con-tracted further. I wasn't sure I could handle rejection from him this close to me when I was fighting every urge to go up on my toes and press my lips to his.

"I didn't want you to hate me or look at me differently. I didn't want to ruin what our families have because I couldn't control myself, but I—"

But I couldn't keep babbling, not when he closed the distance, ducking his head down and pressing his lips to mine.

The kiss immediately set me ablaze. That electric pulse between us at just the touch of our hands together was nothing in comparison to the way it felt with our lips pressed together. It was better than anything I had imagined over the years, better than last night. There was no hiding behind the excuse of alcohol this time. He was kissing me because he wanted to, because it seemed like he couldn't hold back anymore. The feel of his chest against me, his hands on my skin, and his lips moving against mine were like ecstasy. My hands immediately went to his shoulders, fingers wrapping around to hold tightly to his shirt, as his fingers on my chin traveled to cup the base of my head, tilting it farther back for better access.

He moaned into the kiss, his tongue pressing lightly to the seam of my lips, and I had no desire to deny him, my mouth opening eagerly to meet his tongue with mine. Our chests pressed more tightly together, his hips coming forward to bump against me. I could feel the rapid beating of his own heart against mine. Somewhere nearby someone squealed with delight, just as a small firework went off, and that seemed to pull us out of the trance of our kiss for long enough to realize we were doing this right out in the open for anyone who drove by to see.

"Open the door," he said raggedly as he pulled only far enough from my mouth to speak. I bent down to grab the keys I had dropped at some point, unlocking the door and stepping inside, with him right behind me.

LEO

Carmen had gone on that date with that stupid Jeremy Wallingford because I couldn't tell her through text how I felt. Because I wanted to *talk*. How stupid was I to wait, letting whatever sort of rejection she felt, her embarrassment and concern, fester this whole time? Very stupid.

We stepped inside the house, and I immediately closed and locked the door once again, turning back to her. She had taken a few steps into the large, open living space. Her face was still flushed, chest still heaving from our kiss, but when she turned to look at me there was so much heat in her eyes, unwavering desire burning in those green orbs.

I wanted to cross the distance between us and continue what we had started, but there were a lot of things that we should probably say. Things I should have said for years, but I didn't want to risk any part of her.

"Do you know why I asked you to email me?" I asked. Her brows knitted together as she looked at me, shaking her head. "I knew I was going to miss you. More than Benny or my mom. More than anyone here," I whispered, stepping closer again. I was just as close as I had been in that bathroom six years ago, her body only a few inches from mine. My hand reached out, cupping her cheek just as I had then, the soft feel of her skin on my rough hands simultaneously like a balm to soothe me and a torch, lighting a fire within me.

"Why?" she asked, her voice nothing but a breathy whisper.

"You thought you'd ruin everything by sending me that picture?" I chuckled darkly. "I tortured myself for years, yearning for the girl in the window across from mine. My best friend's sister, who I tried but failed to stop myself from wanting. If there was anything to be ruined, I had already done it by wanting you so much it hurt," I confessed, watching as her pupils seemed to dilate farther with my words.

Her hands reached out, grabbing the front of my shirt. She pulled me closer, and I didn't need any further invitation, closing the distance once again, so our lips crashed together. My cock, which had already been hard from the kiss against the door, grew impossibly harder. My hands seemed to roam of their own accord, groping and grasping at her hair, her back, her luscious hips.

A whimper came from within her as I pressed us closer together, my hardness trapped between our bodies and clothes so she could certainly feel it there. She could feel what she did to me. But it only seemed to spur her on, her own little hands hot as they raked over my shoulders and back, traveling down until they clawed into my ass, pressing me even closer.

I let a rumble escape my chest, unable to resist the urge to pull her up by the backs of her thighs so her legs could wrap around my waist, her hot core now pressing directly against my straining erection in my jeans. Could feel her thigh muscles clenching as she tried to press herself against me, the hot apex of her thighs seeking friction, and I was only happy to move my hands just enough under her thick cheeks to press her harder against me while my hips moved forward to meet her at the same time.

She moaned, her head tilting back and breaking the contact between our mouths, but it gave me access to that delicious neck. Teeth scraping and lips sucking only to let my tongue soothe the places that may have stung.

"Leo," she whispered on another moan as her hips bucked forward. The way my name sounded coming out of her like that did something to me. I felt like an animal, suddenly ravenous in a way I had never been before. I stumbled forward, letting us crash onto one of the large couches in the living room. How many times had we watched a movie there after a long day of swimming in the lake? How many times had I pictured how her body would feel under mine? Or on top?

I held myself up on one elbow, so I didn't crush her with my full weight, returning my lips to her, which she greedily took, her tongue chasing mine as her legs spread wide to let me press my still-covered cock against her more fully. We both groaned as I thrust against her, humping her like I was a teenager again.

"Are you wet for me, Little Song?" I whispered against her lips, thrusting against her again and feeling it in her chest against mine as she moaned deeply.

She didn't say anything, instead tilting her hips up to meet my next thrust. I let my hand wander as I returned my lips to hers, fingers brushing over her peaked nipples through her tank top and thin bra which made her let out a little gasp against my mouth, before they continued their descent, brushing over her stomach, which clenched against my touch, until finally I found the waistband of her leggings.

"Should I find out?" I asked, tugging roughly so they were pulled down slightly lower, but still covering that heat between her legs.

Her hips lifted as if giving me permission to pull the leggings down farther, but instead of giving in, I let my mouth trail over her chin and down her neck, tongue lingering along her collarbone before dipping lower to the bit of skin that her tank top revealed just at the top of her breasts. I looked up at her face, her green eyes trained on me as my mouth went lower, licking and sucking one nipple into my mouth through her shirt. She arched her back, panting, and I wondered what it would feel like, how she would respond if I licked her there without the cloth between us.

Too impatient to try, my mouth danced farther, lavishing at her toned stomach, my free hand splaying over the inside of her thigh as I pushed her legs farther apart. Now so close to her core, I could smell her arousal, potent through her leggings. Mouthwatering.

My hand slipped farther up her thigh, fingers pressing into the damp fabric there. The heat and moisture coming through the thin material made an animalistic sound come from my chest, and I couldn't wait any longer.

My hands went back to the waistband of her leggings, pulling them down to her knees so I could feast my eyes on her.

Beautiful, wet, and already swollen, aching to be touched. This pussy, which I had only imagined being able to gaze upon, let alone touch, was more beautiful than the images my mind had conjured. The combination of seeing her, practically dripping for me, and her scent flooding my nostrils made me so much harder than I already had been it was almost painful. I looked back up at her face, just to make sure she wasn't having second thoughts, but all I saw there was an overwhelming need.

"I want to make you sing for me," I said. My voice may as well have been gravel with how rough it sounded.

She whimpered again, the slight dip of her chin as a nod the only thing I needed before I dove in. She tasted like heaven. Lightly fruity with a musk that left a tang on my tongue, and I couldn't get enough. She was more delicious than I had expected. I wasn't sure I would ever get enough of the way she tasted. My tongue traced the angles of each fold, each crevice, coming up to swirl over her swollen bud in a way that made her quiver beneath me, her moans getting louder with each new stroke.

I opened my eyes, looking up at her face to see it flushed, her eyes nearly black with need as her hips moved in time with my movements, chasing the pleasure *I* was giving her. I didn't want her to stop looking at me that way. I wanted those sounds to resonate around me forever. Her hands reached out, threading through my hair and holding me closer as I speared my tongue inside her tight hole, moaning as I felt her channel pulsing around it.

I pressed my aching cock into the couch, wanting friction too, but unwilling to stop until I felt her cum, because she *would* cum for me. I could already feel it building within her, see the way her stomach muscles tightened. I replaced my tongue with fingers. Pressing into her and loving the soft "ahh!" that came from her, her channel spasming more as soon as I hooked them, pumping them in and out as my tongue went back to work on her clit.

"Leo! I'm gonna—I—"

I just went harder, becoming relentless, like a starving man, lapping and sucking at her clit as my fingers pounded roughly, making squishing sounds as her orgasm took over and we were flooded with a fresh wave of her arousal, her mouth open and slack in a silent scream as her body went rigid. I softened my touch, riding out the aftershocks of her pleasure with her, before slipping my fingers out of her pussy, licking away the juices that were dripping to my wrist.

Sitting up, I went to pull her shoes from her feet, so the leggings could finally come fully off, but she sat up too, whipping her shirt over her head and pushing her shoes off with her toes. I pulled the leggings off the rest of the way, so the only thing that was left on her was the thin bra, nipples hard and peaked against the fabric.

But before I could reach to take it off, she was climbing over to where I sat, straddling my lap and tugging at the hem of my shirt. I let her take it off me, tossing it over her head blindly, as she raked her fingers over my chest, her eyes hungrily taking me in. Her movements slowed as the soft pads of her fingers lingered over the tattoos. She hadn't seen them before, and I wondered if she knew what they meant.

It was sheet music that twisted around from my wrist, traveling up my arm and cascading over my chest like delicate vines. There were no lyrics written, only the music, but it was the song she used to sing all the time when she turned sixteen. The song she sang when I was fairly certain I had started to fall for her.

Her eyes flashed up to mine, my body rippling with each swipe of her hands before those fingers went to the button on my jeans. She leaned forward, her lips going to my ear as she slowly undid the button, dragging the zipper down so carefully, I could swear I heard every tooth separating from the other.

"Are you hard for me?" she whispered in my ear, mimicking my question earlier, her voice husky as her hot breath washed over my ear and neck. I had never heard her speak in such a way before. Dirty talk from her was clearly something I had been missing, since my whole body seemed to react to it. My hands gripped her ass, my mouth descending on her neck to lick and suck, because I had to taste her again. Her soft, hot little hand slipped into my open fly, finding my almost painfully hard cock. I couldn't help the moan that burst from me at her touch.

How many times had I fantasized about this very moment? How it would feel for her to touch me this way? More times than I could count.

She scooted down, so she sat more on my knees, pulling my jeans down enough to have my cock spring free, standing proud and long for her eyes to take in. She licked her lips as she did so, sucking her bottom lip in her mouth as she tentatively reached her hand back out to touch. She gave me a slow stroke, getting a good feel of my length, letting her thumb swirl at the top and smearing the bead of precum that had gathered there.

I dug my fingers into the leather of the couch. It was too good having *her* touching me. Just her slowly stroking me had me on the verge of exploding. Her eyes darted from my cock to look me in the eyes, for a moment, like she was seeking permission, before she slid off my lap altogether, going on to her knees between my legs so she could press her thick, pillowed lips against the mushroom head.

My breath caught in my throat at the contact. The kiss was so soft, sweet, yet incredibly erotic. Her tongue slipped out, tasting me, her mouth watering as she let her lips envelop and descend on my shaft. The feeling was magnificent. The wet heat of her mouth, tongue pulsing against the vein on the underside as she slowly started to move up and down, letting her spit and my precum slick my shaft for better access.

Each uncontrollable sound I made seemed to spur her on, taking more of me, sucking harder, until I was panting. I dug my fingers deeper into the couch, willing myself not to plunge them into her hair and force her head down farther, but my hips bucked up on their own accord, pressing myself farther into her throat. She moaned at that, her movements getting faster as my balls drew up, my stomach clenching with the impending orgasm.

"Carmen," I managed to grunt out, trying to get her to stop, but she merely flashed her eyes up at mine, hunger clearly present there, redoubling her efforts and cupping my tight balls, until there was no way for me to stop what was about to happen.

I tried once more to pull her away, but she just seemed to dig in deeper, humming at the back of her throat and setting off the eruption that sent hot spurts of my cum shooting down her throat. She didn't even gag, pulling off my cock with one long suck and swallowing everything I gave her with a satisfied look on her face.

CHAPTER 12

CARMEN

The look on Leo's face was like he was trapped in a state of awe and bliss; I wanted to see that look on his face over and over. I wanted to be the reason he felt that pleasure and no one else. But it was only a minute later that he was leaning over, gathering me into his arms and pulling me back to straddle his lap. His lips found mine, tongues clashing again as if we couldn't get enough. The combination of our releases lingering in our mouths and mixing into an intoxicating cocktail. My hands fisted in his hair to keep him there, while his hands held tight to my hips, fingers splaying down to my ass cheeks.

It was only a few minutes into our kissing that I could feel his cock getting hard again, pressing against my thigh, until I moved, slipping it along my seam and making us both moan at the feel of us together. It was good. It was right, but it wasn't enough. I needed him inside of me. My core was clenching and dripping, needing to be filled by him.

I was just about to reach between us and notch his thick head to my entrance when the sound of another car pulling in the driveway made us both freeze. The sound of Liliana's voice, muffled only by the distance from the front door to the driveway, the indication of who it was.

"Fuck!" I whisper-shouted, hopping off his lap and frantically trying to find the pieces of my clothes that had been carelessly tossed aside.

"Go to your room. I'll just grab your bags from the car," Leo said, quickly tucking himself away and slipping his shirt over his head. I nodded, running up the stairs and down the hall to the room that had always been mine. With the door safely closed, I pulled my clothes back on, rushing to my private bathroom to see if I could pull off looking anything other than nearly fucked on the living room couch.

My face was flushed, my curls in utter disarray and my nipples were still being perilous traitors poking through my bra and t-shirt. I grunted in frustration, throwing my hair into a messy bun on top of my head and splashing cold water on my face.

The door opened and closed downstairs and I could hear muffled talking outside. Since the house was so empty, there was little to keep the sounds from traveling. The living room was so huge, fully open to the dining room and kitchen, that I hoped that the scent of sex wasn't potent enough for them to know what we had been doing.

What we had been doing…

My whole body seemed to light on fire again. I kissed Leo. Leo kissed me. *Leo* ate me out. I sucked his *very* long cock.

I would not be shocked if it did smell like sex in that living room. We did just about everything *but* sex.

I pressed my hands to my burning cheeks. Trying to see if this was real.

The taste that lingered in my mouth, the combined flavors of both of our cum on my tongue from our heated kiss, told me it definitely was real. As well as the throb between my thighs that told me my body would have much preferred if we had just kept going because my pussy clenched like it still wanted to be filled up.

"She's lying down, you said?" came Liliana's voice as the front door opened again. "Well, I'm not surprised. I can't imagine what must be going through her head right now, after having a gun aimed at her."

I crept quietly to the door, opening it enough so I could hear better.

"We'll make her favorite for dinner, and maybe you boys can get a fire going down by the shore. She always liked it when you all sat there together," Mama said shortly after.

"How much food do you think we need, Ma? We're only going to be here five days!" Benny protested. And then there was a crash. "Carmen!" Benny yelled, shaking me to my core. "She just leaves her fucking shoes out in the middle of everything?" he asked, his voice laced with annoyance.

"Benito! Language!" Mama snapped immediately, making me smile.

"Look at this! We all move from home, and she becomes some princess who doesn't have to pick up her shoes?"

"She's been through something today. Give her a little grace," Liliana said in my defense. Goodness, I loved that woman, but she didn't know the half of what I'd been through today.

I went to the closet and pulled out an old sweatshirt of my dad's that I kept there for cool nights on the lake, and made my way back down the stairs to face them. I couldn't hide upstairs forever. Leo came through the door, carrying the last of the groceries and my bags over his shoulder, while Benny was still grumbling, picking up the bags of groceries he dropped, presumably when he tripped over my shoe.

Of course, Leo looked like nothing happened, other than his hair being slightly more tussled than it normally was, and his shirt was a little wrinkled, but it wasn't plainly noticeable.

"Sorry, Benny. I just … got a little overwhelmed," I murmured, pointedly not looking at Leo while going to pick up my shoes and phone from the ground where they were left in our haste to undress me.

I slipped my phone back into my pocket, stowed my shoes in the front closet, and joined everyone in the kitchen to get the groceries unpacked. The moms were going to start prepping for lunch, so I went back upstairs to make sure the beds weren't dusty and the bathrooms were stocked. Mr. Lupo paid someone to clean and stock the house when we weren't there, but sometimes they missed things.

As I was coming from one of the bathrooms, Leo was coming down the hall, his duffle and my bags in hand.

"I can take mine," I said, reaching out to snag them from his grasp, but he pulled back before I could.

"I know which one your room is," he said, the faintest hint of a smirk on his face, going past me and down to my room. I followed, leaning in the doorway while he set my things down beside my bed.

"Thank you," I said quietly, still aware of the chatter down below. He came close, and I moved to get out of his way when he stopped me by bracing his hand beside my head on the door frame.

"You remember where mine is?" he asked. His body heat was radiating out over me, reminding me there was unfinished business between us. I nodded, swallowing thickly.

"Across the hall."

"That's right, Little Song. And my bed is a little bigger than yours," he murmured, his voice a rumble.

He ducked his head down, pressing his lips to mine, and whatever delusions I may have tried to put in my head to tell myself what happened earlier couldn't have been real disappeared. He was just as eager to pick up where we left off as I was. He broke the kiss, both of us breathing raggedly, and pulled himself from my room, striding across the hall and into his room to toss the duffle on the floor.

As Benny and Leo got the wood set up in the stone pit for later and the moms prepped for dinner, I went to the cellar in the guise of choosing wine. Mom had brought some, but we usually shared a reserve bottle with dinner when we all got together for holidays here. As soon as I knew I was out of earshot I called Rory.

"Hey! Daph and I were thinking of coming up tomorrow, if it's okay. She still has work tonight," she said, in true Rory form, starting the conversation off before she'd even confirmed I could hear her.

"I kissed Leo. Well, he kissed me. I'm not entirely sure, but we kissed. And it wasn't a 'he might be tipsy' kiss. This was a 'we were both definitely sober' kiss … and then more," I blurted out as soon as there was a lull in her talking. There was silence on the other end of the phone for what felt like a full minute before an ear-splitting squeal came from the other end.

"I *knew* it!" she sang. "Oh my god. Tell me everything. Was it good?"

"Yes."

"How big is his dick?"

"Rory!" I hissed, glancing around the cellar as if someone would hear.

"Sorry! I mean … it didn't disappoint, did it?"

What we got to didn't disappoint in the slightest. My stomach burned and fluttered at the idea of his mouth on my pussy again, or the taste of his cock on my tongue. God, what I'd do to continue where we started.

"The full deed wasn't done, but I got a pretty good idea that it will more than do," I said, fanning myself with my hand at how hot my cheeks were feeling from just thinking about how much was left that I couldn't take in my mouth, even when it hit the back of my throat.

"So, is this a thing? Are you two finally a thing?"

"I don't know," I said, slumping onto a crate and picking at a wine label. "He said some things that make me think maybe it could be. But then I don't fully know. Benny said something to me the other day that had me thinking he wouldn't hate Leo if something happened between us."

"If they didn't already know you both had a thing for each other for years, they were blind. This has got to be something they saw coming. I mean, you haven't had a serious relationship since high school, and even then, you kept comparing him to Leo," Rory said, and I could practically see the expression on her face, dubious about my brothers' ignorance, eyebrow arching high on her forehead.

"I'm not sure how they'd feel about it if they knew he was eating me out on the couch where we all watched movies as kids," I reminded.

"I'm pretty sure it was Leo who threatened your boyfriend when you found out he was cheating at the winter dance sophomore year," Rory added, as if she didn't hear me. "And I feel like Benny backed him up and was pretty happy about it when Leo danced with you the rest of the night."

"You make it seem so simple, like my brothers could just be *happy* with anyone I chose to be with," I grumbled, thinking about the overprotective way they all seemed to behave around any man I had spent more than one date with.

"I think they'd be *more* happy with someone like Leo, who they know and trust."

"Carmen!" called Mama, clearly leaning down the door to the basement stairs. "Are you okay down there?"

"I'm fine, Ma!" I yelled back. "I need to go," I told Rory.

"Please text me later. Or wait until Daph and I come. I can't wait to hear everything," Rory said, ending the call with a delighted laugh.

I snagged the Barolo I had already decided would pair best with the steak and mushroom risotto the moms were cooking and made my way back upstairs.

CHAPTER 13

LEO

I may have kept my cool exterior, but inside I was freaking out. Those moments when Carmen was darting, basically naked up the stairs while Benny and our moms were getting out of the car, groceries loaded in their arms, were nerve-wracking. I smoothed my hair, steadied my breathing, and checked to make sure the couch showed no signs of what we had just been doing. With a little pride, I found that I had gotten every drop of her orgasm, and the slight wetness she left on the crotch of my pants was hidden well if I kept my shirt untucked.

Before they had an opportunity to come inside, I went out to Carmen's car, her keys in hand, feigning that I was just going to get her bags, but joining in to carry the last of the groceries that were left in the car.

My façade seemed to be working, no one seemed to catch on to anything, even when I brought her bags up to her along with my duffle that they had brought for me. But there was a look Benny gave me at lunch when I sat beside her at the bar top in the kitchen. I had found myself watching her, then feeling his eyes boring into me until I looked over and caught him. Those green eyes, similar to Carmen's, but a little darker shade, were burning with suspicion.

He had seen something there in my face as I looked at her, and I realized I had failed thoroughly in keeping this, whatever it was, a secret for just a little longer. He didn't say anything for hours, waiting until we were alone, gathering wood and clearing out the fire pit to build a fresh stack for later.

He stopped working, looking at me strangely after a few silent moments. It wasn't abnormal for us to go stretches without words, having been best friends for as long as either of us could remember, but this one felt heavy.

"You were pretty upset earlier. At the house," Benny noted, tossing a dried log into the neat pile I had just built and ruining the space beneath that I had saved for kindling.

"It's pretty messed up what happened to Carmen. I didn't think the Irish went so low to target people outside of the life," I said, looking up at his unreadable expression.

"It is. It's a low blow, but I wonder if there's something more Sal and Adrian aren't telling us," Benny said. His words had more meaning than what they outwardly seemed. He was talking about dishonesty by omission; insinuating I wasn't saying something either.

"I'm sure they'll tell us soon. They can't keep it from Carmen if her life is at risk," I said, deciding to keep up with the outward conversation and see how long it took him to spit out what was really on his mind. It wouldn't take him long, it usually didn't, but the tension might get to me before then.

Benny nodded, clicking his tongue inside his cheek for a moment as I fixed the pile and stuffed the kindling we had found in the space.

"I'm just pretty frustrated that our own brothers aren't keeping us in the loop. Especially if it affects us," Benny continued, crossing his arms and glaring down at where I remained crouched. Yeah, I wasn't going to hold out, not with the glint in his eye and the way his arms flexed, like keeping them crossed was the only thing holding back from hitting me.

"What, Benny? What do you want to say?" I asked, letting my forearms drop to my thighs, hands relaxed and dangling between my legs. He needed to see I was physically not being an aggressor, because I didn't want this to be a fight.

"You went to the shop right when you got home," Benny stated.

"I did."

"You've barely seen my sister in six years, and that's the first place you go?" he asked, his voice accusatory, just like his suspicious eyes. I sighed, standing and moving a little around the fire pit so we were only a few feet apart. This was one of the things I feared the most about my feelings for Carmen, how Benny would react. Benny was more than just my friend; he was my brother. And I knew now that Carmen feared this as well.

"I knew you had a thing for her for a while when we were teenagers. It didn't bother me so much, because I knew you wouldn't act on it. Six years you've been gone, Leo," he continued.

So he had noticed it. I was sure I had kept those feelings to myself. Sure that only I knew that she was all I thought about for years. It killed me when she dated someone. I hated watching the way the stupid high school boys would touch her or sometimes kiss that soft cheek that I had so often wanted to kiss.

I supposed, looking back, I could see how some things were obvious. I would purposefully wait to give her a ride or do things like stay up until 3 a.m. making pies with her. I wasn't sure when it changed. When I went from teasing her with Benny to defending her against it, but he had clearly noticed.

"We emailed. A lot, more than you or even my mom the whole time I was gone," I admitted. I wasn't ready to tell him what had occurred today. Perhaps I would leave that for him to imagine, but I wouldn't lie to him about what I felt.

"Then why did she date? Why did she even entertain that dumbass Wallingford, if she was *talking* to you?" Benny asked, his voice even harsher than it was before.

"I—we…" What could I say to explain it? I was in love with her but couldn't admit it? That I didn't want to make her love me if a mission went bad and I never came home. I couldn't stand the idea of her waiting for me, even though the idea of her with anyone else made my heart ache in my chest and my jealousy flare up like an angry beast.

"She loves you, you know?" Benny asked, when the silence stretched on for a few moments and I couldn't find the words. I knew she cared about me, but … she loved me? "She has for a long time. Everything fell apart for her when Mom got sick. She gave everything up, took care of things Adrian and I couldn't, and when I told her how sorry I was that I got to follow my dream while she had to give it all up, do you know what she said?"

I swallowed dryly, shaking my head because I couldn't find my voice.

"She said nothing she had sacrificed was as big or as important as what *you* have. And there was only one dream that really mattered, and she didn't know if she'd ever get to have it."

The breath seemed to be knocked right out of me. She said something similar to me over email when Maria got diagnosed and she told me her plan to stay at home instead of moving out and taking the corporate job she had lined up after graduating. What I hadn't realized, not until Benny posed it the way he had, was that *I was the dream.*

As much as I had fantasized about her, she had about me. As much as I longed for her, she had longed for me too. Hence why she emailed me so much more than I could email her back. Why she jumped at any chance to see or talk to me. Why she sent me that picture.

"You can't hurt her, Leo. It would crush her. And if you hurt her, I don't care how big and tough of a Marine you are, I don't care that sometimes you're more of a brother to me than Adrian, I will hurt you ten times worse," Benny said darkly.

He wasn't in bad shape. He was a physical therapist and kept up with his workout regimen, but beyond that, he was trained to fight. He knew how to hurt someone if he had to, because all the LaMartinas and Lupos had to be prepared for that possibility, simply from the proximity to danger that our families hailed from. But if I hurt Carmen, I would let him hurt me. Hell, I'd let him hurt me now, if I could ensure that he wouldn't hate me.

"I won't hurt her, Benny. I don't want to hurt her or you," I said, finally finding my voice.

"Don't worry about me. Just don't fuck this up," he said with finality, turning and walking back toward the house.

Sal, Adrian, and Enzo got to the lake house just when dinner was being set on the table. I was glad for the additional people. Between the tension hovering between me and Carmen, and the conversation that Benny and I had by the pit, the deflection of attention was a relief. They brought their own tension with them though, and we all knew, just by looking at their faces, that whatever was going on with the Irish was bigger than they were expecting.

Dinner was abnormally quiet. Maria and Mom kept the conversation going with plans for the Fourth, and speculation about what the lake would be like with all the visitors to the area. We all added little bits in here or there, but the usual banter between all of us was solemn.

"You all go down to the beach and relax. We can handle the dishes tonight," Maria said, standing and pulling dishes from the table.

"I packed a cooler to take with you," Mom said, pointing near the back door where our old trusty blue cooler sat waiting for us.

Enzo and Benny took the cooler, while the rest of us hauled the folding chairs down to set them all up. Carmen dutifully carried a few of the chairs over her shoulder, her bare feet moving down the path and through the soft sand once we hit the beach with delicate steps. Odd that such a simple thing, like her cute little feet, could endear her to me more.

I started the fire, and we all settled in as it was built enough for me to stop fussing over it, beers in hand. For several long minutes, we all just sat there, the soft sound of the lake water lapping at the shore and the crackling of the fire the only sounds as a backdrop to the nervousness we all felt about the current situation. The sun set and it was beautiful, orange and red, like the brilliant fire before us. Until it faded into deep purples and finally it was just the darkened sky filled with stars around us.

"Just spit it out," Benny finally said to Adrian, seeming to be unable to keep up this tense silence any longer. I was grateful for it. Sal and Adrian shared a look, while Enzo looked more defeated than I had ever seen him, his usual carefree air replaced with deep concern.

"We don't really know yet," Sal said, running a hand through his hair nervously. "Enzo traced O'Shea around Kansas City for the last few days. It looks like he might have met with Dad once or twice."

A shiver ran down my spine and I looked over at Carmen, who clutched her beer in both hands as she stared at my older brother.

"What the hell does that mean? Did they approve of Carmen being taken out?" Benny asked, his voice hoarse. It might have seemed like a leap, but the evidence being what it was, it wasn't a hard line to jump to. Why would O'Shea be going after Carmen otherwise? Loose ends had been taken out for less, and my father wasn't above letting someone die who didn't deserve it. We all knew that intimately.

Except what would Carmen have done to offend the Irish? She wasn't *in* the Mafia, more like an adjacent and unwilling associate. Maybe scorning Wallingford? But that didn't make sense, he wasn't Irish mob. What could Carmen, of all people, have done to deserve a death sentence?

I felt like punching something. No, like ripping something apart. Like burning the world down. I had to set my beer in the sand at my feet to keep from breaking it in my grip as I clenched my fingers into fists.

"I don't think they were trying to kill her," Enzo said, glancing up at Carmen. "If that's what they wanted, they could have done it at the streetlight when she stopped and first noticed them." He must have gone through all the CCTV footage, so he watched the whole thing go down.

"Then what? Take her?" I asked, my voice barely more than a growl. I already knew what O'Shea was up to with stolen women. If they thought they could make her a sex slave, they were in for a rude awakening.

"Dad said something strange to Adrian earlier. He made it sound like they were supposed to wait, but they went after her early." Sal said, his tone slightly shaken. I looked at Adrian, who seemed like he was about to explode himself.

"He's not telling us more until he comes here," Enzo said, making us all fall back into silence.

Sal pulled out a bottle of whiskey from the bag he had brought down to the beach with him, unscrewing the top and taking a long pull, before passing it to Adrian.

"We get one back and now this," Enzo said sadly when Adrian passed the bottle to him after taking his own drink. He was referring to me, having me back, having the group of us together again for the first time in so long, and we already had a knife poised, only this time it wasn't an impending trip overseas or one of us going off to college, it was the Mafia, my father, holding that knife and threatening to ruin everything.

"We'll figure it out," Benny said quietly, glancing at his sister before he passed me the bottle.

"She's not getting involved with this," I said darkly, my eyes casting around to every single one of the men in the circle of chairs. "I'm not fucking kidding. Anything we have to do to keep her out of it, we do it. You understand me?"

They all looked back and, one by one, as I made eye contact, they nodded.

"Well, unfortunately, you can't keep me out of it, Leo!" she said, louder than any of us were expecting.

"We will make this go away, Car. Whatever we have to sacrifice, we'll do it to make sure you aren't involved," Benny said. His voice hardened with the same resolve I felt settling into my bones.

"You aren't sacrificing shit for me. We'll figure this out *together*. I'm not some wilting flower that you all have to protect," Carmen said, tearing the bottle from my grasp and taking a big drink of whiskey. "Whatever Salvatore has to tell us, we'll fucking deal with it. Emphasis on *we*, boys."

"This isn't the same thing as us getting into trouble as kids, Carmen," Adrian said, his dark blue eyes illuminating with the light from the fire.

"It doesn't fucking matter, *Adriano*. They were after me. Period. You aren't leaving me out because you think I'm some weak little girl who can't take care of myself. I've been taking care of myself and Ma for years. And none of you know everything that I've been through," she said, her voice holding a bit of ominousness that hinted at things that were far darker than simply taking care of their sick mother.

"I don't doubt that you can defend yourself, Sis, but this is different than fending off Jeremy or holding Mom when she was sick," Benny said sympathetically.

She bowed her head over the bottle, shoulders tensing for a long, quiet moment.

"How about when I was almost gang raped for an initiation my sophomore year at UMKC? How about then? Was it so different when I defended myself from six men twice my size? Hm?" Her voice was so full of anger I almost didn't recognize it. Of course, I'd seen and heard her mad before, but nothing like this. "Just because I started training in earnest not long after that, doesn't mean I was worthless before that. Don't you forget I grew up the same as you. The same as all of you. I know how to fight. How to shoot a gun. I'm not some delicate fucking flower. I wasn't made to be a *wife*," she spit the word out like it was disgusting, her green eyes glaring out around the campfire at each of our shocked and horrified faces. She meant a Mafia wife, like our mothers, who were kept safely stored away, protected, and kept out of the life as much as possible. "I was made to be a soldier in Papa and Salvatore's operation, just like the rest of you."

And with that, she stood from her chair, bottle still clutched in her fist, and walked away from the fire, down the beach, toward the long dock that pushed far out into the lake water, leaving us all to just watch her go in complete and absolute stunned silence.

I felt like I was a raging animal, caged within my own chest. I wanted to hunt down whoever hurt her. I wanted to tear people to shreds. I wanted to run after her and pull her close while demanding she tell me who they were. I wanted to go back in time so I could have been there. So I could have protected her. She may have been capable of defending herself, but I didn't want her to ever have to.

"I—I didn't know," Benny whispered, gaining nods of agreement from Enzo and Adrian.

"She didn't tell anyone, it doesn't sound like," Sal said sadly.

"We would have killed them if she had," Adrian pointed out. He wasn't wrong. They would have all been dead.

CHAPTER 14

CARMEN

I sat on the dock, my fingers gripping the edge with one hand, letting the old wood bite into the skin of my palm, while the other held the whiskey bottle by the neck in a death grip. The moon was out, not quite full, but full enough that it showed brightly against the lake water.

It should have been beautiful. It should have felt so good to be here again with all the boys. I should have been feeling elated that something was happening between me and Leo. Instead, I felt the bitter taste of being underestimated, of being pitied. My stomach churned with bile at the resurgence of memories I'd much rather forget.

Growing up like we had was not ideal. Before my Papa died, between soccer games and music lessons, we were trained to fight. Taken to the gun range, so we knew our way around any firearm. Papa taught me how to throw a knife, how to shoot a gun, how to kill a man twice my size with my bare hands.

Before that night all those years ago, I had never had to use it for anything other than play fighting with the boys or fending off kids at school who thought it'd be fun to rough up a girl. One of my brothers, and sometimes a Lupo, normally stepped in if I ever had trouble with a guy. Occasionally, my threats were enough to scare people away, but outnumbered as I was, and all alone, I had no choice that night. I had never been grateful for that training before then, but each broken bone and bloody nose I inflicted on my attackers, allowing me to get away, was because of my father. My father who died because of some stupid Irishman's mistake.

And now they were back, and for some reason they wanted me.

I took a swig from the bottle in my grasp just as I heard the sound of someone coming up from behind. They were hesitant footsteps all the way down the long dock until they finally made it to me. Leo sat down beside me, not touching, but near enough. He didn't speak, just sat there, and I offered him the bottle, which he took from me, taking a long pull of the amber liquid himself.

"We're going to do the wishing game. They say it's not fun without you," he said quietly.

"We haven't played the wishing game since I was fourteen," I said, finally turning to give him a skeptical look.

"Enzo said something like, 'Maybe we need all the wishes we can get.' Or that's the gist. He said it much funnier than I did," Leo said, leaning closer to hand the bottle back over so his shoulder pressed into mine.

This wishing game. We weren't sure where it originated, but at some point, when we were children, we developed it. Any time something bad happened, we would all gather in a circle. Whoever had the worst of the situation, be that Sal getting beaten for talking back to his father, Benny when he wrecked the car, or Enzo when he was caught hacking into the school district's files and changing the scores for kids who paid him. Even when our Papa died, we played the game.

"We wish…" would always start together, then one word at a time, we would build our wish together. I always added subtle little additional words that held meaning just for me, usually laced with my desire for Leo to like me the way I liked him, especially as we got older. Not all our wishes came true, but enough of them did, especially early on, that we continued it until Adrian left for the military.

"I don't make wishes anymore," I said, taking the proffered bottle.

"But you do dream, don't you, Little Song?" His voice was like warm honey as he said it, the words practically dripping from his lips.

I shivered a little, remembering when he told me he wanted to make me sing. And boy, did he. The noises that came out of me this afternoon were pornographic in a way I had never sounded before in my life. Of course, it helped that it was the most pleasure I had ever felt with someone else. No one had ever made me cum like that. It was a full-body experience that made me immediately want to do it again.

I shot him a playful glare as heat flashed in his eyes, clearly seeing a hint of desire on my face with his words.

"Come on. You know you don't want to be left out," he said, pushing his shoulder against mine more playfully this time.

"Fine," I snapped, though I gave him a little smirk, hopping up and walking with him side-by-side back down to the sandy beach.

"You know, if I ever find out who did that to you, I'll kill them," Leo whispered into my ear when we grew close enough that the muffled sounds of my brothers arguing about something could be heard. The way he said it was a promise, like the sweet boy who was once defiant about learning how to shoot a rifle at the range, was now a deadly machine of a man.

I didn't know how many people he had killed over the last six years, but I imagined it was enough that now he wouldn't even bat an eye at killing anyone who threatened me.

We sat back down at the chairs, Sal wordlessly handing me a fresh beer from the cooler, Enzo holding his stomach while he laughed, Adrian looking like he ate something sour.

"That girl has you wrapped around her finger, and you don't even know it," Enzo said, wiping his eyes when his laughter died down to a chuckle.

"She's a pain in the ass," Adrian grumbled, taking another swig of his beer.

"Ah, talking about Ash, are we?" I asked as I popped the top on the beer. Adrian shot me a look at that that had me grinning.

"Don't even start, Carmen. I have so much more material to take you down if I need it," he said, glancing at Leo and back at me with a devious glint in his eyes. I put my hands up in defeat, a smirk still tickling at the corner of my mouth.

"I didn't say anything, Adrian. Besides, you aren't the only one that butts heads with her," I said, glancing at Sal, who stiffened slightly, narrowing his eyes. There was an odd tension between the three of them that I had noticed developing over the years. Ash fought and flirted with both Sal and Adrian, and neither of them seemed to mind that her attention wasn't solely focused on one of them. I was waiting to see who would break the dam first. Only time would tell.

"Did anyone get fireworks?" I asked, moving the conversation away from delicate subjects. The more I prodded, the more likely they would prod back, and I had just given them all a reason to try to get something out of me. The last thing I needed was these five men racing to Kansas City to deal with a handful of gang members that didn't even matter. Besides the gang they were in, I had no clue who they even were after four years.

"Shit!" Benny hissed, pulling out his phone. "I knew I forgot something."

"There will be stands open somewhere nearby tomorrow," Enzo said, though his face filled with similar anxiety, as he also pulled out his phone to locate the nearest places. Usually, the boys put on a huge display off the dock for me and the moms to watch from our spots in the sand. Occasionally I would join them, but for the most part, I preferred enjoying the show.

Sal's phone chimed with an incoming text message, and he looked at it, his brows furrowing as he glanced down.

"Dad's here. Travis just texted me," Sal murmured, bringing the more cheerful mood back to the darkness. "Adrian," he said, standing from his chair and nodding his head in the direction of the house.

The bitterness I felt about that man seemed to curl around me like cellophane, suffocating and trapping me in its clutches. He had something to do with this. He *did* something, promised something, and now he was here. I didn't want to talk to him yet. Couldn't stand the idea of looking at that man's face, especially not when it was so very similar to three men I held so dear.

"We'll go through the basement entrance. You won't have to see him yet," Leo said, standing from his chair and glancing at Benny. They locked eyes for a moment, some sort of silent communication passing between them, before Benny finally nodded.

"Enzo and I will bring in the cooler," he said, as he started dousing the fire with sand.

Leo and I headed back up the dark path toward the house. I could see the main living area windows were illuminated still, and I could only imagine what the moms were dealing with Salvatore having arrived. My mom could barely stand to deal with him since Papa died, but on the occasions she had to see him, she usually handled it like a pro. Liliana, however, loved him helplessly, even if he left her to live without him most of the time, probably cheating on her with whatever women threw themselves at a high-ranking member of the Mafia.

We rounded the corner of the house, heading toward the basement entrance that sat on the side. It was not often used, usually only people bringing in deliveries came through this way, but we had all used it to sneak in and out during the summers as kids. Leo's hand brushed against mine when the path narrowed. That spark between us immediately reignited, and the knowledge that we were essentially alone here seemed to heighten our awareness of one another. His hand took mine, pulling me to a stop and then closer so we were chest to chest.

"I don't want to go in there," he whispered, his head tilted down so his nose could brush against mine.

"Me neither," I said back, letting my hand trail up his other arm to find its home in the divot between his neck and shoulder, fingers splaying and touching the bit of hair at the back of his neck.

Our mouths immediately fused together, lips, teeth, and tongues moving together frantically as our hands roamed. I hadn't put any shoes back on, so when his hands slipped under my leggings, cupping my ass for a moment, before coming back up to tug my leggings down my legs. I kicked them the rest of the way off, fingers ferociously going for the button and zipper on his jeans, but he stopped me, wrapping my wrists in one of his big hands and walking me back so I was pressed to the wall.

His head dipped down, mouth descending on my neck as the fingers of his free hand traveled down my stomach, caressing over my hip, before dipping between my legs. He groaned against my skin as he felt how wet I already was. His rough fingers ran along the wetness, gathering it up, before making quick, tight circles at my clit.

"Soon," he whispered in my ear. "I'm going to get you completely naked and feast on you for hours." He pressed two fingers past my entrance, my pussy immediately clamping around them. "We won't have to be quiet or quick, and I'll make you sing so loud you'll scream my name."

His words were like an accelerant, making me burn from the inside out. He wanted this. Wanted me. And not just once. Not just now, he was planning, in his mind, *hours* of this. I wanted it so much I could barely breathe.

"Leo," I whimpered as I felt that familiar fire building low in my belly.

"Yes," he said, his fingers relentless as he pressed his lips to mine again, his tongue just as insistent as his fingers inside of me.

The kiss and the press of his thumb against my clit were enough to push me over the edge. My orgasm crashed over me, his mouth the only thing there to swallow my moans of pleasure.

He pulled his fingers from me, leaving me feeling incredibly empty, before pushing his pants past his hips, his cock springing free. I went to reach for him, hoping to feel the hot, silky hardness of his cock in my hand again, but he snatched my hand, putting it on his shoulder, before grabbing me by the backs of the thighs to lift me off the ground.

I gasped at the suddenness of it and the ease with which he lifted me. There was no hesitation in the strength of his arms as he pressed me closer to him, so his cock rubbed against my slit. The feel of us pressed together like this was so good, but I wanted him in me. I wanted to feel him inside. I wanted my body to swallow this man whole.

"I can't go slow," he grunted out, his voice hushed as he pinned me with his body against the wall again, my legs spread wide for him, his big hands digging into the skin of my ass so deliciously.

"I don't want you to," I breathed back, gripping his shoulders roughly as I felt the head of his cock slip past my folds, collecting the wetness from my first orgasm. I bit my lip to fight the moan that wanted to escape at the feel of his long, hard length sliding against me.

He stopped, his head at my entrance pressing in just slightly. Our gaze was locked, breathing mingling and ragged. The moment seemed to last forever. I wanted to say I trusted him. That I loved him, but I felt like he could see it in my eyes, because his lips met mine again. This kiss was less ferocious, more tender, but no less passionate.

I tilted my hips as he pressed in a bit more. I couldn't help the groan that came from me as I felt the first few inches slipping in. My body was eager for him, slick and clamping down, as if it wanted to suck him in deeper.

"God … Carmen … you're so tight," he let out with a harsh breath, pressing his forehead to mine as he pulled out just slightly, then pressing in deeper than he had been a moment before. Just the feel of having him in me, the knowledge that this was really happening, had my insides coiling with another climax already.

"More," I panted out, digging my heels into his ass and urging him on. He growled, pressing in even farther until he was fully seated, staying there for a moment, our harsh breathing the only sound.

"I don't want to hurt you. I—"

"Leo," I said quietly, waiting until his eyes were on me. "I said I don't want you to go slow."

His eyes seemed to switch from worried to wild in an instant. His hips reared back, letting me feel each inch of him pulling out of me, before he surged forward, slamming in hard again. My head fell back against the house. I bit my lip to keep the scream that wanted to burst from me inside.

His thrusts were hard and fast, everything I wanted and needed. He grasped my ass so hard, pulling me to meet his thrusts. I could hear the slapping of our skin in the night air, our panting breaths, and the occasional uncontrollable moan.

"I—I can't—" he started, but his hips began thrusting a bit more uncontrolled, the feeling in my stomach starting to tingle and burst as it spread and grew. "Come with me," he grunted, his pounding into me becoming untamed as my third orgasm of the day finally exploded within me. My hands clenched against him, pussy pulsing as his cock got even harder. My orgasm seemed to trigger his. Before I fully came down to aftershocks, I could feel the hot spill of his cum into my core in spurts.

We stayed locked together against the house for several moments, letting our breath return to normal. Leo pressed his forehead to mine once more, eyes closed and face so serene.

"I'd like to say you're mine, Carmen, but the truth is I've been yours for a long time," he finally murmured as he slipped his softening cock from within me and opened his eyes to take me in.

"I think you may have been the only person I've ever wanted," I said back, looking up at those hazel eyes with wonder at what he just confessed to me.

Slowly he set me down, his hands immediately moving from where they had been holding me up to cup my face. When our lips met again, there was so much feeling behind it, so many unsaid words, but with the knowledge we had time for that now, and there wasn't much to hold us back.

Slowly we got ourselves put back together, me slipping my leggings back on before we finally made our way to the door. Leo entered the code on the keypad and opened it for us to go in. The basement had two ways to get down, one from the kitchen, where we could hear the others conversing, and one that opened up directly next to the stairs that led to bedrooms.

We made our way over there, quietly walking up and opening the door. No one in the kitchen would have been able to see us, but not everyone was in there, apparently, since Adrian was pacing in the living room, looking like he was one wrong move away from losing his mind and doing something he could never come back from.

Leo and I stood perfectly still at the top of the basement stairs, not wanting to alert him to our presence.

"How could you do this, Salvatore?" came my mother's sobbing shriek, making Adrian's head whip up in that direction, and in doing so, his gaze passed over the two of us. At first, it didn't seem like he noticed us, too absorbed in our crying mother who I could tell was being consoled by Benny, but then those eyes slid right back, taking us in. His face turned a darker shade of red. Whatever fury he had already been trying to hold down was now unleashed.

CHAPTER 15

CARMEN

"**W**hat the fuck is this?" Adrian demanded, stalking over and grabbing Leo by the front of his shirt to drag him away from me and into the room. Leo didn't look too mussed. His short hair was a little wild on top where my fingers raked through it and his shirt was rumpled. Which could only mean I looked like I had been ravaged.

"Adrian, calm down," I said, following them straight into the living room, thus exposing us to the whole family.

"Calm down, Carmen? Calm down?" Adrian yelled, his chest heaving as his other hand curled into a fist. "First, I find out Salvatore has decided you—yes, *you*, Carmen Valeria *LaMartina*—" He said our last name so pointedly, shooting a glance over at the kitchen that could stop a man's heart. "—are being sold off like some sort of Mafia princess to the Irish, and now *this*," he said, pulling Leo closer so they were nearly nose to nose. "Did you just fuck my sister, Leonardo?"

"What?" came a soft cry from my mother, who I turned to see was being held by Benny.

But I couldn't really focus on anything else that was going on, because the words "being sold off" and "Mafia princess" were swirling in my head like a swarm of bees.

My eyes fell on Salvatore, who was smoking a cigarette, a glass of some sort of amber liquid in his hand, as he leaned against the kitchen island, brown eyes glaring across at the three of us.

"Did you?" Adrian asked again, ignoring our mother, this time bringing his fist up, his strong arms ready to punch Leo right in the face. Leo's arms remained loose at his sides, not even twitching with the need to defend himself.

I whirled around, landing a solid kick to Adrian's stomach, not enough to hurt him but enough to wind him for a moment, causing him to release his hold on Leo's shirt and step back a few paces.

"He did, but that's not the important thing right now. Stop being an asshole, Adriano!" I screamed, glaring down at him where he was doubled over, gasping for breath. "Is what he just said true?" I asked, turning back to the kitchen and letting my gaze land on Sal, because every time I was reminded that his father was in the room, it made me sick.

"Well, clearly you aren't a princess, if that's what you're referring to," Salvatore said with a chuckle before taking another swallow of his liquor. I very nearly growled at him, stepping forward toward the kitchen with my teeth bared and fists readying. I would gladly punch that smirk right off his face. But I didn't get far as strong arms wrapped around me, keeping me firmly in place.

"What did you do?" Leo asked coldly, his voice right in my ear as he held my back to his chest.

"Negotiations had to be made. If O'Shea had any daughters, we may have been able to work something out where one of you married her, but as it is that we both had sons, I had to find a solution somewhere. Thank goodness Bernardo had some female stock for me to pull from," Salvatore said, his voice filled with more humor over the situation and our reactions than anything else.

"This is wrong, Dad," Sal said, hands shoved roughly through his hair as he leaned against the counter over the sink. He looked like he was about to be sick. I felt similarly.

"Wrong? What is wrong about doing what has to be done? We need strong ties with the others, otherwise we're facing *war*, son. Something I've been avoiding since Bernardo died."

My mom released another sob, turning into Benny's chest while he ran his hand gently over her back.

"She's not doing this," Leo growled, still holding me.

"She has no choice. *I* have no choice, Leonardo. And if you just accepted your role, you'd see just how imperative it is for all of us," Salvatore said, his voice growing louder in frustration with each word.

I didn't know all the reasons yet, and I wasn't sure what the terms were, but I had a sudden moment of clarity. Unfortunately, Salvatore was right. If they wanted to avoid a war, which would mean so many unnecessary deaths, I had to go as some sort of offering to the Irish, potentially marrying one of them.

If I didn't do this, I was putting everyone in this room at risk. I was thrusting my family into a war. While every part of being sold off as property rebelled against who I was as a person, one thing I could never do was let anything happen to them because of me.

I took a deep breath, feeling the strong beat of Leo's heart against my back, his arms wrapped around me, no longer to restrain me, but in a protective, possessive way. This man had just survived being out of the country, thrown into dangerous situations that could have killed him who knew how many times over. I would never be the reason he had to die at the hands of a mob member. I loved him too much to put him in that sort of danger after having just come home.

"I'll do it," I said quietly as Sal turned to continue arguing with his father, but he stopped short when he heard what I said. Everyone seemed to freeze at my words, eyes turning to stare at me.

My mom exploded out of Benny's arms, turning to face me with her puffy, tear-filled eyes.

"My *Carmenetta*, my love, no," she said brokenly, stumbling across the room to me. Leo's arms seemed to tighten on me for a moment, before he released me to my mother, who was now clutching me, face buried in my shoulder.

"I can't say no and be the reason any more of us die," I said firmly, holding her back just as tightly. My father was dead because of this life, and I couldn't guarantee Adrian, Sal, or Enzo wouldn't be killed, since they were in it too, but I could save my mom, Liliana, and Benny.

I could save Leo.

"At least *she* has some sense," Salvatore said with a triumphant huff.

Liliana, who had been clutching Enzo this whole time, remaining in shocked silence, seemed to snap, charging over the few steps to her husband and reeling back to smack him hard across the face. His head snapped to the side, the cigarette he had just placed between his lips flying away.

"This should never have even been an option. How could you do this? How could you ruin her life like this?" Liliana demanded. Salvatore turned back to her, his eyes narrowing as he let his hand rub at the cheek that was still red from where her small palm hit him.

"She won't have a bad life, Liliana. Look at you and Maria. Don't you have a good life?"

"I married you for *love,* Salvatore! Maria married Bernardo *for love*! What you're asking Carmen to do is sick! You're treating her like property, like chattel. Sold off so all you men can build your empires bigger and better. She shouldn't have to become an Irishman's prisoner because you and Manzo Morelli need the connection. Find another way!" she screamed.

Very few times in our lives had we seen Liliana burst with anger. My mother was more prone to that than she was, but to have her anger directed at her husband, the one person she never fought back against, was almost as shocking as everything else that had happened today.

Salvatore's eyes seemed to soften, but only slightly as he looked at his wife, the softness turning to utter sadness for the briefest of moments, before his cold mask slipped back in place. The Capo was back.

"There's nothing I can do. If we don't want to fight in a war, she has to go with them. We have a few days, and she'll be sent with Freddy back to Chicago."

A few days?

My knees wobbled a little at that, the weight of my mother on me seeming to become heavier.

"What are the terms?" Sal demanded, glancing at me before pulling his mother into his arms.

"She'll marry Freddy O'Shea. Not right away. They will take her with them and make sure she'll behave." He gave me a pointed look at that, his eyes warning me against any mischief I might have already been brewing inside of me. "This only works because I have told them she's like a daughter to me, because Bernardo may as well have been my brother."

My mother scoffed, pulling away from me to look at Salvatore.

"'Like a daughter to you,'" she quoted bitterly. "You don't even know your own sons, let alone my Bernardo's children, yet you walk in whenever it suits you, demanding we all play our parts and do as you say."

"To keep you all *safe*!" he roared, slamming his hand holding the liquor onto the table, the glass shattering across the counter. Liliana and my mom shared a dark look.

"You keep our sons safe, Salvatore?" Liliana asked, her voice letting on her disgust. "You dragged Junior and Enzo into this life, while our baby went off to be a soldier just to avoid you!"

"My Adriano tried to stay away, but you sank your claws in him, just as you did your own sons. You think we're stupid? That we don't know what you've done, Salvatore? And now you want to take my daughter?" Mama asked, spitting on the ground before her. Salvatore said nothing, crossing his arms over his broad chest and glaring out at all of us. If it weren't for the whole force of the Italian Mafia at his back, we would make a pretty good, united front, but as it was, he still had the upper hand on us.

"What do you get out of this?" Leo asked coldly after a few beats of tense silence.

"An in. The American-Irish have been working with European connections. The money is good. It will boost us more globally and open a door to a new market in the States too." He said it so quickly, without hesitation, letting us know, without the important details, what their organization stood to gain from me simply marrying Freddy O'Shea.

"What market?" Leo growled, stepping forward, his body tensing like a lion stalking his prey.

"You don't want to be in the life, remember, Leonardo? It's better that you don't know," Salvatore said, pulling his cigarettes from his pocket and lighting another.

It was like Leo knew something he wasn't sharing, something about these plans of his father's had clicked in his head. And if I saw it, so did the other boys. Benny stepped forward to our mom, but his eyes locked with Leo's, that silent communication passing between them. If Leo knew something, it was best to not divulge it. Maybe it could be used as leverage later.

But there would be no later. No rescue. I was going to be married off, like property.

"We can talk more tomorrow. You're all upset and have been drinking," Salvatore said with a wicked smile. "I'm sure you'll all feel better about our situation in the morning," he said, moving back over to the liquor station in the kitchen to pour himself another glass.

I couldn't agree more. The weight of the room was too heavy for me to handle anymore, and I turned on my heel, heading up the stairs before anyone else breathed another word.

CHAPTER 16

LEO

I watched her go, warring with myself as she quickly made her way up the stairs. I wanted to go with her, but I wanted to kill my father just as much. The audacity of this man was limitless. He, like always, barged right back into our lives and demanded he control everything. He was going to take Carmen from us, rip her away from everything she knew and loved, to marry an Irish Mafia prince so he could, what? Have a better foothold in human trafficking?

I knew that's what it was. I knew that's why he was doing this. There was a lot of money in the sex trade. He had been dealing in it in small doses off and on over the last decade. Sal had told me when he and Enzo found out, and Enzo had refused to be a part of it.

"Come on, Ma. Let's get you to bed," Benny murmured in front of me, his eyes never leaving my face as he tried to process what was showing there.

"Benito, he can't do this," she sobbed again. He shushed her, steering her toward the stairs as Sal pulled our mom out of the kitchen area.

"Enzo," Sal said, ushering Mom into his arms. Enzo didn't have to be told. He scooped up our mother in his arms, carrying her down the hallway to her room that sat on the first floor.

"Don't worry, my love. You'll see it's all for the best," Dad said to Mom as she and Enzo disappeared around the corner. That just left me, Sal, and Adrian in the room. Whatever rage Adrian had toward me minutes ago was now firmly redirected at Dad.

"Does Morelli know about this?" Sal asked once they were all safely away from the large, open room.

"He'll thank me once it's done," Dad said, sipping the new glass of bourbon he had poured himself. Dad making moves like this without Morelli knowing meant he was not only trying to prove his worth was more than his station, but also to show the rest of the Mafia he was someone to contend with. If it went well, he would be more powerful, perhaps even promoted. If it didn't, he would be feeding our region to the wolves.

He seemed so overly smug, thinking this was airtight, that no one could touch him.

"What are you trying to do, Salvatore? Become his underboss? Consigliere? Being a Capo isn't enough for you?" Adrian asked, his voice so full of venom.

"The higher I am, the better for all of *you!*" he yelled, clearly having enough of being the target of all of our ire.

"What do you want? Hm, Dad? You want us running the organization? You think that's what any of us want?" Sal asked bitterly.

"It's not what we want, Sal. It was never about us. It's always been about him and his legacy," I said finally, my eyes meeting my father's. He looked at me strangely. This man who I hadn't seen in years, who would rather I have become a soldier in his ruthless games than try

to be better, couldn't understand why we all fought so hard against him. He would never understand.

"It's always been for you and your brothers," Dad said, his face turning red with restrained anger.

"So, what are the terms, Dad? Carmen plays her part, marries O'Shea and you get a foothold in whatever this new merchandise is? What are they moving that's so big? A new drug? Weapons?" Sal asked, fists clenching. Adrian moved closer to him, eyes menacing as he backed my brother up.

"You'll know when you need to," Dad said, before slamming the rest of his bourbon and heading toward the hallway where Enzo had just taken Mom.

Enzo came out, putting a hand out to Dad's chest.

"She doesn't want to see you," Enzo warned.

"She's my wife. I'll see her if I want to," Dad growled, before pushing past him and down the hall.

If that wasn't a perfect snapshot of what their marriage was, I didn't know what was. My father barging in on the life she had to create on her own, doing whatever he pleased.

Benny came down the stairs a moment later and the five of us just stood in the large room, like we weren't sure what to do or say.

"Carmen?" Adrian asked Benny, who shook his head.

"Door is locked. She told me to fuck off and then I heard the shower turn on," Benny said as he made his way to the liquor himself. At first, I thought he was going to make himself a drink, but instead, he picked up the decanter of bourbon my dad had been drinking from, moving briskly with it clutched in his hand down the basement stairs off the kitchen.

We all followed and spilled out into the finished basement. To the right was an extensive entertainment room, complete with a billiard and poker table, mainly used when Dad entertained guests. To the left were the stores. There was a room for the wine cellar, a room for shelf-stable stock, a secured door with weapons that we were never allowed in as children, and, of course, a room for hard liquor storage.

Benny stepped into the liquor room, the decanter still in hand, and without warning, he threw the crystal against a wall of glass bottles, an explosion of clear shards of crystal and glass flying everywhere. He didn't look at us as he pulled a crowbar from the wall that was used to open crates and began slamming it into other shelves of bourbon, smashing them all to the ground.

Benny started letting out rough grunts and pained screams as he unleashed what he was feeling on the room. I wanted to release my own rage somehow, but the only thing that would slay the beast inside me was to see death. My father, Freddy O'Shea, hell, even Jeremy fucking Wallingford could die just by association.

But thinking of Jeremy again seemed to spark something in my brain.

Benny finished with the glass bottles, chest heaving, scrapes from shards having hit his skin littering his face and the exposed parts of his arms. Bourbon was Dad's booze of choice, but thankfully, Benny left the whiskey unharmed on the other side of the room.

"You good now, Benny? Ready to make a plan instead of throw a tantrum?" Adrian asked. Benny threw the crowbar to the ground, glaring at his brother for a minute as he calmed himself.

"What the fuck are we going to do?" Benny asked finally, turning to pace, the sound of glass crunching under his feet.

"I don't know yet!" Adrian snapped, pulling a bottle of whiskey from the shelf on the other side of the room and stalking from the room, taking the side entrance that Carmen and I had come through just forty minutes or so ago, although it felt like it could have been hours.

"What are we doing? We need to think of something to get her out of this," Sal hissed as we followed Adrian down the dark path. I felt strange, passing where Carmen and I had just been pressed against the wall, having a moment of complete bliss not but an hour ago, and now her brothers and mine were trudging back to the fire pit where we had been to try to figure out how we would keep her from being sold off like property.

No one moved to light the fire. Instead, the five of us sat around our folding chairs, passing the whiskey around to each other in a slow circle for a few minutes. The reality and gravity of it all was finally sinking in more fully for all of us, and my heart felt like a heavy stone, sinking down to my stomach. I had just gotten her. We hadn't discussed the next steps or what it meant that we had just had sex, but now it didn't matter at all, not if she was going to belong to Freddy O'Shea.

"What does Wallingford have to do with this?" I suddenly asked, breaking the silence that had settled over us. Enzo looked over at me, his brow furrowed.

"That's a good question," he said, pulling out his phone and typing furiously as he started digging things up on the weasel.

"What are our options? What can we do to get her out of this?" Benny asked as the bottle came around to him.

"We need something bigger than the relationship with the Irish to please Morelli. Or we have to find something that the Irish would be willing to take instead of Carmen," Sal said, his eyes almost vacant as he stared off into the distance at the black lake water.

"This wasn't supposed to happen! He promised me when I joined, Sal! He gave his word that Carmen would never even be thought of as a option if I came into the fucking fold and now this?" Adrian exploded suddenly.

My eyes shot over to him as he abruptly stood from his chair, hands running through his hair and gripping like he was about to rip it from his own scalp.

"What are you talking about, Adrian?" Benny asked, his voice quivering. Sal sighed, glancing at Adrian and reaching across the circle to take the bottle from Benny.

"The deal that Adrian made when he joined us three years ago…" Sal said quietly, pulling from the bottle without taking his eyes off Adrian.

"He said she'd never get pulled in. He said she'd be safe and free to live however she wanted. And now—" He broke off with a choked sound.

"He threatened something similar to this and Adrian joined right after. It was the only thing that would keep Dad from pulling her in and selling her off to the highest bidder. Enzo found … pictures of her that he had been passing around to other Bosses in the States," Sal murmured, filling in more than what Adrian's blind rambling did.

I couldn't believe what I was hearing. Not once, but twice now, my father had tried to use Carmen. The mysterious reason Adrian agreed to join? To keep Carmen safe. And pictures of her?

I was going to lose it. I could feel it in the way my heart was beating like a wild drum throughout my whole body.

"Pictures?" came a quiet voice from the path. Carmen stepped out, her hair wet from a shower, loose baggy sweats covering her and masking her body. Enzo cringed when she came farther into the circle, his eyes going back to the phone in his hand as he continued his search.

Adrian released his hair, looking up at his sister as she came and sat in the chair beside me as she had earlier. The agony on his face was apparent as he realized she had been listening to everything. No one said anything for a moment.

"Where are these pictures now?" she asked.

"I made sure they were destroyed," Enzo said.

"So, you thought Salvatore Lupo was just going to let me go when you joined up, huh, Adrian?" she asked, turning her head to look up at her brother. I couldn't see her face through the curtain of wet curls that were hanging down, but I could imagine what she looked at him like. A seething anger burning just below the surface of her eyes. "Don't you think I would have rather made that choice myself than you chaining yourself to him and this organization?"

Adrian's face was pained as he took in her words.

"I meant what I said. I'll do this, because while you all go around thinking you have to make the sacrifices and be the big heroes, the only way to actually prevent your deaths is a small thing. I'll marry Freddy. I'll be sad, I'll hate everything that comes with it, but at least I'll know you all didn't die for me," she said, her voice getting stronger and more resolved with each word.

"You aren't a sacrificial lamb, Carmen!" I said, my voice a rumble.

"And neither was he," she yelled right back at me, pointing behind her to Adrian. "But here we are."

"Let us help you, Sis. If we can find a way that won't mean war, don't you think it's worth it?" Benny asked. She let out a heavy sigh, closing her eyes for a moment.

"Of course, it would be worth it. But I don't think such a way exists," she said, standing and wandering farther down the beach.

I watched her go for a minute, before turning back to Enzo.

"Figure out why Wallingford's involved. I feel like he's the key somehow," I said.

"I need my computers to get a full picture. But something is here," he replied, not looking up from his phone as he stood. "Sal, I want to keep looking, drive me to the office?"

"I'm coming with you," Benny said, standing from his chair the same time Sal did. Adrian stood for a moment as the others passed, his eyes following where Carmen slowly walked away from the cold, dead fire pit between us. I could tell he wanted to go with them. He wanted to be there the moment the pieces came together, but he didn't want to leave Carmen alone. I had no intention of leaving. If I couldn't murder my father right now, or hunt down the Irishmen, the only other place I wanted to be was in her arms.

"Do you love her?" Adrian asked, his eyes flicking back to me. The anger he felt at me earlier when he saw us had dissipated as the rest of this horrible revelation was divulged, but it sat there in his eyes once more.

"I do," I told him seriously.

"For a long time, I'd imagine," he said, more to himself.

"Longer than I admitted to myself," I agreed. He snorted a laugh through his nose, shaking his head.

"I'd say don't fuck this up, but your dad may have done that for you already," he grumbled.

"I don't care what it takes, Adrian. I mean it. She isn't going with that fucking Irish trash," I spat.

"Go take care of her while we try and work this angle," Adrian said, jerking his head in her direction, before turning to follow where the others had just left.

I immediately followed where Carmen went. I couldn't see her anymore in the darkness, but she was easy to track, her bare footprints pressing into the cool sand where the water had lapped at the beach. When she finally came into view, I made my footsteps noisier so she could tell I was coming up behind her.

She paused, turning her head so I knew she heard me, but not facing me completely. The urge to pull her into my arms was too strong to resist. How many years had I kept myself from touching her? Now I felt like I had permission. My hands went to either side of her waist, sliding around to rest against her stomach over the sweatshirt she was wearing. I pressed myself in close, ducking my head down so I could press my lips to the top of her head.

Her small hands came to rest on top of mine, lacing through them. We didn't say anything, merely enjoying being wrapped in the comfort that this simple holding had.

"I shouldn't have stayed away so long," I said as I let my thumb start rubbing slow circles against the top of her silky soft hand.

"You didn't really have a choice," she offered, tilting her head back so she could look up at me. Sadness swirled in those green orbs, as well as regret. The way she was holding me told me she didn't regret what we had done today, that we had crossed the line, but that we didn't have more time. "We are all proud of you for what you've done, Leo. No one was mad that you were gone."

"I missed too much. I should have been where the most important people were, not halfway around the world fighting someone else's battles," I said, my fingers tightening over hers. "I didn't want to be part of my father's life, but I didn't realize until I was leaving, too late, that I wasn't just leaving him. I was leaving you."

Her breath hitched in her chest and for a moment all she did was squeeze me tighter to her, before she turned in my arms, looking up at me. I took one hand from her waist, threading it through the back of her hair and tilting it up farther so we could see directly into each other's eyes.

"I can't let you do this, Carmen. I finally have you. And now I'm supposed to let you go be with another man? A man you don't even love? If you were in love with someone else, maybe I'd…"

She scoffed at me, eyes crinkling with humorous skepticism at me almost saying I'd let her go.

"I don't think there could ever be another man I could love the way I love you." Her words were only a whisper, but I heard every one of them. I felt the shiver run through my body with them.

"I can't let you make this sacrifice, because I love you too much for you to give up anything else," I whispered.

My lips came down to meet hers, her fingers threading through my hair to hold me closer. And even though that knife was still poised over us, in that moment, I felt more whole than I had in years.

CHAPTER 17

CARMEN

This kiss was slow, soft, full of love and promises we would make if our lives were different. I felt the tender press of his lips, the soft tickle of his tongue against mine, the way he gently clung to me like he didn't want any space between us.

I pulled back first, my eyes searching his for a moment.

"Take me to bed?" I asked as my fingers trailed down from his hair to his neck.

He pulled me up by the back of my thighs so my legs could wrap around his hips, holding and carrying me back down the beach to the trail that led to the house. It was like I weighed nothing to him, no tremor in his arms as he effortlessly took me inside and up the stairs.

The house was quiet. We passed by the hallways that led to other bedrooms. The only sound I could hear was our breathing and the thrum of our hearts pressed together. Finally, we made it to his room. I had been in there plenty of times, mostly to see what he and Benny were up to when we were children, but this time I wasn't an annoyance. He set me down, kissing my forehead, before gently closing the door and turning back around to me.

We had already had sex tonight, but something about the way he looked at me in this moment with such love and longing had me feeling heated again, that fire starting low in my belly. The care, as well as the desire, made his eyes molten as they stared at me. It didn't matter that I was dressed in baggy sweats. He had seen me at some of my worst and yet he still wanted me.

"We can just go to sleep," he offered. Taking his shirt off as he moved to the duffel he had left on the floor to dig for sweatpants of his own. But I didn't say anything, watching as he undid his jeans. Letting them slip past his muscular ass and down those thick thighs. He had toed off his shoes apparently, and I missed that, but he turned around, his boxer briefs the only things on his body as he clutched his sweats in one hand.

I pulled the sweatshirt I had been wearing over my head, letting it drop to the floor, as I hooked my thumbs under the waistband of my pants and pushed them enough so they could pool at my feet. I hadn't put a bra on after my shower earlier, so I was only in a pair of black panties.

"Carmen, we don't have to. We already—"

"Do you not want to?" I asked, partially as a tease, but a little insecurity slipped in. He dropped the pants in his hand, taking two steps until he was right in front of me. His eyes looked me over hungrily for a moment before they met mine.

"I don't think there's been a moment since I laid eyes on you again that I didn't want you every second," he said, his voice rough, hands hovering like he wasn't sure if he could touch me or not. My heart fluttered, but I somehow felt so confident in this moment. I pressed up onto my toes, running my hands up his rippling stomach to his chest, where I placed a soft kiss right over his heart.

"Leo, I love you," I said, watching as his face somehow turned more feral and yet soft with adoration. "And I want you to make love to me."

I didn't have time to process what was happening before Leo was hauling me against him, his hand wrapped around my neck, and he was kissing me. He backed us into the bed, so we were tumbling on top of it, his legs spreading between mine so that I opened for him.

"I love you. I just got you and I can't lose you," he whispered against my lips as his hands roamed over me. I didn't say anything to that. Unless they could find a way that didn't involve war, I was going to go through with the deal. I couldn't live in a world without him or any of our brothers in it. But this moment didn't need that.

His lips and tongue trailed down my neck and to my chest, locking onto one nipple with his mouth as his hand teased and pinched the other. I was writhing under him. Biting my lip to stifle my moans. My hips bucked to his stomach, seeking friction on my now-soaking core. He released my nipple from his fingers, letting his hand gently caress its way down until they were pressing at my folds through my panties.

He grunted against my breast that he was still sucking relentlessly, popping off with a loud smack as he sat up between my legs. His hard cock was straining against his boxer briefs as he looked down at me. He ran his hands up my legs, the callouses rough against my calves, over my knees, and up my thighs, before his finger found the waistband of my underwear, tugging them down and lifting my legs to fully take them off.

It was the first time I was completely naked in front of him, my body fully on display, lying on his bed, wet and ready for him. A rumble of satisfaction came from his chest as he took me in.

"Better than I imagined," he said, his voice hushed. He stood quickly, pulling his own underwear off and tossing them haphazardly to the side.

And this was the first time I saw him in his full naked glory. And dear god, it didn't disappoint. His body was stunning, muscles hard and rippling, veins bulging in his arms, arms which were covered in ink that snaked up to his chest. His thighs were thick and roped with muscles, but that long cock was hard, protruding from him like it was begging to find a home inside of me. I was panting at the sight of him, a fresh wave of arousal wetting my now-exposed pussy.

He hunched and climbed back over me, his lips finding mine in a searing kiss. My arms wrapped around him, pulling him closer so his chest was pressed to mine. His cock rubbed against my folds as our tongues danced, catching each other's moans at the contact. I would never get tired of him. He was everything I had been waiting for. Every other sexual encounter paled in comparison. No one else would ever set me on fire the way he did. No one would ever feel so perfect against me.

The friction from his cock rubbing against my clit and the way he was kissing me with such passion, such overwhelming love, had that tension coiling in my belly. I could cum just from this, but I wanted more. I wanted him inside me.

"Leo, please," I begged, my fingers digging into muscles at his shoulder blades.

"What do you want, Carmen?" he whispered against my lips. "Tell me what you want and it's yours."

"You. I want you inside me now," I said, my voice sounding strained and desperate to my ears. He pulled back to look me in the eyes, his own face so full of need as he lined his head up, pressing into me.

After already being opened up by him just a few hours ago, my body greedily sucked him in, letting him press into the hilt almost immediately.

"Fuck! Carmen," he let out on a grunt as his hips hit mine. He came back down, his lips and tongue crashing into mine as he set a slow pace. I dug my nails into his skin, my breath coming out in pants against his lips. There was something ethereal, transcendent in the way we were connected.

That heat building up inside of me started to spread, my pussy clenching down on him with an impending orgasm.

"Little Song, I'm going to cum," he grunted against my lips, his hips starting to slap erratically against mine, pushing me over the edge. I had to press my hand to my mouth to suppress the guttural sounds coming from me.

"Yes, baby," he breathed as my pussy milked his cock, it hardening further, just before he pounded into me a few more times, his cum filling me for a second time tonight. With his final thrust, he pressed as far as he could, almost like we were truly one. His lips came down on mine, this time so sweetly and soft that my heart nearly melted from it, a gasp of a different type of pleasure coursing through me.

He rolled us over, still joined, but with me sprawled on his chest, his arms wrapping firmly around me to keep me there. Contentment settled into my bones as I settled onto him, my eyes drifting closed as I breathed in the scent of him. Despite what cataclysm awaited us when the sun came up, here locked together, I could sleep soundly, listening to the steady beat of his heart.

I woke before Leo. At some point in the early morning hours, we had shifted position, so I was still resting on his arm, but wasn't draped across him anymore. For a moment, I just looked at him as the sun spilled in through the curtains. His face was so relaxed, lips slightly parted. His dark hair was mussed from my hands and sleep, and he had a little stubble on his cheeks already growing in.

I smiled at the sight. It wasn't a dream or something I made up in my head. He had really told me he loved me last night. But then the reality of everything else crashed through the bliss in my brain, reminding me that this happiness was going to be short-lived.

I carefully moved from the bed, slipping on my clothes so I could dart across the hall to my room. It seemed to be early enough no one else was awake, and I quickly showered, pulling on shorts and a red shirt. It was the fourth of July after all.

My phone was still where I left it charging by my bed the night before, and I grabbed it, sticking it in my back pocket so I could go start the coffee in the kitchen. I had no idea if the others had come back last night, but there were still the moms who would most certainly want coffee once they woke up.

It was a little eerie being the only one awake in this big lake house. We spent a lot less time here than we did when we were children, and I usually woke up in those days to a cacophony of noise as the boys and the moms prepared breakfast. Being the only one awake now, waiting for the coffee to finish so I could grab my first cup was strange.

I glanced at the broken glass still shattered across the counter from Salvatore's outburst last night. I started cleaning it up when my phone buzzed in my pocket.

[Rory: We're up! Going to get ready, then head over. You awake, bitch?]

[Daph: I hope there's coffee.]

I grinned, thinking about seeing them, then it faltered. Oh fuck, they were coming here. The idea of my two best friends being in the midst of all this right now sounded awful. I didn't need any more people I cared about being put in compromising positions. But how could I keep them from coming?

The truth was, I couldn't. They wouldn't leave me alone if I tried. They would be there for the day, maybe stay overnight, and then go back to their lives; Rory teaching art at the local elementary school, and Daph with her tattoos. They would know something was up eventually, given that I was about to be shipped off to Chicago, so I might as well break the news in person.

[Me: I'm up, coffee is being made.]

[Daph: Thank god.]

I smiled, imagining my half-awake best friend while her chipper sister pushed her to get herself ready. But the smile faded quickly from my face when Salvatore appeared at the mouth of the hallway that led to the bedroom suit he and Liliana shared.

"Oh good. You made coffee," he said, walking over to the pot behind me and getting a mug to pour some for himself. The way he strode through the room was exactly how he had my whole life, confidence oozing from every pore. He felt like he was untouchable. I remained still, waiting until he made his way around to the other side of the island, before I went to get myself a cup.

I was used to Salvatore, of course. After my Papa died, he became the only adult male authority figure in my life, a fact that he was clearly using now. He was much more present when we were younger, but it was about the time Leo and Benny started high school that he came back to Lee's Summit less and less.

I cringed internally at the strange feeling of pride that his small bit of praise gave me. The inner child in me getting a rush from it.

"Not very talkative in the morning, Carmen? I thought you'd be used to waking up so early since you work at my coffee shop," Salvatore said, his brown eyes twinkling with amusement as I turned around to face him. *His* coffee shop. But of course, it was his. It couldn't have been Liliana's, not when he controlled everything. I hated that he had his fingers in all of our lives, like some sort of puppet master, showing up only often enough to remind us that we were never truly free of him and his influence.

Salvatore didn't see us as people, not even his own sons. They were soldiers for him to use. Stock he had bred from infants, trained to be something more useful to him when they were older. That's why we all learned to fight and use weapons. That's why, despite working so hard to keep ourselves away and apart from the life, we had all been dragged back in one way or another.

I could only imagine the look of hatred on my face, and I turned to face him again, but he seemed unperturbed.

"Just not talkative with assholes. You know how to spot them when you work in service for enough years," I said. His smile widened, but something malicious was hidden behind there.

"Those skills will come in handy when you're dealing with the Irish. Being able to know your place and when to talk will keep you from too much punishment." My skin crawled. "I have some men gathering your things while we're here. I managed to convince O'Shea that you should get one more day with friends and family before he takes you back with him. It helps that it's a holiday. So enjoy today, Carmen. It might be a long time before you see us again."

Like I would want to ever see his face with that smug look plastered there again.

Leo seemed to just appear at the bottom of the stairs at those words, as if his father's declaration summoned him, and while the sight of him in only the sweatpants he hadn't ever gotten on the night before was a beautiful one, I was trying not to choke on the fact that I only had today before I was going to be handed over to the Irish mob.

Leo's eyes didn't indicate any hint of tiredness as he glared at his father, moving over toward my side of the island.

"My boy, you've changed so much since I last saw you," Salvatore said, easily changing the subject. "All grown up."

"Grown and not willing to play your stupid games, Dad," Leo said, not bothering to pour himself any coffee as he came over, leaning on the counter beside me.

"You have to come up with another way, Dad. They can't have Carmen," Leo said, his eyes burning as he glared across the island at his father.

"It's too late for that, Leo, and you know it." As the words left Salvatore's lips, Leo pushed off the counter and stepped forward like he was going to snap Salvatore's neck with his own hands, but the front door banged open, and our brothers came through, tired and rumpled like they had been awake all night.

The look on Adrian and Benny's faces was enough to tell me they had information, but it wasn't what they were hoping for. Leo paused when they came in, taking them in as I was.

"Good morning, boys," Salvatore said cheerfully. "I'll let you all have the kitchen. I should wake up Liliana so she can start on breakfast."

He shot me one last smirk before heading back toward the suite where Liliana was sleeping, leaving the six of us in the great room.

CHAPTER 18

LEO

I woke up without Carmen, and immediately my pulse was racing. I could still smell her on me, the bed was still somewhat warm, like she hadn't been gone too terribly long, and when I quickly pulled on the sweatpants I had discarded and made my way down the stairs, I felt relief at first, hearing her voice, and then immediate fury when I heard what my father said to her.

Today. She only had today, and then she was being taken.

I barely contained myself while he was in the room. It took everything in me not to take his life right there for everything he's ever done, but especially this. I could almost feel the way his neck would give under my hands. He may have been strong, but I knew I was stronger now.

When the others came through the door, it gave me just enough pause before I leaped over the island. Just enough that I knew if I killed him right then, it would cause a whole other load of misery for all of us, because the Boss, Morelli, would not take kindly to the murder of one of his Capos.

We all watched quietly as he left the room, six pairs of eyes glaring at the man who had and would continue to make our lives hell.

"We need to get fireworks," Enzo said. It was so out of left field that it took me aback for a moment, before I looked at him and there was no excitement or playful gleam in his eyes. We couldn't be *here.* They needed me and Carmen to come with them so they could tell us what they had found.

"Let me get a shirt," I said, glancing at Carmen as the same realization came over her face at Enzo's words.

"I need to wake Mom. Rory and Daph are on their way," she said, immediately heading to the stairs.

"Rory and Daph can't come here, Carmen," Benny said, his eyes growing a bit more frantic at her words.

"They were already planning to, I can't exactly tell them, 'Don't come, Mafia business is afoot, and you'll be in danger.'"

"Damnit!" Benny hissed, storming from the front door to the kitchen, while Carmen headed back up the stairs.

I followed her, watching as she turned down the hall to where her mom's room was before I went back to mine. I decided to take a quick two-minute shower, the ice-cold water doing more to bring me back from the heated fury that seemed to be ever-present in my veins. Once I was clean enough, I pulled on fresh clothes and went back downstairs. Carmen was still not down, probably having to calm Maria again.

"Where are we going?" I asked, my eyes going over all the men still gathered in the living room.

"There's a few spots to hit," Sal said, giving a pointed look at me just as Carmen re-emerged.

"Ma will be down in time for them to get here," she said, going to slip her shoes we had discarded yesterday afternoon on, signaling for us all to file back out to Sal's SUV. There wasn't enough room for all of us, and for a moment Carmen stood outside the passenger door, glancing at the trunk and then at us.

"Just get in," Benny grumbled, grabbing her wrist and pulling her in, pushing her over to where I sat in the middle so she could sit on my lap. I tried not to smirk at the way Benny rolled his eyes as she shifted a bit to get more comfortable, my arms wrapping around her middle.

Enzo grinned, leaning forward to catch the eye roll.

"I just want everyone to know I love this, and I wish I had placed a bet years ago. I would be rolling in it right now," he said, gaining a smack from Adrian from the front seat.

Sal said nothing, just pulling out of the driveway, nodding toward the new set of guards that stood watch out front. As the seconds passed, the mood of the car grew somber. I tried to calm myself against the anxiety of the unknown by rubbing slow circles over Carmen's skin. Her hands found my arms, gripping me tightly, I could only imagine for the same reason.

Sal drove a little past a fireworks stand, pulling off on a strip of dirt at the side of the road that sat just outside some woods. We all piled out, eyes cast over to the fireworks stand that wasn't busy yet. We were far enough away that no one would overhear us, but close enough it seemed like we belonged there, just a group of people buying fireworks for the holiday.

"So, what do you know?"

"Jeremy Wallingford is a little more than we thought he was," Benny said, his hands fidgeting like he wanted to hit something.

"It took a bit of digging, but apparently he's the illegitimate son of O'Shea," Enzo offered when Carmen and I clearly wanted elaboration.

"They're brothers?" Carmen asked, her voice a bit harsh. Now that it was brought to my attention, I could see the resemblance. The same dirty-blond hair, classic good looks, but where Freddy had blue eyes, Jeremy's were more of a gray. Jeremy must have gotten just enough of his mother in him to make a difference in their jawline, but the rest of their faces were nearly identical.

"His obsession with Carmen?" I let out with a growl.

"Apparently the pictures that went around a few years ago? Jeremy was shown them," Sal said, glancing at Adrian. Everyone seemed like they were ready for bloodshed, but we didn't have enough to even entertain that yet.

"What else?" Carmen seemed to bark out. She was vibrating with fury. I both wanted to see her rip someone to shreds with that fury and fuck the anger right out of her.

"I saw O'Shea on my last mission. I know exactly what market Dad is trying to tap into. They're sex traffickers," I said, making Sal's eyes go wide.

"Did you know about this?" Sal shot at Enzo.

"They haven't done anything yet, or I would have seen something. I had no idea, though I was going to mention that was something these Irish were into, just to paint a picture of how much we should all hate them," Enzo said, looking a little sick.

"We're so far beyond hatred," Carmen said coldly, and I couldn't agree more.

"So, we have two problems. Carmen being sold off to marry this piece of garbage and the fact that your dad is planning on becoming a sex trafficker. What the fuck!" Benny said, his voice coming out as a harsh burst, trying not to draw attention to us.

"What do we do?" Enzo asked, seeming more lost than I had ever seen him.

"We kill him," Adrian said. His voice was so quiet, so calm, that I wasn't sure at first that I heard him correctly. We all just stared at him for a moment, taking in that he actually said those words, and then a moment longer as they sunk in and we realized he was right.

"I'm being collected tomorrow," Carmen said, her voice hollow. "There's no way to fix this in time."

The truth in those words was somehow so much more terrifying than anything I had faced before. I had been in active war zones; I had fought for my life with my bare hands on a covert mission where no one would find my body if I didn't make it out as the victor. I had been on a remote island off the coast of Sicily where my team and I were caught, the building exploding with us inside. But here and now, the fact that we were absolutely powerless to protect her from a moment of this fate, chilled me to my core. What could happen to her if we didn't get this done immediately?

I looked to Sal, my oldest brother, the leader of us all, and he met my eyes with sorrow. My hand reached out, grasping Carmen's in a tight grip. She seemed to fold into me, letting me more fully wrap my arms around her while she shook a little.

"If we do this, it has to be airtight. Morelli would have all of us killed if we don't do it perfectly," he said. I may have been in shock. The knowledge that she would be gone with the Irish come morning was almost too much for my brain to comprehend. We would have to let her go. *I* would have to let her go, or we would never get her back.

"Fuck no! She's not spending a moment in his custody!" Adrian yelled. A few of the workers in the tent popped their heads out to look over at us. Sal turned to him, bracing his hands on Adrian's shoulders while he heaved in breaths, looking over at where Carmen and I stood.

"Adrian, listen to me," Sal said, shaking him a little, and when that didn't work to get his attention, Sal grabbed his face with one hand, turning him to look in his eyes. "We will get her back. We will find a way to do this."

"It was for nothing, Sal," Adrian said, the pain and vulnerability in his voice something I hadn't heard from him since we were small… since his dad died.

"No. Not for nothing. If Salvatore Lupo is dead, who do you think will be Caporegime?" Sal asked, his dark eyes intense as they looked into Adrian's. "I need you to be my second, Adrian. You're the only man that can." This suddenly felt so intimate and intense that I wasn't sure the rest of us should have been there. They stared at each other for another moment, arms wrapped, and holding each other closely with clenched hands, before Adrian nodded, and Sal released him, standing back.

"How do we do this?" Enzo asked, though I could see the wheels turning in his head. He was amazing with computers, but part of that was because he was so damn good at puzzles. He could fit the pieces of any problem together in his mind, seeing all angles.

"We're going to need more people in on this, loyal to *us*, not Salvatore," Adrian said.

"I have a contact. Best sniper I know," I offered, knowing immediately Kia would be on board. This wouldn't just be helping me; it would be a redemption of our failed mission.

"My crew at the gym, they have no real love for Salvatore," Adrian offered, gaining a nod from Sal. His men were all based here, and though they all fell under Salvatore's leadership, technically, Sal was truly their leader.

"I've been dealing with most of the south side of our territory. I have some men who may be willing to at least look the other way, rather than get involved," Sal said.

"We'll start as soon as she leaves. There's no way it wouldn't be suspicious if we weren't here, knowing this is her last day. Benny will go back to his practice, and the rest of us will—"

"If you think I'm going back to Kansas City to work on old people, you're insane," Benny said roughly, cutting Adrian off before he could say anymore.

"No, Benny. You're not dropping everything you've worked for, for this," Carmen said, her body stiffening against mine. Benny walked right up to us, not seeming to care that he was more face-to-face with me than his sister. He glowered down at her, green eyes alight with determination.

"You think I'm going to let my whole family be in danger and not do something to help?" he asked, quieter than I expected. "You think I'm about to watch you sacrifice everything again and not try to change that?"

"We've always been a team," Enzo said, coming over to clap Benny and Carmen on the shoulders.

"And once I'm in charge, I can promise things will not be the same as they are under my father," Sal said, as he and Adrian stepped closer, as well.

I didn't know if Carmen could feel it, but there was a sense of rightness that happened when a team came together. A sense that, as long as everyone was working together, they could accomplish anything. We had always been that team, the six of us, and now we were all together again. We would be an unstoppable force, even against a gangster as formidable as my father.

CARMEN

We made our way back to the house, fireworks were loaded to overflowing in the back seat. The little stand was so happy with everything we bought; they didn't seem to remember how strange our little argument seemed to them previously. Since the boys had all lacked serious sleep last night, most of them went to their respective rooms to rest, except Leo, who seemed completely unwilling to leave my side.

I was greeted by riotous squeals and hard squeezes from my two best friends. I wasn't sure how I was going to tell them I probably wouldn't see them for a while.

Rory and Daph, of course, noticed Leo's attention while we helped get breakfast ready with the moms.

"You two seem pretty cozy. Care to fill a girl in on any new developments?" Rory asked in a not-so-quiet whisper as she came to the sink, where I was washing the fruit to cut.

"My mother is right there," I hissed back, glancing toward my mom, who was chatting with Liliana near the coffee station.

"He's looking at you like he doesn't want to lose you *and* like he wants to eat you alive," Rory said, drawing my gaze back to where Leo sat, rolling out the dough for cinnamon rolls. His eyes were, in fact, trained on me, a little smirk playing at the corner of his mouth when I caught him.

There did seem to be a war within his eyes over which emotion he was feeling. They seemed to flicker between worry and desire, the present moment, desire seemed to be winning out.

"Oh Leo, I think Daphne can handle the rest. Why don't you get the boat ready?" Liliana instructed more than asked. We all knew the difference in tone.

"Ma, I need to—"

"Boat, please Leonardo," she said, firmly.

Salvatore had left before we got back, having promised Liliana he would return before the real festivities began. No one cared he was gone. It was almost like his absence was a heavy burden lifted off of us, but we all knew it was poised to come crushing down on us again at any minute.

Leo came around to the sink to wash the flour off his hands, prompting me and Rory to move aside. Once his hands were washed, he leaned forward, seemingly unconcerned about all the eyes on him, as he pressed a kiss to my forehead, before walking out the back door to the garage, where the boat was kept.

The silence seemed to last a beat or two within the room, all eyes on me as a blush heated my cheeks violently.

"Oh, I knew this would happen," Liliana said, her voice tearful.

"Our babies, in love," Mama said, her voice just as strained with joy as Liliana's.

"I wonder when we can plan a wedding," Liliana murmured, coming over to push Daph into finishing the cinnamon rolls.

"Liliana..." I grumbled, pressing my cheeks onto my hands.

"What? Look at you two!" Liliana said with a sigh, coming over to squeeze my shoulders. "There's no way he's going to let you go with the Irish."

Well, he was. He had to let me go, at least for a little while. There wasn't a plan yet. There may never be a plan, and they were coming tomorrow, no matter what. My body shook a little with the thought of leaving, of having another man feel like he had any say over my person, my body.

"Let's just finish getting this ready before the boys all wake-up and start whining," I said as she gave me one final squeeze and got back to work, helping Daph with the dough.

The smell of baking bread and sausage must have roused the boys, because not long after we pulled the rolls from the oven, four tired men made their way down the stairs. They had all changed and showered, but greedily took the carafe of coffee, passing it around as the moms passed our plates.

The rest of the day felt oddly normal. The years where Leo hadn't been here to celebrate the fourth seemed like a blink. We went on the boat, swimming and playing like we did as teenagers, coming in to help the moms with lunch and to rest and watch our traditional *Independence Day* midday movie.

Leo settled in one of the corners of the sectional, quickly pulling me to him so I could snuggle in against him. I couldn't get the images of what we had done on this couch from my mind as his fingers gently trailed over the skin of my arm. How many times had we watched this very movie on this day, and I had imagined this happening? And it was happening.

His lips were at my neck off and on, sending pleasure spiking through my body. I glanced around. Most of the others had fallen asleep, all of us wrapped in blankets since the house was so cold with the air conditioning in comparison to the humid outdoors. Leo had draped a blanket that was tossed over the back of the couch over us at some point, and though his hands started to wander away from my arms and to my stomach, no one would notice.

"I fantasized about this for years," Leo whispered in my ear as his hand snaked under my shirt, moving to push underneath my bra, as his other arm snaked under my other side, fingers slipping down between my thighs over my shorts. I pressed back against him, feeling him already hard against my ass.

"Me too," I whispered back, wishing desperately that my friends and our brothers were anywhere else but here right now.

The movie went to the credits, but everyone stayed where they were; Leo's hot body behind me, as his hands wandered leisurely. I got lost in the feeling of his touch, the way our bodies were molded to one another, his breath cascading over my neck and shoulder as he kissed the exposed skin.

"I want to do so many things with you right now, Little Song, but your sounds are only for me," he whispered, pressing his hip more firmly against my ass while his hand that had snaked up my shirt grasped my breast firmly. I stifled the moan that wanted to escape, and it was a good thing too, because a moment later we heard the moms come back in from the deck where they had been chatting.

"Okay, kids. We need hands to prep for dinner," Liliana said, her voice rousing the others from where they had fallen asleep across the furniture.

Nothing could realistically happen in a room full of our friends and family, but what we had done certainly made it difficult to right ourselves and move to help with the others. My blood on fire, need for him pulsing within me, I somehow made my way from the couch with a quick kiss to begin chopping things while Sal and Adrian wandered out to get the grill started and Benny helped the twins pull the things needed from the pantry.

Leo stayed out a moment or two longer in the living room, picking up the blankets everyone else had tossed haphazardly around, and presumably giving himself a moment longer to calm down.

I could have almost forgotten what would happen tomorrow, until Salvatore returned, but this time he wasn't alone. Normally we would eat dinner on the patio, everyone camping out and chatting casually while we munched before fireworks, but now that Salvatore was back, and had company, we were forced to sit at the table.

Freddy O'Shea stared at me from where he sat directly across. His eyes were hungry, predatory as his gaze moved over my features and my chest. Leo sat beside me, his hand reaching over to firmly grasp my thigh, though only he and I knew it was there.

"Freddy wanted to see a truly spectacular fireworks show. Living in Chicago means he only gets to see the professional displays from a distance, but I told him you boys always do such a good job of making it amazing," Salvatore said.

"Such a fitting thing, a big display as a sendoff to Miss Carmen," Freddy said with a sickening smile.

"Sendoff?" Daph asked, her head snapping up from her plate. She never missed anything, that one, and she began eyeing everything so much more suspiciously.

I internally kicked myself for not finding a way to tell her and Rory what was happening earlier in the day. There was a slip here and there, someone mentioning

I was leaving, but the conversation was always moved along to the next topic before either of my friends could inquire for more. Now they were both alert, their eyes absorbing everything and scrutinizing, trying to determine exactly what was happening.

"Oh, yes. Carmen's coming back to Chicago with me," Freddy said, not even granting Daph the courtesy of a glance.

What could I have said that wouldn't have put them in danger? They both looked at me in that creepy twin way, where their heads seemed to move in a synchronized motion, eyeing me strangely as I gave them my most subtle "not now" look.

Salvatore kept talking, pointedly asking one of us a question, which was the only way he seemed to draw any of us out of the cold silence that had fallen. The remainder of my food sat untouched, as did Leo's, his hand on my thigh getting increasingly tighter with each pass of Freddy's eyes over me.

After dinner, when the sun had finally set, and the sky was good and dark, we all wandered down to the beach. The boys were all loaded down with fireworks, and there was a moment when Leo and I stopped just outside of the little fire pit area, letting everyone else pass.

"Come on the boat with us," he said quietly, his tone full of concern. I glanced at Rory and Daph, who were still seeming to try to make sense of everything.

"I can't leave them," I said, gesturing to my friends. He looked over at them for a moment, letting out a deep sigh, before nodding.

"It will be fast. None of us want to leave you too long," Leo said, before leaning over to kiss my head and heading over to the dock with the others.

I walked the last few steps to the fire pit, when I noticed Freddy staring at me, some combination of anger and amusement in his eyes. I quickly moved to settle beside Rory and Daph.

"What is going on?" Daph whispered as she leaned over to hand me a beer.

"It's not safe," I murmured back, trying not to be too conspicuous.

"So, you're going to Chicago? What about the pastry chef program?" Rory said loudly, not seeming to care that Freddy and Salvator could hear the clear anger in her voice. That made me sick. I had worked hard to get into that program, the only glimmer of hope of the future I had for so long, and now, like everything else, it felt like it was slipping away.

"She won't be doing that," Freddy said, before I could even open my mouth to respond.

"Excuse me?" Daph asked, sounding much more brazen than normal.

"She worked her ass off for this. Of course, she's going!" Rory said.

"I'm sure we'll find something suitable in Chicago. I won't be having my future wife coming back here regularly to attend classes," Freddy said, eyes flicking to the twins briefly before resting back on me. "We don't need you forgetting who you belong to."

Behind those words were so many promises. Promises of loneliness, anger, sadness … pain. He couldn't wait.

I couldn't seem to turn my head to take in Rory or Daph's reactions to his response, but I could see my mother shaking with silent tears to my left somewhere, while Salvatore looked at him with only a mild look of disgust on his own face.

A pop rang out, and the sky behind me bloomed with red fireworks, painting Salvatore and Freddy's faces with it. Freddy's face lit up with amusement, actual pure joy, and I hated him for that.

"Oh wow! I've never seen them so close!" he said with a grin, standing and moving past the circle of chairs to get a little closer on the beach to where the boys were on the boat.

Rory stood too, abruptly grabbing my arm and dragging me and Daph in the opposite direction from where Freddy stood near a tilting tree where we had all played as kids at one time or another.

"Carmen, what the fuck is going on?" Rory demanded once we were far enough away that there weren't prying ears.

"Mafia stuff," I hissed, making them both stiffen a little. They knew to some degree that my Papa was in the Mafia when he was alive, and that Salvatore was also involved. They suspected that Adrian was now too, along with Sal. I wasn't sure if they knew Enzo was involved, but that really didn't matter. They were daughters of a cop, so we tried our best to not discuss that, if at all possible, but there was no other way to explain to them the strange suddenness of this situation without it.

"Is this a 'we know, and we die' situation?" Rory asked, mild excitement coming over her features. She was always the one that liked talking about it, like those parts of my life were an exotic part of me she could peek at every so often.

"Yes!" I said in a harsh whisper. "So, please! Stick with the moms and just … don't do anything. Try not to react," I finished, feeling a bit defeated at having to say it that way. I just didn't want them in harm's way.

"Carmen! Come watch with me!" Freddy shouted over his shoulder.

"Go back to the fire pit," I said to my friends, looking in both of their eyes for a moment, before slowly heading over to where Freddy stood.

"You were missing the show, whispering to your friends over there," he said quietly, eyes still up toward the sky above the lake while more explosions sounded. I could tell they were getting to the big finale, since they were only shooting off one at a time. My eyes fell to the boat where all five of them were. Enzo seemed to be the only one lighting anything, because the rest of them were staring out at the beach. They were all looking at me.

Leo was yelling something, but his words were lost in the distance between us, and the noise of other people around the lake shooting off their own fireworks. I stepped forward, wanting to see if I could make out what he was saying by reading his lips, but Freddy's hand shot out, grasping my arm with a bruising grip.

"I can tell there's something going on between the two of you. Salvatore's son is off limits to you from now on," Freddy said, his mouth right against my ear.

"I'm not an idiot," I said back, trying to keep the shake out of my voice. I wasn't helpless, but there was a heightened sense of danger in this whole situation. It wasn't just me who would be affected if I fought back. Everyone I cared about could be targeted.

Freddy chuckled. The sound was more frightening than I anticipated, invoking an involuntary shiver through me. "I would certainly hope you aren't stupid. Much fierier than I was anticipating though. Which means you'll be fun to break."

"Don't count on breaking me," I said in a whisper. My gaze locked with Leo's at our distance, wishing I could somehow get there and replace the repulsive touch of Freddy O'Shea with his.

"Oh, you'll break. They all break eventually," he said, his voice a rumble. "You should wave goodbye now; it's the last time you'll see them until the wedding."

It took a moment for those words to sink in. Leo's yelling looked like it grew more frantic, just before he dove off the boat right into the water. As I turned around to find out why, the words clicked in my head. Freddy still had a hold on my wrist, but that man, the same large, scarred-faced man who had pulled a gun on me, was suddenly right there beside us, his gloved hands covering my mouth and nose. The shock of everything had me taking a deep inhale, and with the chemical scent burning through my windpipe and into my lungs, I knew I messed up.

My body slumped, eyes dropping down as Freddy's arms wrapped around me, and then, with one final look at the lake, I could see Leo's dark head rise out of the surface of the water, just before it all went black.

CHAPTER 19

LEO

I should have just stayed on the beach. I couldn't concentrate or be helpful to the others at all with the fireworks. My eyes trained on Carmen the entire time we were on the boat. But as she came up to stand beside O'Shea it became abundantly clear that they had no intention of letting her have the rest of the evening. With all five of us indisposed on the water, there was no one there to stop what happened next.

The men came out of the shadows of the trees, guns at the ready, trained on the moms and the twins. If the rage I felt at seeing guns pointed at the two women who raised me wasn't enough, a huge hulk of a man came up behind Carmen, pressing a cloth to her face before she could react.

I watched in horror, knowing it didn't matter how fast I swam to them; it would be too late. My lungs burned with lake water, but I could barely feel it. I was nearly there, almost at the beach, when she turned, now being carried by the man who had placed the cloth on her mouth, and looked back at us—at me, before her eyes closed.

I fought through the water, making it to the beach and racing as fast as I could through the sand. Every moment felt like an eternity as I rushed past the fire pit, the moms and twins screaming something at me, but I couldn't hear them. O'Shea and his men had already made it around to the front and were pulling off in their vehicles. I kept going, my arms pumping as I pushed myself to keep up with them. I couldn't lose her. Not like this. Not without the goodbye and promises I wanted to make her. She needed hope, and I couldn't give that to her now.

The taillights of the vehicles got farther ahead of us as they wound quickly through the lake streets, bursting to full speed as soon as they breached the main streets ahead, and I was too far behind now. There was no way I would ever catch up to them on foot.

I slowed and came to a stop, hunching over; my lungs and diaphragm rejecting the idea of contracting as I tried to suck in air. I lost her.

I heard the loud sound of others running behind me after a minute. I turned to look behind me, seeing Adrian and Benny as they slowed and stopped beside me.

"Fuck!" Benny screamed.

"Fuckers couldn't wait until tomorrow," Adrian said, his voice rough from the exertion of running as well as his anger.

"This plan better get figured out quick, Adrian, or I'm just going to start killing everyone until I get her back," I said, my voice flat. Neither of the brothers said anything to that, their chests heaving as they regained control of their breathing and watching me as I turned to head back to the lake house, pulling my phone from my pocket.

"Didn't think you were particularly patriotic, but happy Independence Day, Leo," Kia said when she picked up the phone.

"I need your help," I said without hesitation. I didn't have time for pleasantries, not with Carmen in the hands of the Irish.

"Does this have anything to do with how that Irish mob guy knew you at our last mission?"

"Yes. Can you come to Kansas City?" Fireworks still showered through the sky above me. People were cheering and celebrating, but I could barely see it. The only thing going through my mind was the look on Carmen's face before her eyes finally closed.

"I don't have anywhere better to be. Give me two days?" she asked. Two days seemed like too much time, but we didn't have a plan yet, and hopefully, by then, we would have some semblance of one.

"Two days," I agreed with a grunt, hanging up and turning back to Adrian and Benny.

"Your sniper?" Adrian asked as we got closer to the lake house again.

"Kia. She was on my team," I said with a nod, now turning my thoughts to the man responsible for all of this, who was still at that damn house, having watched everything that just happened and didn't do one thing to stop it. My rage was palpable, and my pace picked back up as the house came into view.

The front door was still wide open, and every light was on, bringing a strange cheerfulness to the darkened exterior that was so opposite to how everyone was feeling. It felt like a jab. I marched back into the house, the scene similar to last night, with my dad leisurely sipping a drink at the kitchen island, must have resorted to whiskey since Benny had destroyed all his fancy bourbon, as the moms cried against Sal.

Enzo was busy on his laptop, no doubt tracing where they were taking Carmen.

"What the fuck was that?" I yelled, pointing at my father so he knew exactly who I was speaking to.

"He wanted to get back early. What can I say?" Salvatore said with a shrug. His nonchalance and the smug look on his face made my nostrils flare with anger.

"She didn't even get a chance to say goodbye!" Maria screamed, her voice thick and raspy. Suddenly my mom pulled from Sal's arms, leaving Maria to cry into his chest, her tear-filled eyes glaring at my father with such intensity he looked surprised, stepping back a bit as she approached.

"Get out!" she said coldly, her voice lower and rougher than I had ever heard it before.

"Lili—"

"Get the fuck out of this house! I don't want to see your face right now!" she screamed. My father's face turned red, eyes wide with anger.

"This is *my* house!" he said, crossing his arms defiantly.

"You bought it, but since you have so many, please go to the one you spend the most time in. I know that's your favorite. It comes with Celia. Or is it Joanna? I can't remember. They change so frequently."

At that, his face seemed to pale. He lifted the drink to his lips, throwing back the liquid, before slamming the glass down on the countertop.

"Liliana, I—"

"I don't want to hear a word of your lies, Salvatore. Save it for someone who actually believes them," Mom said, her voice giving away a little of the pain as it wobbled near the end.

"You heard her," Sal said, his voice ice cold as he glared daggers at our father.

"This changes nothing. You all know that, right? Carmen is still gone and you," he punctuated the word with a pointed finger at Enzo and Sal and then Adrian, "you still work for me. You have the weekend and then I expect you back to work." And with that, he sauntered through the large open room and out the front door.

He was lucky I didn't cave his face in with my fist, which I had barely held myself back from. The room was silent save for Maria's whimpers and soft cries as we listened to his car and the guards he had brought with him turn over, drive down the street, and fade away.

"Tell me you have a plan," my mom's voice cut through after several long minutes.

"Ma—" Sal started, but she cut him off with a sharp wave of her hand.

"This is it. This is the last unforgivable thing he has done and believe me, there have been many. I know the only way to get Carmen back is to make sure he is gone. Permanently," she said, her shoulders rolling as she straightened herself. "So, I will do whatever you need me to. Whatever you have planned, I want to help."

Sal's eyes slid over to mine, and we shared a dark look. Our mother not only approved of us killing our father, but she also wanted to help us do it. There was something sinister in the air, a darkness creeping in all of us as we realized that what we had talked about doing just hours ago needed to be made a reality as soon as possible.

The twins came in from the back door at that moment, Daph had clearly been crying, her head slumped as she was supported by Rory.

"I put the fire out," Rory said, her voice flat. Of the two of them, Rory was much better about being stoic, but I could see it unraveling there. They just watched their best friend get kidnapped in front of them. They were not okay.

"I need to get to my computers," Enzo said suddenly.

"We'll pack your things. Just go," my mom said, finally looking up at me. I'm not sure what she saw in my eyes when she did so, but the sharp intake of air and the way her own eyes widened in surprise made me assume it was something she had never seen there before.

My throat felt thick. I wasn't sure what would come out other than a scream if I talked again. I needed to be doing something to get her back, because every moment she was in O'Shea's hands was a moment he could be hurting her.

I gave her a quick nod, before turning on my heel to head out the door, Adrian and Benny right behind me.

CHAPTER 20

CARMEN

My head was throbbing. That was the first clue something wasn't right. I didn't recall drinking too much. In fact, I wasn't quite sure what I did recall. My eyelids felt too heavy to move. My whole body felt too heavy to move. It smelled of stale cigarette smoke and leather wherever I was. Not a scent that was found anywhere I would associate with familiarly.

The sound around me was loud. It vibrated in my skull, making the throbbing of my head even more intense. I furrowed my brow as I tried to figure out what it was.

"I think she's waking up," came a gruff male voice that I didn't recognize.

That's when I realized the vibrations weren't just in my head, we were in a car. Several things seemed to click in my brain all at once; the memories flooding into my mind again. Leo's face as he screamed from the boat and jumped in the water. The press of the chemical-laced fabric to my face. My attempts to fight off the huge brute of a man. And then, as Leo's face re-emerged, eyes darkened like a shark's, as a beast I never saw before lurked there, rage emanating from him as he tore from the water. That's when everything went black.

"Good. We're nearly there." This voice I did remember. The same voice that whispered in my ear right before it all went to shit. Freddy O'Shea. But then the laugh that followed chilled me to the core.

I knew that laugh. It had been in the background of my high school experience, in the shop where I worked, in the grocery store where I shopped, on the worst date of my life. I was suddenly very happy that my eyes were still closed, though the heaviness of my lids and limbs had lifted enough that I knew I could move if I wanted to. Very happy, because Jeremy Wallingford was currently sitting closer than anyone else to me, and if he knew I was awake, I am not sure what he would do, or what I would do to him.

But I couldn't stay like this forever. At some point, I would have to "wake up" and deal with the men around me and my new circumstances. I was stuck with O'Shea, and apparently Jeremy, for the foreseeable future. I wasn't sure how long I'd have to wait for Leo and our collective brothers to help me get out of this, and in all honesty, I wasn't sure if they ever would. At the moment, I was on my own in this situation.

What would Leo do?

He'd gather as much information as possible, try to keep himself alive at all costs, and take opportunities when they present themselves.

I was not an opportunity taker in my normal life, but keeping myself safe was something I was well versed at, and gaining information was something I could definitely do.

So what did I know?

We were heading to Chicago, where O'Shea lived and his father was based. I already knew I was supposed to be heading there, which meant, if we were close, I had been out cold for more than six hours at least.

What else?

We were in a car. There were three men, two I knew, one I didn't, but I assumed it was the brute who drugged me, seeing as how he was the same man who pulled a gun on me out front of the gym.

I let myself become more aware of my body. The headache was dissipating, but now that I was becoming more alert, I realized my wrists were sore, as well as one side of my hip, but fortunately, there was nothing more. Probably just bruising from moving my limp body around.

We hit a bump in the road, and I couldn't help the startle that went through my body, using it to fain waking. I opened my eyes a bit, my vision still bleary, but I could see Jeremy looking down at me, his eyes eager as he took me in.

"Hello, sunshine. You slept for nearly eight hours. We're almost to your new home," he said, as though those words were a comfort and not a nightmare. My legs were on his lap, his hands resting on my calves tightened as eagerness washed over his face.

I shot him a glare, which only made his smile widen, before maneuvering to sit up, pulling my legs away from him as quickly as I could.

"You'll love it here, Carmen. I always thought that little suburb was too shitty for the likes of us," Jeremy said, letting his gaze go back over to the front of the car. Signs on the highway indicated Chicago exits.

"You act like I've been sold off to marry *you*, Jeremy, but I'm fairly sure your *brother* is the one I'm supposed to tie the knot with," I said indignantly, my gaze hardening at the back of Freddy's head in the seat in front of me. Freddy laughed this time, turning his head to look at me.

"Sold off may be right, Miss LaMartina. I can share my *property* with whoever I'd like," he said, his words sending a shiver through my body. No wonder Jeremy was so pleased.

"I told you, you should have just given me a chance. I get my way no matter what, but you may have liked it better if you got to choose," Jeremy said coldly.

I chose to remain silent for the remainder of the drive, holding my limbs as close to myself as possible, as not to give Jeremy any leeway to touch me unnecessarily. The car got off at an exit and, after a short drive through tall buildings, it pulled into an underground parking garage only accessible with a keycard. I turned around as we passed through, watching as the large iron gate came down, sealing us in, before turning back to watch while the car was maneuvered through toward another area that was sectioned off, only accessible by the keycard.

The brute finally parked, and I hesitated as they all got out.

"Don't make this more difficult than it has to be," Freddy said from his still-open door.

"How am I supposed to trust you when you drugged me?" I asked, my tone clipped.

"Would you have come without a fight?"

"Physically? Yes. There may have been some words," I said with a growl.

"I'd rather not. Get out or Hamish will do it again," he said, glancing at the brute who was now standing beside my door.

I pushed the door open, stomping out and slamming the door as best as my still weak limbs could, before coming around to the back of the car. Freddy was already there when I came around, and before I could register it, his hand was at the back of my neck, fingers pressing lightly at pressure points there.

"Do not think for one second, Carmen, that you have any pull here. You are my property now, and until you can behave the way I want you to, you'll be treated like an untrained dog," Freddy hissed into my ear. I didn't move or say anything, letting him steer me by the neck toward an elevator a few paces away from where they parked.

The keycard once again gained us access and then allowed Freddy to press the button for the penthouse. This security was serious. No way of sneaking out of here, or anyone sneaking in undetected. There were cameras everywhere; the corners of the hallways, above every door. A sick feeling of being trapped started taking over my body. I couldn't control the thundering of my pulse or the way my breath came out in panicked little pants. Freddy's fingers tightened on the back of my neck, as if feeling my body struggle only made his grip harder. And I realized in that moment, that was true. The more I fought this situation, the worse it would be for me. He basically said those exact words to me.

CHAPTER 21

LEO

My fists slammed into the bag over and over again. In my mind the bag was faces, so many faces of people who needed to come down. Their bones were crunching under the power of my knuckles, blood spurting from breaks in their skin, their mouth, their crushed noses. My dad, Freddy, Jeremy, that fucker who drugged Carmen before dragging her away.

Fuck!

Even Morelli.

"Still nothing?" Ash asked, pulling me from the rage-fueled haze I had been in moments ago, causing me to catch the bag as it swung back to me, my breath coming out haggard as my eyes turned to look at her.

"It's just going slow," I said, my voice rough.

"It will come together," she said, wrapping her own knuckles in tape.

"Not fast enough."

She looked at me sharply, her eyes boring into me like she was trying to figure out whether she wanted to chew me out or try to comfort me. I'd spent nearly every day here, every single day of the last ten days since the Fourth, pushing my body and pouring out my aggression when I couldn't do any more to help Carmen. Kia arrived and was helping Enzo in his quest to find faults in the security of the penthouse we were fairly sure they took Carmen to and dig up information on my father and the O'Sheas that might help us negotiate, but I wanted blood.

"She agreed to this because she didn't want any of you in danger, right? So rushing this is only going to backfire and cause exactly what she was trying to avoid."

Though her words made sense, my mind couldn't help but pull everything it knew about men like O'Shea that I had come across in my time in the military. Sex traffickers were sick, scum of the earth that didn't view people, especially women, as anything more than toys to play with. My imagination couldn't help but run wild with all the horrible things that could have been happening to her.

"And what is she going through in the meantime?" I let out, not sure what she saw in my eyes as my body tensed, but her eyes widened. Fear took over her features for a moment before her gaze turned back to her hands.

I liked Ash. If the circumstances were different, I was certain I would like her far more. She was clearly close with Carmen, knew way too much about the Mafia business, and, though tensions were high and I didn't see any of the banter that the others had teased Sal and Adrian about between the three of them right now, she was definitely putting herself out there to be of help to all of us. I just wasn't capable of being my normal friendly self. Not after having finally gotten Carmen, only to have her torn away from me.

My phone rang from the bench where I had set it when I got to the gym, and I released the bag, striding over to see it was Rory calling. Carmen hadn't wanted her friends involved, but there had been little stopping them when they realized we were trying to figure out a way to break Carmen free.

"You got something?" I asked, too impatient for formalities.

"Well, hello to you too, Leo. Good to know your nice boy goes away when there's a crisis," Rory said grumpily.

"Hello, Rory. Do you have something?" I asked, pinching the bridge of my nose in frustration.

"Benny said Kia got something about the building. A weak point, I think? She didn't want to stop to call, and Benny is currently stitching up Adrain's face from when he had to fight to gain loyalty last night, so I'm calling," Rory finished. Always so wordy, that one.

"On my way," I said, hanging up the phone. I turned to Ash, who had finished her wrapping and heading to a different bag. "Kia found something," I told her as I started pulling the tape from my fingers.

"It's going to come together. Carmen is strong. She'll hold out," Ash said, giving me such a confident look from where she stood behind the bag that I was struck for a moment.

Ash was right, of course, Carmen was strong and smart. She would have been trying to find a way to survive and escape just as much as we were on the outside. The difference was Carmen was alone. An island with no resources was incredibly vulnerable and at a definite disadvantage.

I left, heading to the base of operations for this little gang, Maria's house. Of course, some of us overflowed into Ma's house, but it was less likely that Salvatore or any of his men would bother Maria than my mother.

When I walked in, it was much the same as it had been for the last ten days. The dining room table was spread with laptops, papers, and coffee mugs. Rory was at the table next to Enzo and Kia pouring them each fresh cups of coffee, Daph was doing dishes with Maria in the kitchen, while Benny and Adrian were on the couch, a bandage finishing being taped to Adrian's forehead.

Adrian's fight for loyalty the night before was apparently for respect. Several of the local gangs in Kansas City were big enough to be potentially hazardous to the likes of a new and unbacked Capo in town but done the right way, they could be persuaded to either look the other way or even be allies and partners. As Sal's second, Adrian often took the brunt of these sorts of things. The fight for loyalty was showing strength. Adrian, being able to hold his own, told them that Sal was not someone to be trifled with. And Adrian did just that the night before.

"Oh good. You're here," Kia said as I tossed my stuff on the side table and made my way over to them.

"You stink," Rory said as she came past me.

"So do you," I said back, watching a small smile come to her lips, but it faded quickly.

"I found the schematics for the penthouse and Enzo is about to break into their camera feed," Kia said, glancing away from her screen to where Enzo was typing furiously.

"I don't know who's doing their computer work, but they were definitely a hard nut to crack," Enzo said, clearly impressed with the caliber of the security measures. "But not as good as me," he said, a satisfied smile coming over his face as the screen changed, multiple windows popping up with video feeds.

The whole apartment complex was open to us now, but I was only interested in one. My eyes immediately found her. She was in a room, her curls pulled back in a bun, face lined in determination as she went through the motions as if she were hitting a punching bag.

"Looks like she's still got some fight in her," Rory said proudly from behind Enzo's shoulder, watching the feed as well.

"Didn't doubt it for a second," Daph said as she came over, her hands still soapy, to look and see the confirmation that the person we all cared about was still alive.

"Can you get me into the feed?" I asked, tearing my eyes from the image and quickly grabbing my phone from where I tossed it. Enzo snatched it from my hand as I got closer, quickly patching my phone into the feed.

When he handed it back, my eyes couldn't stray from her. I watched the way her body moved, the wrinkle between her brows as they knitted in determination. She didn't show any outward signs of trauma, but simply from the look on her face, I knew things had been hard for her. What had happened to her in these last ten days?

I didn't get an answer to that question, but I certainly got a good look at the way she reacted when the door opened. She tensed up, her body coiled as if she were preparing to strike. Had they hurt her, or was she just being cautious?

A man, one of O'Shea's guard dogs, said something to her, and she let her hands drop, nodding and waiting for him to leave again. As soon as the door was closed, she hurried to get herself ready, a look of panic written all over her face. Just as she was finishing slipping a dress on, Maria's phone rang from where it sat on the dining room table.

"Mom," Benny said, looking at the phone as the number listed was not someone she knew.

She answered it, putting it on speaker.

"Hello?" she asked.

"So lovely to hear your voice, Maria. How are you this fine evening?" came the voice of Freddy O'Shea.

"I would be better if my daughter was joining me for dinner," Maria said, her voice sharp as she also realized who was on the phone. He laughed, the sound making me want to reach through the phone and tear out his throat.

"Well, luck would have it she's been behaving the last few days, and I thought I'd reward her with a little chat."

Behaving? Part of me was filled with satisfaction, knowing she had been putting up a fight, but the idea of her "behaving" chilled me. My eyes flashed to see Benny and Adrian stiffening at those words as well.

"In fact, you'll get to talk to her, but I also wanted to extend an invitation for you to come to Chicago with us for a few days. A girl can't buy a wedding dress without her mother present." My heart felt like lead in my chest at those words. Maria looked up at me, tears filling her eyes as she took in whatever my expression was.

"I–I would love to," Maria said, her voice shaking.

"Good! I thought so! I'll talk to Salvatore and get your travel plans arranged."

"Carmen would want her friends to come with me," Maria said quickly, looking at where Rory and Daph were standing together, hands clasped tightly.

"Oh yes. Wouldn't want her friends to miss such a big moment," Freddy said, though his tone suggested mild irritation. "Whomever you'd like, but her brothers will need to stay home. They'll be able to attend the wedding."

"Of course," Maria murmured with a nod. "Can I speak to Carmen now?"

"Here she comes," he said. I looked down at my phone, the feed still on her room, but she was no longer in there. I moved through the different cameras until I saw her again. In a living room, from the looks of it, she was being escorted by the behemoth of a man who had drugged her the night they took her. Freddy was sitting in the middle of the couch, legs and arms spread wide as he held the phone to his ear.

"Come here, darling. Your mom is on the phone for you," Freddy said, curling his finger for her to come closer.

Slowly she stepped around her guard, walking toward Freddy. He didn't hand the phone to her, but as soon as she got close enough, he grabbed her wrist, pulling her down roughly onto his lap. Her face twisted in disgust as his arm wrapped around her, pulling her against his chest so he could press his nose to the soft flesh of her neck. He pressed a button, presumably muting their end of the phone all, his lips murmuring something in her ear that made her body stiff as a board.

Then he handed her the phone, taking his free hand to position her more firmly against him, his hands roaming over her.

"Mama?" Carmen's voice came over the phone.

"Carmen!" Maria cried, tears unable to stop from spilling over. "Are you okay? *Cosa ti hano fatto, piccola mia?*"

"I'm okay," Carmen said, but between the strain of her voice and the way she held herself like a statue against Freddy's chest while his hands wandered unabashedly over her body, she was anything but.

"We're coming to see you. Me and the girls," Maria said, brushing the tears from her cheeks.

"When?" Carmen asked, but before Maria could say anything more, Freddy ripped the phone from Carmen's hand, placing it to his own ear once more.

"I think that's enough for now. Carmen and I have other plans this evening. Salvatore will be in touch soon, I'm sure," he said, before abruptly hanging up.

A roar ripped through my chest as soon as the line went dead. My eyes were unable to turn away from the image of him groping her. He better pray that was all he had done to her, because if he…

I couldn't go there. My mind could not take that dangerous path, or I would end up going on a murderous rampage now, and we had to plan it perfectly.

It didn't matter too much though. Freddy O'Shea was dead, no matter what.

CHAPTER 22

CARMEN

I paced the front room nervously as I waited for my mom. She was supposed to be here any minute. Freddy was escorting her from the airport with most of his men, meaning I was left here in the penthouse practically alone. Not that I could go anywhere. The two guards were stationed in such a way that it would take a miracle for me to escape.

I went back to my room, still not feeling completely comfortable being in the main spaces. Three and a half weeks here, most of them as a prisoner of this room, didn't lend well for feeling safe, but the room was where I had spent most of my time, and the four walls were more familiar than anywhere else here.

When I stepped back through the door, a figure stood at the foot of the bed, and for a moment I wondered if I was dreaming. Tall, broad shoulders, sun-kissed skin, and hazel eyes that snapped up to meet mine. Leo.

I closed the door with a snap, my body pressed against it as I looked at him.

"Am I dreaming?" I asked, trying not to let the tears that were clouding my vision fall. Leo took two long steps over to me, his hands coming up to cup my cheeks.

"You aren't dreaming, Little Song," he said quietly, his voice hoarse. "We only have twenty minutes. The cameras are looped, so it looks like you're still pacing the living room," he whispered.

"And then?"

"We're close. The plan is almost in place, but I couldn't go another moment without seeing you." His own eyes, I noticed, looked so tired, filled with tears. "Has he… did he hurt you?"

I couldn't tell him about how Freddy starved me the first few days, or the way he made me strip for him so he could admire what he'd soon be getting. I couldn't tell him how Freddy would touch me, never to penetration, but as if my body was his to possess. I couldn't tell him that Freddy would hurt me, force me to kneel for long stretches of time, or hit me when I didn't respond how he wanted me to, never in a place that was obvious, or could be seen when I was dressed, just in case he decided to take me somewhere.

And of course, the torture of the little mentions of my friends and family, telling me how wonderful they were all doing without me, not that I believed he had any true idea, it was all just to torture me and break me down.

I wasn't a person to him, but an object that he would soon be able to do anything he wanted to.

"He hasn't done *that,*" I said honestly, knowing Leo was worried I had been raped, but Leo could see there was more simply by looking at me. He let out a pained sound, pulling me farther from the door and pressing me to his chest. His scent flooded my nostrils, his heartbeat was in my ear, and I couldn't help the way my body relaxed against him. *He* was safe. *His* touch was gentle.

"I can't leave you here," he whispered as he pressed his lips to my hair, his hands gripping me tightly, but only out of concern, not to hurt me. This was the only man who ever could own me, body and soul, and he didn't want to possess me. He wanted to hold on to me so we could fly together.

"You can, because the plan needs to go forward," I said, pulling back so I could look up at his face.

"Carmen, I—"

"Kiss me before it's too late," I whispered, pushing up on my toes while my fingers twisted in the front of his shirt. He hesitated for a moment, as if he thought he'd hurt me, but he must have seen the need in my eyes, because he groaned, leaning down and pressing his lips to mine.

Desperation, that was the only way to describe this kiss. It was like we were trying to consume each other's souls. Lips, tongues, and teeth clashed together. Hands grasped frantically, fingers bruising and nails scratching. I needed to be closer to him. I needed his skin on my skin. I wanted his scent surrounding me. I needed Leo to erase any trace that O'Shea had ever touched me.

My fingers trailed down his chest, pulling at his belt roughly.

"Carmen…"

"I need you, Leo," I whispered against his lips, our ragged breathing the only thing to be heard in the quiet penthouse.

He pulled me off the floor, wrapping my legs around his waist.

"You're going to have me dripping from you when O'Shea comes back. You'll know, if he touches you, that you and I?" He tipped us over, bracing himself above me as my back fell on the bed. "We can't be torn apart. We were meant to be. I've been in love with you for so long, Carmen. I don't plan on letting you go."

I couldn't help the moan that was pulled from me at his words. The promise in them hit me so hard, and I needed him even more than I had a moment before.

"I love you," I whispered, pulling him back down so our lips could meet again. Leo's hands moved from my hips, down my thighs to the hem of my skirt, pushing it up. The feeling of his hands on me was burning a trail over my skin and through my veins. His fingers fumbled with his belt and fly for a moment, pausing and halting our kiss again to look in my eyes.

Within those hazel depths was the question. He didn't want to continue unless I was sure. I didn't say anything, reaching down and letting my fingers touch the hard skin below his navel, traveling down and pushing past the waistband of his briefs so they could find and wrap around his hardened length. We both moaned at the contact, my core pulsing with need as I felt him.

"Leo, please," I whispered. We didn't have much time left, and I wanted him so badly. I needed him. If I was going to survive however long it was going to take to free me of this, I needed the reminder of his touch.

He pushed his pants and briefs down his hips before pulling my panties down my legs, quickly returning to where he was hovering over me before, his lips finding mine in another searing kiss as his fingers found my folds. The amount of wetness there would have been embarrassing if it weren't for who was feeling it. A rumble sounded in his chest as he felt me, his slicked fingers moving to circle my clit, as his cock rubbed through my folds, brushing at my entrance and making me shiver with the combined feelings.

I was wound so tight, I knew it would take no time before I was falling apart. I tilted my hips up as his tip met my entrance again, and he pressed in just a little bit.

My back arched at that, his mouth trailing wet kisses down my neck to the part of my chest that was exposed.

"I can't go slow, we don't have enough time," he murmured.

"Leo, fuck me hard," I managed to say through pants. His head snapped up, looking at me with an expression that was so hungry and feral, I was surprised I didn't fall apart from that alone. He pressed in farther, the feel of him stretching me almost too much pleasure for me to handle.

Inch by inch, he pressed slowly farther until he was fully seated within me, our hips flush. He reached up, his hand moving softly from my brow to my cheek, down my neck, and to my chest. His hand pressed a bit right where my heart was before he pulled out, letting his hips snap back to slam into me.

"I'm yours and you're mine, Carmen," he whispered roughly, each word punctuated with another thrust.

"I'm yours!" I said in a moan, my hands moving to grip his ass, feeling the flex of his muscles through my fingers.

I knew it wouldn't take long, and I was right. I could feel that heat building within me, that tightened burning low on my belly. As if Leo could sense it, his thumb found a home at my clit, pressing in tight circles in rhythm with each thrust.

"How close are you, Little Song?" he asked, his voice like gravel.

"I'm so—I'm gonna—" I couldn't even speak anymore, the waves of pleasure wracking through me. My pussy was pulsing against his cock as it moved within me.

"Fuck!" he hissed, his grip on my hips tightening as his thrusts became more erratic. He tilted my hips farther, the new angle hitting me so deep and so hard that despite just having cum a moment earlier, I could feel it building again.

I gripped his arms, my nails digging into his flesh as he pounded into me. And it happened, like magic; the dam broke, my second orgasm washing over me as I felt him hardening further, a few rough thrusts slapping against me as he filled me with his hot cum, before he slumped over me.

His lips found my neck, traveling to my lips, and we kissed sloppily, panting through it. I didn't want him to pull out or move from me. I wanted him to stay with me forever. Just the two of us here together in this happy little bubble of peace. But it couldn't last.

Leo pulled out and off me, taking my hands to pull me up with him. He tucked himself away, moving to grab my panties from where he threw them and kneeling to help me step back into them. He wasn't kidding about the cum staying in place.

I was expecting him to stand again, but he remained kneeling, pulling me closer so his face pressed into my stomach.

"I don't want to leave you," he said, his voice muffled as his breath pressed through my dress and against my skin.

"Soon, right?" I asked, raking my finger through his dark hair. He pulled back, looking up at me, his eyes swimming with worry.

"Soon," he said with a nod.

I heard the rattle of the front door, which meant one of the guards was planning on checking on me, or Freddy had returned with my mom and the girls.

"Go," I whispered, leaning forward to give him one more kiss, before he stood, heading to my window.

"I'm getting you out of here, Carmen. I promise," he said quietly as he paused.

"I know," I said back, watching as his face seemed to inflame with determination, before he opened the window and slipped out.

CHAPTER 23

CARMEN

I went to my bathroom as soon as Leo was gone, making sure that my hair and clothes looked okay. He didn't leave any marks on me, but my skin was flushed, and I could feel his cum slipping out of me and collecting in my panties. There was an odd sense of satisfaction I felt with that.

The sound of commotion in the penthouse reached my ears, and I did a final look at myself in the mirror before heading out to greet whoever had come.

There was a decently large group of people that came through the door, but I only had eyes for my mom. As soon as she saw me, she moved hurriedly across the space, her arms outstretched as she pulled me into a tight hug.

"Oh, my *Carmenetta*," she sobbed, crying as she tightened her arms around me. I hugged her back just as tight, reveling in the feel of her once more.

"Mama," I whispered, trying not to cry as she sobbed into my shoulder.

When she pulled away, I let myself look at the whole group that had accompanied her. Of course, Liliana was here, as well as Rory and Daph, but there was a woman I had never met standing with them. Her skin was dark, beautiful brown, eyes like honey, and hair in tight curls framing her head and shoulders. Her body was toned and definitely lethal.

Liliana came to hug me once my mom released me, and Rory and Daph followed closely behind. The mystery woman came last, hugging me like she had known me for years.

"I'm Kia. I worked with Leo," she whispered quickly before she released me from the hug. Somehow, that made me feel both better and worse. She was strong and utterly beautiful. Was she who he had been with him during his time away? Did sleeping with her make him such a god in bed with me?

"What a wonderful reunion," Freddy said loudly, breaking me my from my thoughts. His voice made my stomach lurch uncomfortably. "I'm sure you're all tired and hungry from the flight. These men will show you to your rooms. Go freshen up while I order us some food."

It didn't look like any of the five women standing in the living room wanted to leave me, but they reluctantly turned, following the men who showed them down the opposite hall to the guest rooms.

"Are you going to behave while they're here?" Freddy asked after they were all down the hall, his gaze not lifting from his phone where he was ordering dinner for all of us.

Behave. That was what he kept calling it when I didn't fight back or resist. When I kept my mouth shut. He would hit me, deprive me of food, keep me locked in my room, or have me strip in front of him, humiliated and naked, if I didn't *behave.*

He had promised me that he would do far worse once we were married, as far as my punishments were concerned. I was honestly surprised he hadn't raped me yet, but apparently, he liked to prolong the torture. On one particular evening, after his men discovered I had been taking notes on the guards, he had me stripped.

Freddy sat on the couch, sipping whatever liquor he had decided to choose for the evening. His blue eyes glared as he watched his men tear the fabric from my body. I tried to cover myself, but he stood abruptly, wrenching my hands away and glaring down at my exposed flesh.

"I could do anything to you right now," he said, oddly calm as he took another sip of his drink. The grip of his other hand was bruising my flesh.

I didn't say anything, watching him as I tried to will my heart to slow down and my breathing to become less erratic. He continued to stare, eyes drifting over every inch of me, until they landed on my face. I'm not sure what he saw there, but abruptly he released his hold, turning and moving to return to his seat on the couch.

"Do you know why I have been so kind?" he asked.

I held back the scoff that rose to my throat. Kind? Starving me, beating me, and shaming me was not kindness. But I knew what he was implying. Why hadn't he taken it one step further yet?

"I want this deal to go through. If I do what I want to you before you're my wife, that might be cause for the Italians to pull out of the deal. Even start a war. Mafia wars draw attention, and I don't want the wrong kind of attention set my way."

He stood again, taking two quick strides until he was right in front of me, hand grasping my throat forcefully and making me look up at his snarling face.

"I need this to go smoothly. I don't need questions for why you're here. We need you, but when we're done with you I could kill you, or—" He loosened his grip a little on my throat, thumb stroking almost sensually at the skin there. I fought back the shiver of disgust, but the goosebumps weren't something I could control. *"—you could be a good little wife and live a comfortable life."*

The face I was making must have not sat right with him, his eyes narrowing and his grip getting harder, cutting off most of my air.

"Once you are my wife, you'll do whatever I say. Whatever I want. If I want to watch you be gang raped by my men, you'll do it. Your life is in my hands either way, Italian whore," he spat out, shoving me backward so I stumbled on the tattered remains of my clothes around my ankles, hitting the cold marble floor with a resounding smack that echoed across the penthouse.

Since then, I had been much more careful about how I logged information. Not that I had any way to get that to my brothers or the Lupos, but I had to feel like I was doing something, or else I'd go mad.

So, I behaved, because the tiny freedoms I started being permitted to have only aided my task, and if I didn't… I shuddered to think of him deciding to go a step further, risk of war or not, because of something stupid I had done.

"Why wouldn't I behave?" I asked, trying to keep the sharp edge from my voice as I said it. He looked up at me from the food order, those blue eyes full of anger and hunger. If only he knew Leo's cum was still soaking my panties as we stood there. He would certainly have a reason to be angry about that. But that was a risk I hadn't been able to hold back from.

"Go shower. I can tell you didn't after you worked out. Your hair is a mess. You'll have to figure out a way to make that less unruly once we're married. I'll let you back out once the food has arrived," he said dismissively, turning his gaze back to his phone.

The boutique we were in was beautiful. Handmade and designer dresses hung artfully around, antique furniture and decor set strategically here and there, and there was champagne poured for all six of us women as I was brought back and forth from the dressing room.

This should have been an exciting moment. I, like many other girls, had fantasized about when I got to go dress shopping for my wedding. Except there had only ever been one man that I was picking the dress out to walk down the aisle to in my dreams, and it wasn't Freddy O'Shea.

Each dress, while beautiful, held with it the heavy reality that it couldn't possibly be my wedding dress. Not *the dress,* because I wouldn't waste that on this. If whatever plan the boys had come up with didn't work, if I had to marry Freddy, then this dress would be as good as a shackle.

"*Carmenetta,*" my mom said through tears as I stepped out from behind the heavy curtain and into their view.

I tried to smile as she looked at me lovingly through her tears, but it was hard. Kia looked at me sympathetically from where she sat beside Liliana, and I turned to face the wall of mirrors.

Dammit!

This was absolutely beautiful. So beautiful, I couldn't stand that I was wearing it for this purpose.

The bodice cut low, all the way to my belly button, but it was covered in sheer lace that traveled up and over my arms. The skirt hugged my wide hips perfectly, flaring out about mid-thigh with a slit just to the side that showed off my legs as I walked. It was *the dress*, and it took my breath away when I saw it in the mirror.

"We can just make a slight adjustment here, so it fits you like a glove," the woman who had been helping me with the dresses said, pulling a little more at the clip holding back some of the fabric at my waist. I glanced through the mirror at the women behind me. My eyes pleading. I wanted this dress, but not for this wedding.

Rory's eyes seemed to harden with determination when she saw my face.

"I think maybe the third one was better suited," she said, standing and pulling Kia up along with her to get on the podium with me. Kia flashed a smile at the salespeople, but when she turned back to us, her face became shadowed. I saw the same sort of thing happen with Leo before. They were trained for this, after all.

"Let's get you out of this," Rory said once up there with me. The two of them led me back to the dressing room, shooing the attendant away when she tried to push in with us.

Silently, they started helping get all the little buttons undone.

"I have something for you," I whispered when Kia moved to get the ones on my wrist. Her eyes met mine, searching for what I meant. "In my shoe."

Kia went to dig through my stack of clothes I had set on the bench when I got undressed, while Rory took her place, watching my face as I tried very hard not to let the tears that were threatening to spill over my lashes fall.

"We're going to get you out of this, Carmen," Rory whispered, though her tone was worn and sad. I wasn't sure how much Rory and Daph were kept in on the plan, but based on what I heard in her voice, the boys weren't getting very far. I couldn't say anything, either to the affirmative or not. I had no way of knowing how they would truly get me out of this without blood being shed.

Kia stood, having gotten the note I put in my shoe with all the small details I had accumulated over the course of my time in the penthouse. The lightest guard times, what I had overheard about deals, important names that were mentioned, and, of course, the time and location of the events leading up to the wedding that I had heard.

Kia quickly snapped a picture of it with her phone, sending it off to Enzo, I presumed, before tearing it up and putting it in the trash can that sat in the room.

"You've got it?" Kia asked, looking up at Rory, who nodded quickly before she turned back to me. Her face broke into a sad smile looking me over, before she reached out and took my hand. "Carmen, he talked about you so much. The others may have given him shit for it, but I knew it was love from the moment he opened the first email in my presence. We're going to get you out of this. He isn't going to let you go."

Those tears that had been threatening to spill over did. I took in a shaky breath, willing myself to not burst out in sobs. She squeezed my hand one more time, before leaving the dressing room to join Daph and the moms.

Rory stayed in the room as I put my clothes back on. I was fine with the third dress, as Rory said. It wasn't perfect, but why would I want to look perfect at a wedding I didn't even want to participate in? As I turned my back on *"the dress,"* Rory stepped close to me, holding a small rectangle less than the size of a deck of cards in the palm of her hand, before she put that hand down the front of my shirt into my bra.

"What—"

"For you to contact us. No calls. No sound. Enzo made it untraceable," Rory whispered directly into my ear.

I gulped back the questions on my tongue as she stepped away once more, fussing with my hair, which had become unruly after having changed my clothes so many times. More tears threatened to escape, but this time because I was so overwhelmed with the level of love so many people had for me. The boys, the moms, my two best friends, and even Kia, who I wished I knew better, were risking an awful lot to try to free me from this situation.

I took Rory's hand, looking down at the way our skin tones differed, hers so much paler than the olive tone of mine. Her gray eyes sparkled with that love as she watched me pull myself back together and once I felt like the tears were safely tucked away, I nodded before the two of us walked back out to buy a dress I didn't love.

CHAPTER 24

LEO

I was sitting in the back of a car with Benny beside me. Enzo and Adrian were up front while we pulled out to follow the car Sal had just entered with our father. Sal had been brought up to Chicago to see what forming this alliance with the Irish would gain them. We had simply followed along, even though only Enzo and Adrian were officially there with Sal.

Their presence in Chicago was a distraction for O'Shea and his men. It was how I was able to sneak into the penthouse and see Carmen, which I was itching to do again after weeks of not seeing or hearing any-thing from her, to have her in that room, to smell her and touch her, was overwhelming. But what was worse was when I had to leave again, and I couldn't take her with me.

The only solace I had, the only way I could have left her, was knowing that the girls would be getting the phone to her that Enzo had modified. We'd be able to contact her and vice versa, so it would no longer be simply the feed of Freddy's penthouse cameras to indicate that she was still alive and breathing.

The car with Dad and Sal pulled off the highway toward a shipping area, but Adrian didn't follow, instead taking an exit to head back toward the city.

"What are we doing?" Benny asked, sitting up more in his seat, his eyes frantically looking around.

"I just wanted to make sure where Sal was in case he needed us. We have a different mission," Adrian said, glancing at me in the rearview mirror.

"We have a date with the Russians," Enzo said, his voice far too chipper for what came out of his mouth.

"Russians?" I asked, my voice barely more than a growl.

"They are not too keen on the Irish in this city. Just wondering how far their hate goes and if it will help us here," Adrian said. It made sense. The enemy of my enemy is my friend. Right?

We pulled up across from a nightclub. The line wasn't too long since it was still rather early in the evening, the sun having just set a few hours before. Mom had been allowed to stay one night with Maria and the others visiting Carmen, but Salvatore had insisted she stay with him in a hotel during the remainder of her stay. Dad had waited until she was back to the room from dinner with them, safely guarded by his men, before he headed out with Sal for the show and tell from hell. Her being home provided us with the cover we needed to slip away for this purpose. Travis, who came with us as Sal's guard, thankfully stayed with her so she wouldn't be alone and vulnerable.

"Sal and I contacted him a few days ago, so he should be expecting us," Adrian said as he killed the engine and opened his door.

I was dressed in a black t-shirt and jeans, which I supposed was good enough to seem like a guard or something, behind Adrian, who had dressed up from his usual gym attire to slacks and a button-down. Enzo was similarly dressed, and Benny, he was dressed more like me. I guess we were the muscle.

As we approached the entrance, the security there immediately went on alert, one talking into a headpiece while another was glaring at us, flexing menacingly.

"Adrian LaMartina, here to see Gregor Stepanov," Adrian said, letting his glower compete with the statuesque guard.

The other murmured into the earpiece and they both seemed to stiffen after several moments.

"He's expecting you," Earpiece said, pushing back from where he stood in front of the door to let us by.

We entered. The place wasn't quite full, but the music was loud, bass thumping and rattling in my chest. I had been to plenty of places just like this across Europe. It was easy to launder money with so much cash and booze flowing. Easy to deal drugs too. But instead of being unnoticed or undercover, like I was on missions, the people watching us like hawks as we walked through knew exactly who we were. Some of them probably knew why we were there.

We were led up to a second level, where there were lush couches placed here and there, as well as a private bar. There was only one person here, except for the bartender.

Gregor sat on a red, crushed velvet couch that overlooked the club, taking in his domain. Those deep-set brown eyes slid across everyone in attendance tonight like a predator until they landed on us. He was young, probably not much older than Sal, but you could see the weight of his experience in his eyes. He had been made into the Pakhan, the boss of this particular area, after his uncle died a few years ago.

"Adrian. I was expecting to have Salvatore here with you," Gregor said.

"Sal," Adrian corrected, having stiffened at the use of my brother's full name.

Adrian was just as protective of my brothers as I was, but somewhat more when it came to Sal, I was realizing. I supposed I was more protective of Benny for similar reasons. They had been friends for a very long time, firstborn of their families. It made sense that they had a strong bond with everything we had all been through.

"He had an errand with his father. I'm sure you understand," Adrian said, coming to sit across from Gregor, leaving Benny, Enzo, and me to stand behind him.

"Of course. Can't say no to your Capo or your father," he said, his voice laced with resentment of previous experience. He snapped his fingers, and the bartender came around from behind the counter to take Adrian's order. She held herself well, though the way her fingers tightened in front of her as she waited for the gesture from Gregor to speak showed her nerves.

Adrian asked for a whiskey and Enzo nodded, taking one as well, but Benny and I kept up with our appearance of security, refusing with shakes of our heads, as she wandered to the bar to collect their shots.

"Sal mentioned a mutual hatred, but he didn't say what when we talked," Gregor said, sipping his own drink as he watched Adrian.

"O'Shea," Adrian said simply, watching as Gregor's face changed, fury burning in his eyes.

"That fucking Irish trash," Gregor hissed, spitting on the ground before his feet as he sat forward with elbows on his knees. "How are you mixed up with that?"

There was no true bad blood between the Italians and the Russians as of now, not since Gregor had taken over. They mostly worked parallel with a mutual respect rather than disdain. This was clear in the true concern that flashed across Gregor's face.

"My sister is being sold to Freddy for an in," Adrian said, his fists clenching as he said it. I could barely contain my own visceral rage, my nails biting into the flesh of my palm as I worked hard to keep myself in check. If I could see Adrian's eyes, I'm sure they would be burning with that same fury he'd shown since they learned this was my father's plan.

"An in…" Gregor murmured, eyes drifting over all four of us now. "That one is your brother," he said, pointing to Benny. Adrian's body stilled a bit, but after a moment, he nodded. No point in lying to someone we wanted as an ally.

"He is."

"And those two, Sal's?"

The resemblance between us was easily recognizable. We were definitely brothers. Enzo was a bit thinner and leaner than me and Sal, and me a bit taller than both of them, but not by much.

"Does it matter?" Adrian said through clenched teeth.

"Your sister was sold off to O'Shea, you said. Why her? She's not Salvatore's to sell," Gregor asked. No truer words had been said. She wasn't my fathers to sell, and yet he certainly did it.

"Our families have been tied for quite some time."

"Ah, yes. The infamous Lupo and LaMartina families. So tight-knit." Gregor's eyes swam with amusement at what I was sure was all our grim faces.

"We're here to talk about your relationship with the Irish," Adrian reminded, raising an eyebrow at the man across from him. A scowl briefly adorned Gregor's features.

There was a moment where tension was all that was holding back the knife of potential upset. This could go very wrong, or exactly how we wanted it to, and we were all waiting as the bartender came back with the drinks for Adrian and Enzo, setting them on the table between us and Gregor.

"What are you wanting?" Gregor asked, his lip curling up once the bartender scurried back to where she belonged.

"We have a common enemy. Our motives are different. I want my sister back without bringing war down on our heads, and you—"

"War with the Irish is inevitable. I've been biding my time for the perfect opportunity to take back what they stole from us," Gregor said with a scowl.

"What is it you want to take back?" Adrian asked, curiously. Gregor eyed him for a moment, taking a sip of his drink as he considered what to tell him.

"I do not believe we are good enough friends for that just yet, LaMartina," Gregor said, his voice barely a rumble.

"We pay back our debts, Gregor. If you help us, perhaps we'll help you," Adrian offered, finally picking up the glass of whiskey and taking a drink. Gregor's face broke into a wide smile at that.

"I'll contact you and Sal to discuss plans."

The clear omission of whatever it was that drove a stake between the Irish and the Russians was noted, but so was Gregor's acceptance of helping us. Even without us knowing what he stood to gain from this partnership, we couldn't say no, and we didn't need to pry.

"We have a timeline we must keep to. She can't be in his custody much longer," Adrian warned.

"Soon," Gregor said, nodding, before waving his hand dismissively, indicating we needed to go now.

As we left the club, some part of the bitter defeat that had been growing within me dissipated. Somehow, knowing we weren't alone in this made it all seem a lot more possible to get Carmen back where she belonged.

Sal, Enzo, and I stood in an alley, rain drenching us as we waited. Two more days had passed since we saw Gregor. He had only reached out to Sal to set up a meeting, one that would take place tomorrow night, but we needed a way to distract our father for that to happen. He barely wanted any of us away from him during our time in Chicago, not that I particularly blamed him. A Capo in a territory that was not his own was easy pickings for rivals. The Irish weren't Salvatore's allies just yet.

The best distraction happened to be someone we wanted to try to recruit anyway. Uncle Romolo was the Capo here, and though he was our blood, my father's older brother, they had long since stopped being friendly toward one another. Something had gone terribly wrong, and the only reason one of them wasn't dead was because of Morelli.

Romolo's restaurant and base of operations sat on just the other side of this alley, the muffled sounds of laughter and music coming through the brick before us. The alley on the other side was where employees came and went, but this alley was where Romolo liked to come and smoke, off limits to anyone who wasn't a guard or family.

The metal door creaked open, the sound from within echoing off the walls and momentarily drowning out the sound of the rain, as the man himself stepped out, chuckling as he pulled a cigarette from his pack, placing it at his lips before he looked up and finally noticed us.

He paused, dark eyes darting between our faces for a moment before he sighed, pulled his lighter from his pocket, and lit it. He looked like us, could have even been our father if someone didn't know the relation. Lupo blood was strong, that was clearly evident in all our features.

"What are you boys doing here?" he asked once he took a drag and let it out slowly.

"Salvatore," Sal said. Romolo's eyes flashed up at met Sal's, searching them for a moment.

"Your father and I don't mix well. You know that."

"We aren't here for you to mix. He needs to be taken out. We need your help to do that," Sal said, watching as the cigarette's cherry illuminated our uncle's face just as his eyes flashed with interest.

"What has he done?"

"The LaMartinas. You remember them?" Sal asked.

"Bernardo and Maria may as well have been my blood." Before our father and Romolo's falling out, he was just as close with Bernardo LaMartina as our father was. Bernardo was the one that Salvatore sent to Chicago most often when the two territories had to work together on something.

"Carmen, Bernardo's daughter. Salvatore gave her to the Irish," Sal said.

Every time one of us said what had happened to Carmen, my blood turned to fire. It didn't matter how many days and weeks passed, my rage burned just as strong, if not stronger. But what did change was the reaction of others as the news was broken. Romolo ripped the cigarette from his mouth, at first a look of disbelief there, quickly followed by his own rage. Romolo had known Carmen's parents; he had seen her as a child. The falling out between our father and him happened after Bernardo died, and before that, he had been just as connected to our two-family unit as anyone.

"Figlio di puttana!" Romolo hissed, throwing his cigarette against the bricks and raking his hands through his hair.

"She's been with them for a month. The wedding should be happening in a few weeks. Salvatore's plan is to join with them in the sex trade. Supplying the Irish with girls to send overseas," Enzo provided, only to be met with a series of additional curses in Italian.

"We need a distraction so we can meet with an ally and plan our next steps," I said, finally speaking up when his curses quieted, and the only sound was the patter of rain.

"When?" he asked, pulling a fresh cigarette from his pocket and lighting it.

"Tomorrow," Sal said.

"I can manage that," Romolo said, nodding. "Morelli will not be happy about this. He is firmly against trafficking that material."

This was news. We weren't sure, of course, if what we had planned would end up getting us all taken out. If Morelli didn't approve of the death of our father, he would most certainly make our lives hell. We'd all have to flee from the country, something I had been using my former contacts to make as quick and painless as possible if it came to that, but was certainly not preferable. Knowledge that Morelli was against anything of this nature seemed to spark all of us.

"Will our familial connection make your council to the Boss moot?" Enzo asked, his voice giving away the hope there.

"Morelli knows how I feel about him. If I tell him you've taken him out and avoided this catastrophe… well, he won't be happy, but he won't send you to the grave either. Be prepared for punishment, *nipoti,* but Carmen." He sighed heavily, rubbing his chin. "She is worth the risk," Romolo said with a nod.

"I'll text you tomorrow," Sal said as Enzo tossed a burner phone to Romolo.

With nothing more than a nod, we turned and left the alley, heading back to the hotel before our father would be able to notice our absence.

CHAPTER 25

CARMEN

My fingers hovered over the keys of the tiny burner phone Rory had stuffed in my shirt just days ago. I had seen the girls and moms a few more times, but they were sent back to Kansas City just yesterday, and I was once again trapped in my prison.

Following their leaving, I was punished. I hadn't done anything to deserve it, but I hadn't eaten anything since our fairwell breakfast, and my stomach protested angrily at the lack of sustenance.

I wasn't sure who would be at the other end of this text, the only name listed was *"Amici,"* Italian for "friends," but I knew I couldn't do nothing while they were all working tirelessly to get me out of this situation.

[Me: Guard duties switch every four hours. Looser constraints in the midday shifts starting at noon. Mickey is young, he sneaks me food sometimes. He's usually the first midday shift.]

I sent it before I could lose my nerve.

[Amici: Mickey, huh? Should I be worried?]

My heart fluttered a little. Only one person would reply with a comment like that.

[Me: Only if you plan on not providing me with snacks.]

[Amici: I'll make sure we are never low on any snacks.]

Somehow, I believed Leo was both playing along while also being completely serious. I could almost imagine a cabinet solely dedicated to snacks of various kinds. Anything I may crave would always be available at my fingertips. The strange joy that brought me made my heart swell, and also made my despair at the possibility that it wouldn't happen crash down on me.

[Amici: Not much longer, Little Song. I promise.]

There was no date mentioned, no time frame I could point to, but that was to be expected. If, for some reason, Freddy or one of his men got ahold of this, Leo wouldn't want them to have any reason to thwart their plans. Even if I wanted to type a dozen different things to Leo, asking for details, for the time, hell, even to just tell him I loved him, I couldn't really. So I typed the only thing I could that would hopefully tell him everything I wished I could say.

[Me: Goodnight.]

[Amici: Goodnight.]

Tomorrow.

Tomorrow I would marry Freddy O'Shea.

Tomorrow my fate would be sealed.

I knew the boys tried their best. I knew they tried everything, but now that the date was here, Freddy having moved it up from September to August, I was feeling the small rope of hope slipping through my fingers.

The texting had been sparse in the last week. It wasn't always Leo on the other end, but the last person to text me tried to tell me not to worry, even though I had been forced to go dress shopping for a rehearsal dinner happening this evening with a woman named Scarlett.

The dress we got was beautiful, but the entire experience had left me off balance. Scarlett was clearly someone Freddy trusted, but the entire time she had been sickeningly kind, overly so, and forced. It was only at the end, when we were in the car with my guard, that she finally turned to me and showed her true colors.

"You won't be offended then, when he always chooses me," she said, turning to me where we sat in the back of the car, her face showing a bit of smugness hiding behind a bright smile.

"Chooses you?" I asked, only mildly confused. The pieces had all been there, the way she clearly kept mentioning Freddy's preferences throughout the day, and how much she wanted to please him, as well as the cutting glares she sent me when she thought I wasn't paying attention.

"If it wasn't for this little deal with the Italians, he would be marrying me," she said, her voice a little clipped with annoyance.

I wasn't sure how much Freddy told his mistress. Perhaps he would have married her, but either way, for men like Freddy and Salvatore, people, no matter how much they are supposed to mean to them, are all disposable. She was no different.

"I'm sure you'll still get your chance." The idea that I would be living a long and miserable life with Freddy was not something I could picture. He had told me blatantly that if I misbehaved once we were married, there would be no stopping him from what he would do to me. I was under no illusion that I would make it out of this arrangement alive if the boys didn't help me. Alone and adrift here, I would be helpless to his forces.

But if I was going to die by his hands, I'd be sure to leave a mark. The only reason I hadn't fought back this far was the possibility I was going to escape. Hurting Freddy or Jeremy when they had guards at their disposal to take me out the next moment wasn't smart if you were hoping for salvation.

And now here I sat, in my room that was both my safe haven and my prison cell, staring across the room at the dress Scarlett had picked out. It was a beautiful dress. The dark silky fabric had melted against my skin when I tried it on, hugging my curves in all the right places, while simultaneously seeming to flutter and drape in places that accentuated my form.

Tonight, I would have to play a happy bride-to-be for all the O'Shea Clan, including the Boss, Colin O'Shea, Freddy's father. I certainly would look the part of a beautiful fiancée.

"Carmen!" came a voice, startling me out of my thoughts.

Jeremy.

For the last month and a half, I had been here, not only had I been subjected to Freddy and his tortures, but Jeremy had mostly stayed in Chicago. I had gotten a brief reprieve from him for the last two weeks when he went back to Kansas City for something. I assume his real job, but apparently he was back. Just in time to make this nightmare even worse.

"Carmen!" he singsonged again, this time closer to the door of my room. My heart rate picked up. The idea of being trapped in this room with him was frightening in a way I wasn't sure I could handle now.

The door burst open and there Jeremy stood, a grin stretched maliciously over his face.

"I brought you something, but only if you're going to promise to be a good girl," he said, striding closer to where I sat on the bed. I tried to control the flinch that wanted to instinctively wrack my body at his movements, but it was impossible. I was cornered, and he was a predator.

"What is it?" I asked, managing somehow to keep my tone pleasant, if not eagerly inquisitive.

"Your makeup. Thought you might want to get a bit more dolled up for tonight. Are you excited?"

Was I excited to be paraded around the O'Shea Clan, pretending to be happy with my situation, when I was actually a prisoner and would most likely die before Freddy and I had our first anniversary? No, not particularly.

"Of course," I said, but my voice came out monotone to my own ears.

"Just think, after tomorrow, there's nothing to keep me from having you in all the ways I've all wanted these years," he said, setting the bag of my makeup on the bed, only to reach out his fingers grasping to a lock of hair that dangled in front of my face. "Ever since I saw that picture of you, I knew I had to have you, Carmen. You were hot in high school. No one would have said otherwise, but I had other interests then. But once I saw you grown up… This body—" He took in a shaky breath, letting it out with a disgusting groan as his hand moved down, fingertips brushing against the exposed skin at the base of my throat. "I can't wait to get a taste."

"It will be worth the wait, Jer," Freddy said, causing my eyes to snap up to the open doorway. Freddy was leaning there, watching the interaction with a heat in his eyes I had seen many times now. He was imagining all the perverse things they were planning on doing to me.

Jeremy sucked in another ragged breath before pulling his hand away and stepping back. The erection was obvious in his pants as he adjusted himself in his suit, before stepping toward the door where Freddy stood.

"You have two hours to make yourself presentable. My father won't tolerate anything short of perfection from you," Freddy said as Jeremy brushed past him.

"Perfection," I scoffed quietly.

"What was that?" he snapped, halting as he turned away.

"I said, of course," I murmured, looking at his scowling face, the one I would be graced with for the rest of my short life.

He stormed across the room, his hand grasping my chin roughly and turning my face forcefully up toward him.

"You better behave tonight. If I get even a whisper of defiance from you, tomorrow following the ceremony, there will be little to keep me from tearing you to shreds. I think my brother would rather play with you more than one night, after all the time he's had to wait. So keep that in mind as you whisper and scoff to yourself.

Your big Italian mouth will only hurt you if you don't learn how to tame it," he hissed, before throwing me back against the bed and storming from the room, slamming the door so hard it shook in its frame.

CHAPTER 26

CARMEN

Gatherings like this were risky for any Mafia. To have all the important players in one place was a recipe for disaster, hence why the guard around the venue was so heavy as I stepped out of the car, my hand trapped in Freddy's. Not one man I came across as we moved through the lavish hotel lobby was without a gun. Most of them were concealed, but I, having been raised in this life, could see all the subtle signs. The way a pant leg would sit just a little oddly at the ankle or how some of them would tuck their hand in their jacket, touching the gun at their hip as if to make sure it was still there.

I recognized the guards hovering nearby us, the ones that Freddy must have trusted enough to let them in his home, all seemed to circle us, staying just far enough away that it wasn't terribly obvious if one didn't know, but close enough to jump in if anything seemed suspicious.

Given this gathering was mostly for the O'Shea Clan, it didn't seem terribly concerning, but then again, Italians would be in attendance tonight. This was supposed to be a show of alliance. Once I was married to Freddy tomorrow, Salvatore and the O'Sheas could officially start their partnership and I would only need to stay alive long enough to solidify that deal, but alive and thriving were two very different things.

Freddy steered us through the crowds, thanking people for their congratulations to us both, while I merely smiled and nodded.

"You are far from mute, Carmen. I expect you to speak to our guests," Freddy murmured through clenched teeth in my ear as we moved deeper into the ballroom, heading toward a table that was set apart from the others.

"I took your words to heart, Freddy," I said back, barely keeping the scathe from my voice as I said it.

My big, fat Italian mouth knew when to adjust for the audience. I just didn't know how to actually get the words "thank you" from my lips when all these people were congratulating me on my own imprisonment. The engagement ring Freddy had forced on my finger in the car felt like a shackle. It was large and gaudy, something to show off the wealth and power the clan held, not a show of love like an engagement ring should have been.

"Behaving includes talking to our guests," he whispered, his fingers digging a little harder into my waist as we got closer to the table.

That's when I finally noticed who was sitting there. Colin O'Shea sat at the center of the oval table, the biggest one in the room. It was easy to see the resemblance between him and his sons, now that I finally got a look at him. The dirty-blond hair that Freddy had matched the man before me, though he had far more gray running through it than Freddy did. His face was similarly shaped, though his skin was a bit looser and riddled with scars. The piercing blue of his eyes was the same though, and so was the maliciousness behind them.

"Ah. The people of the hour," Colin said, standing from his seat. Everyone else sitting at the table stood as well. "Freddy," he said, nodding at his son, before his eyes turned back to me, a smile that sent a shiver down my spine spreading across his lips. "And Carmen. So good to meet you. I hope the party here shows you how happy we are to be welcoming you into the clan."

I had heard similar words before. Being a child of a man so close to a Capo, meant I had gone to my fair share of gatherings for the Italian Mafia. The number of times I had heard Morelli say the words, "Welcome to the family," was long. However, Morelli always seemed to be genuine when he was saying it. O'Shea's words sounded like a death sentence.

"Thank you, Sir," I said, lowering my head in respect. He barked out a laugh, causing me to look back up.

"You've managed to get the bitch to heel, son. Good work," he said between chuckles at Freddy, who grinned in response. I bit my lip to keep myself from snarling at him. This *bitch* was far from a heeled dog, but I wasn't going to risk snapping here and now. I was waiting, not stupid. If I was going to die by Freddy and Jeremy's hands, I wasn't going to go down without a fight.

The party continued; the minutes passing and I was becoming acutely aware that Salvatore was nowhere to be seen yet. In fact, I heard as much murmured on the lips of several guests, eyeing me oddly, before going back to talking loudly behind their hands, as if that would somehow make their words quieter.

Jeremy approached and Freddy withdrew his arm from mine, though the bruises his fingers had left there remained a reminder of his touch.

"She's yours while I figure out what's taking Lupo so damn long to get here," Freddy said, pushing me toward his brother.

LEO

I could see her from my vantage point at the neighboring hotel, my scope set right on her and never wavering. Kia was right next to me, watching as well with her hawk eyes.

"The plan will work, Leo," she said, as if she could read the worried thoughts flitting through my mind.

"I know," I murmured back roughly.

"You going to be okay with everything you had to do and agree to to get here though?" she asked, making me take in a deep breath.

What I had to do and agree to…

It took watching Carmen being dragged off that beach and driven away faster than my legs could chase after it for me to realize there was little more that I was concerned about than her. A month and a half, Carmen had been in the hands of the Irish. It was too long, but it took far longer to navigate the intricate web of underground politics. Trying to save someone from another Mafia was a delicate balancing act when trying not to start a war.

I had been on the outside of all of this. I had wanted to stay out, stay away, like Benny and Carmen, but like it was fated to be, I had to become something different if I was going to get her back. It had been Uncle Romolo

who told us what would happen. Of course, it made sense once he said it.

"You know the Boss will only accept Sal as your father's replacement if you agree to step into the family where you belong."

Like he had just slapped me in the face, I took in air sharply, and looked in his eyes for any indication that he could be joking, but I found none.

"Why's that?" Enzo had asked, his voice laced with the outrage we were all feeling.

"To take on what you plan to, to accomplish this feat of pulling Carmen out safely, you'll need not only allies and manpower, but you'll need the strongest by your side," Romolo said, now looking at Sal. "You might just pull this off with Leo at your side, Sal, but he will need to remain there if you plan on keeping any of your heads."

My brothers looked at me then. I'm not sure what they saw on my face, but sadness filled their gazes for a moment, as well as understanding. They were waiting for me to decide if we would continue. Giving me the choice, even if it meant losing ties with the LaMartina family forever, making enemies out of our friends.

At that moment I couldn't have loved my brothers more.

I turned back to Romolo.

"It's not even a question. I'll be at my brothers' sides until the end," I told Romolo, as much as my brothers. I would do anything, even become part of the Mafia, if it meant getting Carmen back.

Romolo had come in handy, forcing a meeting with my father in the guise of spotting him in his territory. Two Capos should be on good terms and subsequently should be meeting with each other when they encroach on each other's territory. The fact that Salvatore hadn't reached out wasn't a good look for him, but declining a meeting with his brother would have been a far worse insult.

This gave us ample opportunity to meet with Gregor a few weeks before and a second time just days prior to this dreadful excuse for a rehearsal dinner. Everyone in that ballroom knew what kind of wedding this was. It wasn't a marriage of love, it was a transaction between two powerful men. The whispers behind hands, while their eyes darted to Carmen were enough to make my blood boil and my finger twitch against the trigger on my rifle, but I had to wait. If everything went to plan, I wouldn't even be using my rifle on anyone who landed in my scope. That would be for Kia to handle.

Romolo already went above and beyond, aiding us by not only providing us the time we needed to meet with Gregor but also the one task we weren't certain how to pull off, incapacitating our father.

Drugs were a common item the Mafia handled. Anything illegal, the Mafia had their hands in. Most were smuggling weapons, technology, people—not for trafficking, but those who needed to cross the border and were willing to pay the price—and of course, drugs. That was more Romolo's wheelhouse, so when he handed Enzo a little brown packet, we looked at him with cautious interest.

"Give it to your mother. If she is serious about taking your father down, as you say, she can keep him asleep for you, if that will help you any," Romolo said with a shrug.

No name given for what was held in the tiny packet, but then, we didn't really care. Putting our father to sleep would avoid making his guards suspicious and give us enough time to keep him incapacitated while we secured him and set our plan in motion.

We just needed the signal from the Russian before we could move. And finally, it arrived.

"There he is," Kia whispered, tapping against my arm to give me the direction I should aim my scope if I wanted to see. Reluctantly, I moved from my view of Carmen to where Kia indicated, and there he was, stepping out of his car, six of his men moving to surround him. Gregor oozed confidence as he stepped up to the doors, the security outside seeming to puff up, hands itching to draw the guns at their hips.

I couldn't hear what was said, but whatever Gregor said to the guards, accompanied by a very intimidating group of armed Russians, the men at the door seemed to freeze in shock, allowing Gregor to pass by and through the doors to the party beyond.

I pulled out my phone, calling Benny.

"Gregor's in," I said.

"It's time," Benny said, I assumed to the others. "We're moving, Leo. Get to your position."

"We? You're supposed to stay with the moms, Benny," I said, eye back in the scope and searching once more for Carmen.

"Enzo has to be watching the cameras and scrubbing as we move. He's staying with them. I'm coming."

My heart thundered in my chest for a few moments as I looked for her. Between losing sight of Carmen and the fact that Benny was going to be in the fray with the rest of us, I was feeling a sense of panic I hadn't felt even in all the compromising situations I had been put in during my time overseas.

"That wasn't the plan," I growled, scope moving perhaps too quickly over the faces of all the guests, only vaguely aware of the shock and horror on some of their faces as Gregor moved through the crowd.

"Get over it and get your head in the game, Leo. My sister is counting on us," Benny snapped right back, before the call disconnected.

And then I saw her.

CHAPTER 27

CARMEN

"What the fuck?" Jeremy hissed out in a whisper, pulling me closer to his body in a way that made me fight back the urge to shove him off of me. I fixed my gaze where he was looking, watching as a man I had never seen before walked into the large banquet room with a very intimidating entourage. Dark hair was slicked back on his head demurely, his suit black, but clearly expensive and tailored perfectly to fit his muscled body, while his deep-set eyes scanned the room.

Power and dominance radiated from him. I had seen this sort of display many times before, but it was somehow so much more intimidating when I had no idea who they were. He fixed his stare at me for a moment as he passed by, a look of acknowledgment there in his eyes that was so fleeting, I would have missed it if I hadn't been looking, before he moved on, his men following behind watching everyone around them with an air of hostility.

Jeremy had seemed to be frozen as the man walked by, but as soon as we were out of his line of sight, he pulled me roughly farther away as I watched the group approach the table where Colin sat.

"Where did Freddy go?" Jeremy hissed under his breath, clearly to himself, as we moved more toward the main lobby of the hotel. Guests from our party had spilled out there as well, chatting in groups, and honestly, I was fairly pleased to be away from the main room where people were openly gawking at me, but less happy to be trapped with Jeremy, of all people.

I couldn't see Freddy either, but I suddenly felt a bolt of excitement. This was not according to their plan. No, I wasn't privy to what they had originally had in store for tonight, but between Salvatore's lack of appearance and the dramatic entrance of that strange man, I knew something was up.

Freddy seemed to appear out of nowhere, his phone clenched in his hand, blue eyes wide with panic and rage.

"What is the Russian doing here?" Freddy practically growled as he came up to us.

Ah.

So that man was Russian Mafia. His dark Eastern European looks made so much more sense. I knew the Italians, at least the midwestern ones, didn't have too many dealings with Russians, but his presence here meant we certainly did now.

"I-I don't know. I came to find you," Jeremy said stupidly.

"Salvatore isn't answering and now this?" Freddy ran his hands through his hair, making his once pristine dark blond locks much more rumpled with the stress.

"Maybe he's just appealing. Weddings and all that," Jeremy said, though his tone gave away the concern that this was for a very different reason.

Freddy seemed to waver for a moment, his eyes darting from Jeremy to me and back toward the main room, where we could see the group of Russians still at the table where Colin O'Shea sat.

"We need to go to our new guests," Freddy said after several moments of contemplation, taking my arm and roughly pulling me from Jeremy's grasp, before dragging me through the crowd.

The heels I was wearing slipped on the marble floors and the skirt of my dress kept making me trip as he walked far too quickly, pulling me along with him.

"…I would be invited to an event such as this. But no invitation. Not to this or the wedding I hear is tomorrow. You wound me, O'Shea," came the deep voice of the Russian man as we finally approached the table. Now that I could see Colin, I took in the strain, as if he were trying to hold back a scowl.

"This is for family," Colin said.

"What are we, if not an extension of family? Those of us who do what we do must stay together. That's why your son is marrying the Italian girl, is it not?"

With his words, his head turned toward us, eyes once again looking at me with an odd sort of acknowledgment I wasn't sure how to interpret.

Colin's eyes narrowed as he looked at the Russian, giving an almost imperceptible nod toward Freddy at my side.

"Of course," Colin said, standing from his chair and buttoning his jacket smoothly. "But my son and Carmen were just about to head home. Wouldn't want her to get too tired before the big day."

"Pity. I wanted to have a chat with her," the Russian murmured, a smirk drifting across his lips, his eyes continuing to look into mine intensely. "I thought you might wait until Salvatore got here to celebrate."

The outward acknowledgment that Salvatore wasn't in attendance was clearly like a slap in the face to both

Colin and Freddy, who both seemed to clench their hands, though Freddy's was more of an increase to the force of his already bruising grip on my arm.

"Yes, this impression he's leaving doesn't bode well for our future collaboration. Maybe we'll send them a message through her," Colin said, turning those cold eyes onto me. The look on his face turned from tense, like a lion preparing to strike, to merciless greed as he looked at me, clearly imagining all the ways my body could be used to send a message. I was scared to look at Freddy, knowing I'd see the same expression on his face.

"I'll take Jeremy with me," Freddy said, and I watched in horror as Colin's eyes brightened with interest. I had wondered if he knew what Freddy's plans were for me, now I knew he not only did, but he clearly condoned it.

"Before you go," the Russian said, still looking at me, but obviously talking to Freddy. "Perhaps you would like to be present for my proposition."

It wasn't a question. Colin's eyes darted from the Russian to his son.

"Just go," Colin said to Freddy, as a chuckle tumbled from the Russian's lips.

Freddy didn't hesitate, immediately pulling me with him as he turned away, his other arm eagerly waving at his men, wordlessly telling them to prep for departure.

"What's going on?" I asked, unable to help myself. I had no idea what was going on there, no idea what the relationship between the Irish and the Russians was. Clearly, there was history that was about to be brought back from the grave, and I almost wished we would have stayed so I could know what it was.

And where *was* Salvatore? Not that I wanted to see him, but I expected him to be here, expected to have to look at him and watch him gloat about his victory and alliance, despite the misery he was subjecting me to.

His absence was a red flag. I just wasn't sure if it was in my favor or not.

"Fucking Gregor Stepanov," Freddy hissed, spitting as we broke through the final guests and pushed into a back hallway that led to an employee entrance to the hotel. "He's going to demand my father give him something equal to what we took. But there's never anything he accepts. He's holding a grudge, no matter what we do," Freddy continued, mumbling, I assumed mostly to himself as we moved swiftly through the back corridors that were more industrial and sterile than the fancy furnishings and decor that the guests were supposed to see. Oddly there didn't seem to be any staff roaming around here.

The muffled sound of a silenced gun went off not far from where we were, echoing off the barren walls and tiled floor. Freddy stopped short at the sound, his fingers flexing and tensing against my now very sore arm as if he were using it to help him think. He glanced down at me, a moment of fear showing in his eyes and the quieted *bang bang* of additional shots followed and didn't seem to stop.

Whatever he saw in my eyes, perhaps a sliver of hope that maybe whoever was shooting back there was to rescue me, seemed to make him reign in that fear, cold determination taking back over. He pulled a gun that must have been tucked in the back of his suit pants, and held it at his side, before he continued forward, pulling me along behind him at his fast pace.

I didn't fully understand what happened next. My heart was beating wildly in my chest, the pain from his grip nearly unnoticeable to me anymore as the sound of the fighting got louder. We approached the large, metal back door, the sound of a struggle happening just beyond its dented steel. Freddy paused, listening, before he pushed it open violently. The scent of gunpowder and blood filled my nostrils and I saw a battle raging behind this hotel.

Freddy's men had moved the car around to get us, but there were far fewer of them than usual. Hamish was the main shooter, seamlessly dropping clips and reloading in seconds. Jeremy was crouching on the side of the car that faced the doors, while the guards did all the work, I only looked at him briefly, seeing the cowardice of his shaking, disheveled form was not surprising, and not worth my attention when there was still so much more to absorb around me.

Adrian, Travis, and Benny were poised behind a car that was blocking one entrance to the alley about three hundred feet from where we were. My breath caught seeing my brothers there, their burning rage channeled into cold, calculated shots toward their enemies. They were heavily outnumbered by Freddy's men but clearly had better aim and perhaps the advantage of a better location, since they were more shadowed than the Irish were, given Freddy's car was bathed in the bright floodlights that illuminated the alley.

Time seemed to snap back into place when we burst through the door, my mind having taken all this in in moments. In quick succession, three of the guards in front of us dropped to the ground with lethal headshots, blood and brain matter flying everywhere, some even landing on my face and chest. I must have made some sort of sound, because both my brothers and Travis turned their heads, their gunfire stopping as their targets were no longer their focus.

Freddy raised his gun, pulling the trigger before any of the three could react.

"No!" I screamed, watching in horror as the bullet whizzed through the air, striking Adrian's shoulder, the force causing him to drop behind the car and out of sight.

Benny screamed incoherently, the sound more like that of an enraged animal than a human, turning his gun toward Freddy, finger already tightening against the trigger, but all Freddy had to do was pull me in front of him, like a shield, and he knew Benny wouldn't fire.

We stood like that for a moment, silence taking over the whole alley that once had been so loud, despite the silencers on most of their weapons. My breath came out in short gasps, Freddy's hand now wrapped around my throat as he pulled me tightly to his front. I watched the conflict move over Benny's shadowed face.

"Is Adrian okay?" I asked. I couldn't help it. I had to know. Benny said nothing, his jaw clenching as he continued to look between me and over my head at Freddy.

"You made a mistake here, LaMartina. Salvatore is lucky his son isn't here for this or your dear sister," he leaned down, his nose dragging over my cheek as he took a loud inhale, "she would be paying quite the price. She's already going to be sending a message to him for his failure to make an appearance tonight. Just be glad you didn't drag him into this, or we might break her a little more than we were already intending to."

Freddy's fingers tightened on my throat, and I could almost feel the way he must have been staring over my head at Benny, daring him to do something. But he didn't. Benny's finger pulled away from the trigger and he waved at Travis to do the same beside him.

"We're taking the car now," Freddy said, pushing me in front of him away from the door to the hotel to where Jeremy still crouched like a cowering child. As we got closer, I realized he even had a gun clutched in his fingers. What a pathetic excuse for a human.

"You won't follow us if you want her to live," Freddy said loudly, keeping me between my brothers and himself before he quickly shoved me through the driver's-side door, following a moment later and forcing me to crawl over the console to the passenger seat, Jeremy already having crawled in the back.

Freddy started the car, his remaining men stepping in front of it and blocking my view of Benny and Travis, as Freddy began backing us out the other side of the alley so quickly, I wasn't surprised when a side mirror was ripped off on the dumpster. He whipped out into the street, immediately stomping on the accelerator and speeding through the city.

"How the fuck did that happen?" Freddy roared, clearly his question was aimed at Jeremy.

"Most of the men came on to guard Dad when the Russian arrived. Only ours went out to move us," Jeremy said, voice shaking slightly as he tried to brace himself through each of Freddy's sharp turns.

"They are either plotting together, which sounds ridiculous. Stepanov wouldn't sink so low to help Adrian. He isn't even close to being in any position of power," Freddy said, eyes darting between the road before us and the rearview mirror, making sure we weren't being followed. I was sure being in the situation, now completely without his protection, was making his latent fear rear its ugly head.

He didn't have his guards.

It would be difficult, but I realized I could take these two. They had guns, but clearly, Jeremy wasn't well versed in using one, and Freddy was distracted with driving. It would be risky. I could easily die or be severely injured, especially at the speeds we were going down these city streets, but to me, it was worth it.

They took me against my will. They stole and tortured women and children regularly. They shot, maybe killed my brother, and certainly wouldn't stop with just those men I loved. I thought of Leo, certain that whatever this plan was, they were implementing, he would be involved somehow. If I could take Freddy and Jeremy out now, I could hopefully spare Leo. A world without him in it… it wasn't worth living anyway.

"It was like they were waiting," Jeremy said, opening his mouth once more to continue, but being cut off as another car seemed to come out of nowhere, their front end just tapping at the back end of our car. It wasn't a huge or hard hit, but it was enough to have Freddy frantically trying to pull us out of oncoming traffic and avoid spinning out.

It could have been a coincidence, a car that didn't stop for the madman driving ours, but once Freddy corrected the car, the other car caught up beside us. I looked over to see who was driving and there was Sal.

I hit the automatic button to roll down the window, happy that for once, since I had been held by Freddy, I wasn't trapped in the child-locked back seat. The satisfied smile Sal threw my way was all I needed before I ducked down, hugging my knees as I heard the sound of a gun go off. I felt the hot splash of blood and whipped my head back up as I felt the car swerve.

I was disappointed when I looked over, seeing that the bullet seemed to have grazed his right shoulder, tearing open his suit to the flesh before hitting his left arm that had been on the steering wheel. A string of curses flew out of Freddy's mouth as his right hand fumbled to grab his gun from his lap. Both arms were injured, but not fatally.

"Jeremy! Use your fucking gun!" Freddy bellowed, trying to aim out the window in front of my face toward

Sal. His arm didn't quite seem to be able to raise high enough, and I certainly wasn't going to let him shoot Sal. Immediately, I pressed my fingers into the wound on his shoulder, making him let out a pained cry as Jeremy struggled with the locked back windows.

"I can't roll them down!"

Freddy's gun dropped in my lap, and I grabbed it, aiming it at Jeremy while Freddy struggled to control the car with his damaged arms and the added pressure of Sal continuing to follow behind.

"You want to fucking die, bitch?" Freddy screamed, his gaze searing into me for a moment that felt like it lasted forever.

Insanity. That's all I could see there. Somewhere between the stress, the pain, and his own pride, Freddy seemed to snap. He slammed on the breaks. Sal's car, which had slowed to follow behind us to avoid hitting oncoming traffic, surged forward. The impact was nearly instantaneous, the sound so deafening I couldn't even hear my own screams, though I could feel it in my throat.

The last thing I saw before it all went black was the streetlight, glowing orange and flickering, right before it teetered and came crashing down with us.

CHAPTER 28

CARMEN

I woke to a sharp pain. My head felt heavy, my eyes didn't want to open, but something in me reminded me I wasn't safe. That intuition was only solidified as I felt myself being dragged, sharp things biting against my skin, and the feeling of my flesh being rubbed raw on my back as I moved against … what? Pavement?

The tinkling sound of glass falling away, the hissing sound, like pressurized steam escaping all clued me, slowly, into where I was, but it was the harsh grunt of a man and the adjustment of a grip on my wrists that made me keenly aware that I was being moved away from the crash site.

It all snapped back in my mind and my eyes flew open; the light-polluted night sky of Chicago above me and the upside-down face of Jeremy as he dragged me away from the car.

I immediately began trying to resist, willing my body to have enough strength, since I still felt groggy and uncoordinated. I must have hit my head in the crash.

I wondered if Sal was okay, though I couldn't stop my fighting to look at the actual damage.

"You fucking bitch!" Jeremy screamed, releasing my wrists only to round on me, straddling my legs and wrapping a hand around my throat. His blue eyes were wild. He had a cut down one cheek, still actively bleeding, and splattering onto my face as he leaned over me.

"My brother isn't dead yet, but nothing will save you from what I have in store for you. You know where we are, Carmen?"

I shook my head, which was hard considering he was pressing me roughly into the ground.

"Freddy drove exactly to the right place. There's no one here for blocks. No one heard the crash, and no one will hear you scream," he said, the anger on his face transforming to lust.

"No!" I choked out as I realized what he planned.

What sick person decided that raping someone was more important than getting help for their own brother? Who knew what condition Freddy was in? He could have still been alive, but bleeding out, and only Jeremy could help him. Instead, Jeremy decided having his way with me was far more important.

"I told you I'd have you either way," he said, his other hand coming to tear whatever remained of my dress from my body. I was struggling to get air with how tightly he grasped my throat, so all I could hear was the whoosh of my blood in my ears, my shallow breaths, his heaving breaths as he looked at my now mostly exposed body before the sound of him undoing his belt and pants hit the air.

He had me well and truly pinned. Even if I hadn't been battered by the car crash, I would have strug-gled to get out of this hold, but I managed to pull my arms up, nails scratching into anything I could reach. He screamed out in fury at my attempts, but I could feel him lining up. Everything in me tensed as I waited for a new pain, for this new torture that had been held over my head for the last month.

Bang.

Jeremy went still above me, his hand loosening from my throat before he fell right on top of me. I began scrambling to push him off, managing to get out from under his weight and to my feet. Adrenaline seemed to be the only thing keeping me upright, as I whirled around look at whoever belonged to the footfalls coming up behind me.

Though whoever it was clearly shot Jeremy, I couldn't be sure they were friendly. I couldn't be sure of anything but my need to survive at this moment. But it wasn't one of O'Shea's or even Salvatore's men coming, it was Leo, gun raised and pointing at Jeremy as he approached with more smooth speed than should have been possible while wielding a gun.

I was still breathing raggedly, my heart pounding in my chest and body shaking with the instinct to fight, but I knew as I saw those hazel eyes burning with fury that I was safe now. Even as I felt the hand snake around my ankle.

"You're mi—" Jeremy started to choke out, but I didn't want to hear his pathetic voice or feel his disgusting touch for another moment. I tore my eyes from Leo who was quickly closing the distance between us, using my other leg not clutched by Jeremy to stomp once on his wrist, freeing my ankle with a sickening snap. He screamed, his voice echoing off the surrounding warehouses. The bullet had gone through his shoulder. Blood was pouring from both the small entrance at his front and the massive exit wound that was once his scapula, but somehow the pain of my breaking his wrist had him howling.

I raised my foot again as he rolled onto his back, clutching his arm, and kicked him square in the jaw to shut him up. The satisfaction in the crunch of his bones under my foot seemed to breathe life into a beast I had kept hidden inside of me. I raised my foot twice more, bringing it down on his nose and cheekbone. His skull gave away, caving under my strength alone with a sickening crunch.

"Carmen," Leo said quietly, his voice letting me know he had finally reached me and bringing me from the haze of fury and gratification I was in as I made sure Jeremy Wallingford was truly dead.

Leo shuffled his feet, a warning before he touched me, since I knew he could be silent with his steps. His fingers quietly slipped over my hand, asking, not taking. I wanted to hold his hand, to let myself fall into his embrace, but, instead, I waited, watching the tremors of Jeremy's body for a few moments as his blood flowed freely from his face and the wound in his shoulder Leo had given him until he finally went still. Only then did I tear my gaze from the mangled remains, letting my fingers twine with the familiar warmth and strength of Leo's, before turning to look up at him.

As his face came into my view, the rest of the world seemed to go black.

LEO

I knew Adrian and Sal, and even Benny, to my dismay, had moved into their positions as soon as Gregor stepped foot into the hotel. His presence there would put the O'Sheas on alert, pulling more of their guards into the building to keep watch of him and his crew, instead of on the perimeter. That was the point. My task was to meet up with Sal and follow if Adrian's team didn't stop Freddy first.

I had torn through the hotel across the street, racing to the point where I would meet Sal as I put the comm in my ear that would connect all of us. By the time I reached the street corner, turning down to the side street where Sal should have been waiting, I heard the commotion over the comms. Gunfire, glass breaking, and then the unmistakable scream of Carmen, and just after Benny's roar of rage, making my skin crawl. That was not a sound I had ever heard come from him before. Full-on anguish.

"What was that?" came Sal's voice in my ear.

"I got shot," came Adrian's voice quietly. It was very quiet, too quiet on the other end. Firing stopped.

"Are you okay, Adrian?" Sal asked, his voice panicked. "Adrian?"

But the muffled voice of Freddy could be heard on the other end. Not loud enough for us to understand what he said.

We heard car doors slamming, and then the rev of an engine.

"They got out," came Benny's voice a moment later.

"Adrian!" Sal yelled, his own engine revving.

"I'll live! Go before you lose them!" Adrian snapped.

"Fucking gushing," Benny growled as the sound of fabric tearing came over the comms.

"Get him in the car before the rest of the Irish come out here," Travis said.

"Where are you, Leo?" Sal asked, his voice only barely showing signs of relief at the sound of Adrain's voice.

"He's four minutes out," Enzo said through the comms. He was still at the hotel where Maria had been staying, having whisked Mom out of the one she had been staying in with our father before the guards caught wind anything was going on.

"Just go, Sal. I'll find another way," I said, feeling as if the blocks to my brother's car would've been a moment too late. Everything felt too late. "Get out of there before the other guards come down on you," I grunted to Benny and Adrian, changing my trajectory to the car park I spotted across the street.

"There's movement at the front of the hotel," Kia said as I used the handle of my gun to shatter the window of a Dodge Charger.

"In the car, Adriano," Benny hissed.

It felt like ages of listening to Sal's breathing and the engine of his car as I hot-wired the car I had selected, but as I got it started, I heard the unmistakable sound of a collision.

"Found them," Sal grunted, before Enzo gave me the street they were traveling down.

"*Cazzo!* He drives like a fucking madman!" Enzo hissed. I was certain he was watching and trying to scrub footage of the cars as he went. Based on the sounds, and how fast Enzo liked to drive, it was clear Freddy was making quite a scene through down-town Chicago.

I punched the accelerator of the Charger, whipping out of the car park and heading to where Enzo said.

"What's happening?" I asked, tearing through the streets and trying desperately to catch up. If Freddy was going in the direction Enzo suggested, I knew exactly where he was heading. He was taking her to the warehouse district, probably to the slew of buildings the O'Sheas owned, several of which held their human merchandise for periods of time. Sal had just gone there with our father and told us all about it and the depravity he witnessed there. His disgust wasn't limited to the women and girls and what they were being put through though. It was the excitement of our father that made our brother so revolted.

Following directly behind them would be asking to be pulled over by cops, though a high-speed chase through city streets wasn't likely to be something the cops would actually do. Too many civilians at risk.

"Carmen is so fucking smart," Sal said, a grin in his voice just as the sound of his gun being fired went off over the comms. "I shot him, but not to kill. Hopefully, it will be enough to have him slow down. She saw me and immediately rolled down the window and ducked."

This woman.

She was all mine.

"I'm coming from the east side," I said, finding my own mouth spreading into a smile. Fucking smart wasn't even the half of what Carmen was.

"How long? We're going deep in. He's still going fast," Sal said. I whipped through the streets as fast as I could, but there was no telling how quickly I'd make it there.

"Five, maybe ten," I said reluctantly.

"Take the next turn. It will cut the time," Enzo said, his voice low with his concentration.

"Oh, shit!" Sal hissed, just before the sound of screeching tires and the unmistakable crush of metal and glass could be heard, before silence.

"Sal?" I yelled.

"Sal!" came Adrian's voice. The confirmation that Adrian was okay was only a sliver of relief in the new sea of worry I felt for my brother and Carmen.

Sal was silent on the other end as I raced through the remaining streets, my breath coming in pants as I fought the urge to roar. I had no idea what just happened, no idea if my brother and Carmen were alive or dead, but I had to keep pushing with the hope they were still breathing.

"How close are you, Leo? I'm a few minutes behind you," Kia said. Her voice over the comms for the first time during what felt like the most torturous half hour of my life was what I needed. The panic gave way to calm determination. I had a mission. My mission was Carmen, and I wasn't going to give up or let my fear of what had just happened get in the way of getting to her.

"I'm here," I said, pulling up a little under a block away from where I could see the smoking wreckage of the two cars.

"She won't be long. Maybe five minutes," Enzo said, though there was a strain in his voice. Whatever he was seeing through those cameras was affecting him.

I flew from the Charger, pulling my gun and aiming it toward the wreckage, but then I heard the unmistakable sound of Carmen's voice, choked but it was hers, desperately saying, "No!" My gaze fell to a distance away, seeing red as I watched Jeremy Wallingford tearing at her clothes as he pinned her to the ground. I could see her fighting; the anguish in her movements as she clawed at him, trying anything to get him off her.

I picked up my speed, getting as close as I could before I pulled the trigger, my bullet flying and landing in Jeremy's shoulder, causing him to slump and fall on top of Carmen.

I was in awe as I watched her push the man nearly twice her size from her and get to her feet. Like some sort of warrior goddess, she stood, bloody, torn clothes, but eyes wild as she spun to face me, ready to fight off yet another attacker.

"Carmen," I said, not lowering my gun from where Jeremy was, but unable to look at anything but her. And then I watched as she stiffened, turning back to Jeremy, who was now weakly clutching at her ankle. She didn't even say a word as her foot came down on him. The sound of his bones and flesh giving way under her rage-filled stomps was nearly as satisfying as if I had done it myself.

She was beautiful, deadly.

She was mine.

When I touched her and her fingers curled between mine, it was then that her body seemed to finally relax, crumbling against me. I scooped her into my arms.

I turned as I heard the screech of tires. Kia pulled up just before the wreck, jumping from the car, handgun poised over the hood, and aimed toward the smashed cars.

"Check Sal!" I yelled, turning to head back toward her. I looked down at Carmen. Her eyes were closed, body limp in my arms, but she was breathing. We'd have to get her to a doctor immediately but we suspected that would be the case. Romolo was already on standby at a location not far from here, with his guy at the ready.

Kia had already moved over to the driver's-side of Sal's car, pulling the damaged door open with a screech of metal on metal.

"He's breathing. Get her in the car. I'll start on him," she said, nodding to the still-running vehicle behind her.

As soon as I got Carmen placed in the back seat, I ran back to where Kia stood, her knife out, cutting away the seatbelt from Sal's body. He was breathing, with no visible sign of trauma as his head rested against the now deflated airbag. Hopefully just unconscious. He was finally freed from the restraints, and I pulled the large frame of my oldest brother from his seat, slinging him over my shoulder and taking him to the car to place carefully beside Carmen.

"Head to the medic," I said to Kia as I pulled the back door closed, taking Carmen back into my arms while Kia resumed her position in the driver's seat.

Adrian was alive and had been talking over the comms, which were all now strangely silent, except for the quiet directions Enzo was giving to Kia. Sal and Carmen were breathing and with me. Now if they could all keep breathing just a little longer. This wasn't over, but for the moment, I had everyone back where they should have been.

CHAPTER 29

LEO

The remaining hours of the night were a flurry of chaos. We got to the Italian-owned warehouses, Romolo's men descending on us with guns drawn, only to quickly change their minds as they saw me emerge with Carmen in my arms.

"Get Sal," I said, without pausing as I rushed into the open docking bay. There was a plastic enclosure created at the center of the mostly empty warehouse, bright light illuminating it from within like a white glow stick. Romolo saw me coming and pulled the plastic curtain aside, letting me bring Carmen through uninhibited.

"What happened to her?" Benny asked from where he stood next to Adrian. Adrian was sitting on a table, white gauze wrapped around his chest and shoulder.

"Car accident," I said, placing her gently on one of the empty tables. I didn't feel I needed to mention the attempted rape by Jeremy. If the man wasn't already dead by Carmen's hands, I would have finished the job painfully and slowly.

A man in his sixties immediately came forward, his gloved hands going to her face, pulling back her eyelids to look at her pupils as he placed a hand on her bare and bloody chest to check her breathing.

She was still breathing.

I just kept reminding myself of that. As long as she was breathing, she was with me.

The curtain flew to the side once more with Sal being carried by two of Romolo's guards.

"He was just knocked out," I said, my voice coming out mechanically, as I watched them set him on another table. My words were just as much truth as my will that it was the case.

Adrian quickly slid off the table where he had been sitting, coming up to Sal and putting his ear to my brother's chest.

He was still breathing.

They were both still breathing.

A woman moved to him, shining a light in his eyes.

"Just unconscious. No concussion," she said as the doctor working on Carmen began cutting away what remained of her dress, checking wounds that were littered across her body.

There were old bruises accompanying the new ones. A large one was forming on the right side of her forehead. Cuts from glass and road rash covered her skin all along the back of her upper arms and shoulders from Jeremy dragging her. She had a deeper cut on her left side near her shoulder blade that the doctors seemed to suspect was from pulling her from the wreckage, which he quickly cleaned and began stitching.

"How long until he wakes up?" Adrian asked, staring down at Sal, concern still etched into the creases between his furrowed brows.

"We can use salts to wake him," the woman said, gesturing to the guard by a small, wheeled cabinet.

The salts were brought over to her, and she waved them in front of Sal's nose. He startled awake, sitting up and nearly head-butting Adrian, who stepped back away from him.

"Carmen!" Sal said, his voice harsh as his eyes darted around the room.

"Alive," the doctor working on her said as he made quick work of closing the wound on her back. Sal's eyes snapped over to where I was, still standing over her while the doctor worked. Relief in his eyes as he looked at her peaceful, unconscious face.

His eyes slid back to Adrian, who was only a few steps away from him. They looked at each other, assessing any visible wounds they saw, before they both nodded toward one another.

"He's here?" Sal asked, turning to look toward our uncle who had stepped in behind the guards carrying Sal.

"He is," Romolo said with a nod.

"Stay with her," Sal said to me and Benny, who had joined me by Carmen's side. I glanced down at Carmen for a moment, every fiber of my being wanting to stay by her side, while a little voice at the back of my head told me I needed to go with my brother and Adrian. I had to face, and end, the beast that did this to her.

"Don't leave her side until I come back," I said to Benny, who shook his head, eyes never straying from the work the doctor did as he bandaged the now stitched cut. Leaning down, I pressed my lips to her hair, taking in the scent of her, before I turned to follow Sal and Adrian out of the plastic enclosure.

"I'm coming," I murmured.

We walked through the warehouse, passing by crates and boxes stacked over our heads. Guns and electronics were most likely held within them. Following Romolo, he took us through various twists and turns until we came upon a small clear space surrounded by crates in a far corner. There he was. Salvatore Lupo Sr. His head was slumped down, chin to chest, but I could tell he was starting to rouse from whatever Romolo had given us to drug him.

"Do what you need. I'll make sure he ends up with the crash," Romolo said, as he turned and left us there.

"Did you bring those salts?" Sal asked, turning to Adrian, who held out his good hand, the salts resting in his palm.

Sal stepped closer, taking a handful of our father's hair and pulling back roughly so his face was now turned up toward the crude, harsh light that hung from the high ceiling of the warehouse. He pushed the salts into his face, and we watched as his eyes snapped open, jerking violently against the restraints we had him strapped down in the chair with.

"What is this?" he yelled as Sal backed away a few paces, dropping the salts to the floor as Adrian and I stepped closer, flanking him.

"The end for you," Sal said darkly.

Salvatore looked at all of us, his eyes flitting over our faces for a few moments, before he burst out laughing.

"You had your fun. Now untie me, boys. I'm not playing games with you," he said, struggling once more against his restraints.

"This isn't a game, and we aren't children anymore, Pa," Sal said, stepping forward once again. "You fucked with us one too many times. You used us—all of us— like a pawn in *your* games. It ends now."

But somehow, despite the seriousness of the situation, Salvatore wasn't picking it up, laughing once again in his oldest son's face. Without another word, Sal reared back, his fist flying through the air to land a powerful punch to the jaw. The sound echoed off the crates around us, Salvatore's laughter quieting with the blow. His head still turned, he spit blood that had filled his mouth to the floor, before turning to glare.

"Salvatore, let me out of this chair now or—"

Another punch to his face shut him right up.

"What? You don't like the monsters you created?" Sal asked, his chest heaving with his harsh breaths. Adrian stepped forward, his arm still bandaged, but he used his other to pull Salvatore back upright.

"You promised me when I joined, you'd never use Carmen again," Adrian growled, glaring inches away into Salvatore's eyes.

"Everyone has a part to play, Adrian. You should know that by now," Salvatore said, his words slightly garbled as blood oozed from between his lips.

"You made a grave mistake," Sal said, as Adrian pushed my father roughly back against the chair, his good arm rearing back before landing a crushing blow after blow to Salvatore's stomach, ribs, and then finally his face, breaking his nose and splitting the skin there so his face was coated with blood.

"You just couldn't take no for an answer, could you?" I said, stepping forward and grabbing his throat, which was now slick with crimson.

"You all finally grew backbones. I'll put them to good use, don't worry. Once this deal is final, we'll all be better for it," Salvatore said. I could tell there was more worthless babbling he was planning on doing, but I couldn't care less. He was never going to bring this pain and chaos down upon us again. Never.

He didn't deserve any more of our words. Not one more breath from our bodies should have been wasted on this man. With the full force of my rage and anguish at almost losing the lives of Carmen, Adrian, and Sal in one night, almost losing Carmen forever to the likes of the Irish, almost letting Salvatore Lupo continue to use us for the rest of our lives, I unleashed upon him.

Skin and bone gave way under my fists. At some point, the chair fell over, but I merely let his new position aid in my strikes, feeling the way his head stopped bouncing off the concrete as his skull caved under my blows.

"Leo," Sal said, placing a hand on my shoulder, which finally seemed to snap me out of the rage-fueled blood lust I was unleashing upon our father. I pulled back my fist, which was still lodged in the mangled flesh of what once was my father's face, standing once more and letting Sal and Adrian pull me away.

"It's over," Adrian said.

"Just beginning," Sal murmured beside me as we made our way back through the mazes of crates to where Carmen and Benny were.

CHAPTER 30

CARMEN

The scent of my mother's perfume filled my nose and the sound of muffled voices I recognized filtered through my dreamless sleep, making me think of lazy summer afternoons at the lake house. But just as I tried opening my eyes, the voices around me became clearer. Adrian talking about taking an exit off the highway, and Benny arguing with him. I became aware of the soreness in my body. I felt like I had been hit by a bus.

It all seemed to come flooding back, the weeks of being held by O'Shea, the starvation, the party, Gregor Stepanov, Adrian being shot, the car chase and crash... Jeremy afterward. And Leo.

I sat up, vomit filling my mouth before I could even warn anyone, but another set of arms on my other side flew out, a bag at the ready for me to unleash the meager contents of my stomach.

"Good morning, Little Song," Adrian said from the front seat.

"It's afternoon," Benny corrected from the driver's seat, gaining a smack on the arm from Adrian.

I wiped my mouth with the tissue provided by my mom, before turning to where my savior sat and there he was. Leo was unflinching as he closed the bag, tossing it out the back window onto the highway.

"You're here," I said, reaching out a hand to him and touching his face with just the tips of my fingers. I had dreamed of him so many times over the last few weeks, dreamed of moments like this and others much more private, but as I felt his skin on mine and the faint stubble on his cheeks, I knew it was real.

He turned to me, grasping my face in both his strong hands and pulling me in until our foreheads touched.

"I'm here. You're here. You're breathing," he whispered.

"Cool it back there. Mom is in attendance and we're like ten minutes from home," Adrian said, though his voice held a lightness I hadn't heard in quite some time.

We chuckled as we pulled apart, one hand holding my mom's, while the other was threaded through Leo's fingers, my head resting against his chest. I had questions about what happened while I was out, and how it was safe for me to be coming home, but that could wait. For now, all I wanted to do was bask in the fact that I was out of Freddy's clutches. Away from the Irish and all the pain and suffering that came with them.

We pulled into our neighborhood, passing by the familiar streets. The coffee shop was there, closed for the time being, since Liliana and I were not there to keep it running smoothly, Ingrid, being a single mom, could not be a one-woman show running that place alone.

We got to the house, Benny pulling into the driveway of our home, and shortly after Sal pulled into their driveway with Liliana, Enzo, and Kia with him. I moved to get out, but Leo held me to him.

"We're just grabbing some things and heading to the lake house. None of us want to be separated for a day or two," my mom said.

Of course, part of that was due to the increased security we would all need. I wasn't sure what happened just yet, but I was certain it wasn't over, not completely. Jeremy was dead, and I wasn't certain about Freddy, but it was safe to assume. If I was home, I imagined that Salvatore must have been killed as well, and now we had even larger targets on our heads. Staying together wasn't just what we needed, it was a necessity.

The others went into the houses, presumably packing things up for our stay, while Leo just silently held me in the back seat. It was only a few minutes before they were all joining us back in the cars and we were on our way to the lake house. It was odd, knowing I had been taken by Freddy from there, but still only feeling fondness for the place. As it came into view, I felt the comfort it always brought me before we all moved to get out and go inside.

I was weak on my feet, something I wasn't accustomed to at all, but I managed to make it inside. At some point while I was unconscious, I was cleaned of the blood and brain matter I had been covered in and dressed in loose sweats, the fabric soft against my skin as I slowly moved more into the living room. The couch was my target, but Leo's arms wrapped around me, easily lifting me from the floor and turning toward the stairs.

"Carmen needs more sleep," he said as he started climbing them.

"You better actually let her rest, Leonardo," Benny said from where he stood in the kitchen helping the moms unload the groceries from their house that they had brought with them.

But as soon as he brought me into his room, shutting the door before moving me toward the bed, rest was the furthest thing from my mind. He set me gently down against the comforter, lying beside me and looking at me everywhere but my eyes as his hands wandered from one hidden wound or bruise to the other, like he had memorized their placement on my skin.

"Leo, look at me," I whispered, reaching up to touch his face and turn his head toward mine.

"I am looking," he said, continuing what he had been doing.

"No, at me," I said, trying to jerk his face up. Finally, he lifted his eyes. The depth of sadness there was something I had never seen before.

"I–I could have lost you," he whispered, searching my face like he was trying to memorize it.

"But you didn't," I said back, letting my fingers trail over his cheek and up into his hair. He looked tired, as if he hadn't slept in weeks. I had no idea what I looked like, but given how sore and tired I felt, probably not good.

"Sleep, Carmen. You're safe," he said, leaning in to kiss me so gently it felt like his lips barely touched mine.

"Stay with me."

"I'm not leaving," he said, curling his body around mine and pressing his face into my neck.

When I woke again, I didn't feel great, but I felt better than I had when I woke up in the car. It was dark out, the house quiet, so I was fairly certain everyone else was asleep. Leo was. Still and even breathing beside me, his arm trapped beneath my body but splayed on his back. I wanted to cuddle against him, but the knowledge that

I was still covered in a thin layer of blood and dirt and who knew what else from the events of the night before had me feeling ready to crawl out of my skin.

Carefully, I moved off the bed, wincing a little as I twisted the spot on my back that hurt the most. Leo's bathroom was attached. We both got one. One of the perks of being the youngest of our families was that while we got a slightly smaller room in the house, both our rooms had their own bathroom, while our brothers each had to share a Jack and Jill. His was styled in dark blues and gray.

I closed the door, turning on the shower water before finally turning to the huge mirror that sat over the sink and counter. My reflection astonished me. It could have definitely been worse, but I couldn't help the way my mouth dropped open in horror at the bruising over my face, even the part of my arm that got exposed when I raised my hand to touch the small lump at my hairline was marred with bruises and cuts.

"Carmen?" came Leo's voice from the other side of the door, his tone mildly panicked.

"In here," I said, not taking my eyes off each new piece of flesh I saw as I took off the sweatshirt.

He came in, stopping for a moment and breathing a sigh of relief when he saw me standing there. But then he took in the look on my face. I tried to cover my torso from his view with my hands, unable to meet his eyes in the mirror as he came up behind me. Normally his touch and presence would have either put me at ease, or excited me, but this time it filled me with fear that he would reject the way I looked. Some of these scars would never go away. I would be marked by this forever.

"Carmen, look at me," he said, gently placing his hands on my bare shoulders. I slowly lifted my eyes in the mirror, which was starting to fog with the steam of the shower. "You are beautiful. Even with all of this. My warrior goddess. My unforgiving queen. You fought, and you won, that's what these show," he said. At those words alone, I felt myself relax into his touch. "If I could take all these from you, I would, but what I did do was make sure you wouldn't have to face this again."

"You can't promise that, Leo," I whispered, turning around in his arms to look up at his face more fully. "We're part of this world. There's no way you can guarantee I won't be put in danger again."

He let out a pained noise, his hands ghosting down my back until they rested at my waist which seemed to be the only place free of injury.

"I can't—"

"You won't, Leo," I whispered, knowing what he was going to say, knowing he couldn't lose me, just as much as I couldn't lose him. I placed my hands on his shoulder, tipping onto my toes and bringing my lips against his.

Without another word, we began pulling off our remaining clothes and moving into the shower together. Tender kisses were peppered in with soft strokes as we washed one another. It was as he was gently massaging my scalp with shampoo that I couldn't resist the moan that escaped my lips.

He rinsed the shampoo from my curls, and it was as if he washed away the last vestiges of everything that had come to pass since we last were together like this. Our lips met with unrestrained passion, the power of our kiss making tears spring to my eyes as we clung to one another.

"I love you," he whispered against my lips when we broke away to take a breath.

"Take me to bed," I whispered back, pressing myself against him.

He leaned over, turning off the water, before lifting me in his arms so my legs could wrap around him.

He sat on the bed, my legs straddling his while we resumed our kiss. I could feel his hard length pressed between us, my hot core involuntarily grinding against him and making a low groan come from him in response.

"Carmen, we should wait," he said, though his hands tightened on my hips as if he wanted to press me even closer.

"You'll be careful with me," I said raggedly, letting his tip find my entrance and pressing down ever so slightly. He grabbed me tighter, spinning us and pressing me into the mattress.

"I'll be careful," he repeated, his eyes burning as they looked down at me.

I expected him to just line up and push in, but instead, he kissed my neck, traveling down to my chest and laying soft licks and sucks to my nipples making me gasp and shiver before he traveled lower, swirling his tongue over my navel and farther until he reached the apex of my thighs.

"My warrior. My Queen," he murmured, looking up my body to my face and holding my gaze as his mouth descended on me, tongue sweeping through my now soaking folds. He moaned at the taste of me, making me even wetter.

His fingers joined, plunging into me and curling as his tongue swirled over my clit with just the right pressure. I couldn't have controlled whatever sounds I was making even if I tried and he seemed in no rush to quiet me either. The pressure was building, my muscles tensing as I neared that peak.

"Leo! I—" but he only went harder, two fingers diving into my center roughly, curling and hitting that spot just right as the wave finally crested, and the cacophony of pleasure swept through my body, sending shivers wracking my body.

He pulled his fingers out, his tongue softening as he lazily lapped at my release, before he crawled back up my body, peppering more kisses over my torso as he went. He lingered more over the finger-shaped bruises that Freddy and Jeremy had left on me, as if the sweet touch of his lips was erasing the hurt they caused.

When he finally brought his lips back to mine, I was dying for him. I needed him to fill me, to complete me, to make me whole.

"I love you, I love you, I love you," I chanted through panting as my hips tilted up, his tip barely touching me as it slid through my swollen pussy.

"I'm never letting you go again, Carmen. Never again," he whispered to me, pushing in and groaning as he slowly slid home, my greedy channel contracting and sucking him in inch by delicious inch.

"Never," I said back, threading one hand's fingers through his hair while the other clutched roughly at his back.

Once he was fully seated within me, he just paused there for a moment. The two of us just held each other, breathing in each other's air, looking into each other's eyes. It felt profound, looking at those hazel irises, seeing the love, the worry, and the undeniable pleasure that he felt being within me.

We started moving together, slowly at first, sending trills of sensation throughout my body. Our breathing grew ragged; his pace picked up, his cock rubbing my walls and filling me just right. When he sat up on his knees, tilting my hips and changing the angle he was hitting inside of me, I couldn't help but close my eyes, the sensations becoming too much, my second orgasm building with each thrust against that spot within me.

Leo's groans filled my ears, his hips moving yet even faster as my inner walls began contracting as the first wave of this orgasm cascaded over me, speeding it through my body until I could feel it in my toes and fingers.

As I came down from that wave, Leo released one side of my hips, his fingers finding where we were joined, and beginning to rub tight circles against my clit. My orgasm immediately flared back to life. A fresh and more powerful explosion seemed to burst from within me, making me unable to restrain my cries of pleasure as his hips slammed into mine over and over.

Leo let out a cry of his own, a sound so feral and full of unrestrained pleasure I nearly went into a fourth orgasm from just that sound alone. I felt him filling me, my body greedily pulling it in, clenching to keep him there as he pressed one more time as far as he could within me and back down with his hands on either side of my head, breathing harshly as he pressed a hot kiss to my lips.

CHAPTER 31

LEO

The days passed at the lake house, like our own little protective bubble. We all enjoyed the time together, while also waiting for the inevitable fallout of what we had just done. Sal and Adrian left a few times to meet with their men and establish within those who were still loyal to our father that Sal was in charge now. There was only one time that I had to go with them, a night when it became obvious that those who were closest to our father would not be taking Sal's new position well.

Carmen was still healing; the stitches in her back still holding her skin together, the bruises still looking fresh across her body, and I didn't want to leave her, even if Benny, Enzo, and several guards were staying with her and the moms at the house.

"I'm coming with you," she said, pulling on her shoes.

"Carmen, we might have to—"

"Kill them? Yeah, you probably will. I'm still coming," she said, not even hesitating as she stood from the bed where she sat, looking up at me with those bright green eyes, full of determination. "I'm not some wilting flower, Leo. A little bruised, but I'm not leaving you."

She had proven several times over that she could protect herself, that she was smart and resourceful, keeping herself as safe as possible in situations she couldn't control. This was not a situation where she would be alone without backup, she would have me, our brothers, and many of Sal's men beside her.

And I certainly couldn't accuse her of being a woman who couldn't handle death. She grew up in the life as I did, she beat back a slew of gang members, and she killed Jeremy herself.

"Let's go," I said, reaching out and taking her hand.

We all got in Adrian's SUV, only Benny staying behind with the moms. The trip to the city was quiet, only Sal answering the phone a time or two and giving short instructions, while Enzo watched our target location on his phone.

"Like clockwork, they're at the restaurant," Enzo said as we got closer to the plaza, and our father's house there.

"Perfect," Sal said, straightening a little in his seat.

We pulled up in front. Sal's men had been waiting to get out when we did. The restaurant wasn't very busy. It was a Monday night and close to close. Adrian and Sal went in first, and were clearly immediately recognized by the staff, who seemed to scurry around, trying to get a table ready the moment we entered.

"No need for a table, just wanting to talk to Julian," Sal said to the hostess, who had turned pale.

"He's at Salvatore's table," she said, pointing to the corner booth.

It was the biggest booth in the restaurant, slightly raised on a platform, the large round table was the best vantage point across the restaurant, making sure one could see everything happening within this space easily, as well as being the quietest space for having conversations.

"Please let the remaining guests know this restaurant is closed for the night. Anyone who hasn't paid, their food is on the house, and they should leave as soon as possible," Adrian said to the host as Sal stepped forward heading to the booth where Julian sat with several other men who had been closest to our father. Many of them were the guards who had somehow let us sneak his unconscious body past them the night everything went down.

We all followed, and I realized as the few guests that remained in the building watched us as we passed, how intimidating this must look. Sal was dressed in a suit, looking every bit the Mafia Capo he was now, his hair slicked back, deep brown eyes scrutinizing, with Adrian at his side, also in a suit, but having forgone a tie, letting a bit of the tattoos that were on his chest and neck peek out.

I had opted for a dress shirt and slacks, my gun tucked at my back, but easily visible, and Enzo was wearing dark jeans and a black shirt. Carmen, though still bruised, was wearing that sheer green shirt she wore to dinner on my first night back, her hair down around her shoulders like a mane. She didn't have a gun or anything on her, but she was oozing confidence as she walked with us.

"Sal!" Julian said, not bothering to stand as we approached the table.

"Julian," Sal said with a nod, looking around the table at the handful of men who were sitting with him. It was clear that Julian was thinking he had taken over. The ease of his posture and of the men surrounding him was indication of that by itself, but it was also the strange sense of superiority he was exuding as well.

"I think you're in my seat, Julian," Sal said, gaining a laugh from the man, and subsequent chuckles from the others.

"And what makes you think that? Salvatore is dead and I, being his second, take his seat. Isn't that how it works?" Julian said smugly, his eyes glinting with challenge.

"His second? You? Funny… I was certain you were born and bred for that title, Sal," Adrian said, rubbing the beard at his chin.

"You're all just children, Sal. You don't know what to do with all of this now that your *daddy* isn't here to take care of it," Julian said with a smirk, bringing his glass of wine to his lips.

Sal glanced around. Several of the tables of guests had already left, only a lingering table or two remained with the staff buzzing around, clearly trying to clean up so they could also bolt as soon as the dining room was empty.

"Carmen, Enzo, could you help our last few guests move along?" Sal asked as he turned back to stare Julian down.

Carmen released my hand, turning and heading to the older couple that still slowly ate their food, while Enzo stepped up to the couple clearly on a date to talk to them. I watched as a few of the men loyal to Julian, who were not in the booth, moved a bit closer with the dispersal. There were three of them, one stationed strategically around the dining room to be able to swoop in at a moment's notice if necessary. I had taken out a force twice this size easily in missions before, clearing a room so we could get to our target.

"So that's your plan, Julian? You are the new Capo now? Does Morelli know that?" Sal asked as Carmen and Enzo escorted the two groups of diners out, Travis and Paolo stepping into the restaurant just after. Paolo moved toward the kitchen doors, standing next to a man who was nearly in his fifties. He looked a little nervous as Paolo's brutish form towered beside him.

"Morelli will see it's the natural succession," Julian said, eyes taking in the movement within the restaurant more than Sal.

"Do you know what happened to my father?" Sal asked as the last front-of-house staff members moved to the back, where the rest of them were all leaving.

"Does it matter?" Julian snapped, finally meeting Sal's eyes once more.

Adrian grinned and a little smirk flitted over Sal's lips, looking more sinister than amused. Carmen came back to my side, not taking my hand, but brushing against me. It was like she knew that my hands needed to be free in case I needed to jump into action. Any trepidation I had about her being here was dulled slightly, knowing how smart she was, even in moments of crisis.

"I assume the deal went south with the Irish, seeing as how the LaMartina bitch is standing there with you," Julian said, his eyes sliding over to her.

"Oh, Julian." Adrian shook his head. "I'd watch how you speak to her. She's in the new Capo's inner circle, after all. Wouldn't want disrespect to cost you your head, like it did Salvatore," Adrian said.

The choice of words had Julian going still. He kept looking at Carmen as if somehow she would tell him it was all just a misunderstanding, a joke, even, but whatever he saw in her face instead made him swallow dryly.

The sound of the back door of the restaurant closing seemed so ominous now that the restaurant was devoid of staff and patrons. The music had been switched off, and now it was only us and them, and what Julian didn't know was that he and his men were quite out-numbered by what Sal had waiting outside.

"I'll try to make this as simple as possible for you, Julian," Sal said, dragging a chair from a nearby table noisily over to be centered with the corner booth, moving to sit. "My father is dead. We killed him. The details of why and how don't really matter, because you are no longer privy to that information."

"But—"

"Ah, ah," Sal said, raising a finger and shaking it a bit. "Nothing you have to say is going to change my mind on this one, unfortunately for you."

"If you're the new Capo—"

"Like I said, nothing you have to say will change my mind. You are not loyal to me, that much is clear, and from the looks of things, Julian, you weren't particularly loyal to my father either. Here you are acting like you've won the lottery when you haven't even confirmed your position. You played king when you thought your boss was dead, instead of doing what a loyal man would have, finding out who killed him," Sal said, staring darkly at the man across from him.

The men on either side of Julian seemed uneasy, shifting in their seats like they wanted to bolt, but they were trapped in the booth right along with Julian.

"What does that mean?" the man directly beside Julian asked, his voice shaking a little.

"It means my enforcer here," Sal said, gesturing to me, "will be making sure you aren't around to cause problems for us as things change."

Julian started to protest, the other men bursting with arguments, but I didn't hear any of them. All I saw were opportunist rats, men who followed along with my father's disgusting plans only because it would fatten their own pockets, while never really caring if the Capo himself lived or died. No wonder it had been so easy for us to take Salvatore from where he was staying. No one closest to Salvatore cared what happened to him. Not his guards or any of these men seated at *his* table.

I didn't hear anything they said as I pulled my gun from my back, smoothly and methodically shooting each of the men in the head before the other three guards dispersed about the room even had a moment to consider drawing their weapons. Adrian quickly took out one of them, while Paolo and Travis got the other two.

The silence that came over the restaurant after that was filled with so many emotions. Relief that at least some of the men that would cause problems for Sal were gone, frustration that we had to resort to these methods, and for me, fear that when I turned to look at Carmen, she would look at me differently than she had before. I had just murdered four men in front of her. I would have done it again if it meant she would be safe, but I couldn't stand it if she was afraid of me; disgusted by me.

But before I could muster the courage to look, her small hand found mine, the softness of her touch letting the fist that I had formed while shooting loosen. I turned to her then as our fingers wove together and saw no fear in her eyes, but pride.

"I'll send the crew to clean this up," Travis said as he pulled the body of the guard he'd killed toward the middle of the room.

"We're heading back for now, but I think it's time that Adrian and I start staying in the city," Sal said, standing from the chair and glancing at Adrian with a saddened expression.

"We'll have to move closer too," Carmen said, following behind our brothers as we made our way through to the entrance.

"What about the coffee shop?" I asked, watching the little smile play on her lips. I knew I had to be in the city when Sal and Adrian were. If I was their enforcer, I'd have to be around when they needed me, but I didn't want Carmen to have to change her life so drastically. I thought I'd start to figure out a way to make it work between here and Lee's Summit, at least for the time being.

"The pastry program is here in the city. I thought we'd move here together before it starts," she said with a shrug, before getting in the SUV.

Move here together.

The idea was tantalizing. Unlimited, unfettered access to Carmen with no one to be quiet for?

"I think she just said she'd move in with you, Leonardo," Enzo said, clapping me on the back and startling me out of the frozen state I had been in for a moment or two as I imagined the possibilities.

"She did. You're all lucky I have self-control," I practically growled, getting in beside her and pulling her to me for a kiss, which made her laugh against my lips. If we weren't surrounded by our brothers, I wouldn't care that we were in public. This woman would be naked in this car while I showed her exactly how good an idea I thought moving in together was.

CHAPTER 32

LEO

The next day we had decided was our last at the lake house. Maria and Mom had decided to move in together, which would be easier to protect, even though their houses were right next to each other. The other house would be kept up and used for guests. Enzo's computers and base of operations were at Breakers, so his situation wouldn't have to change. Carmen and I had some apartments and houses we were set to look at in the city the next day, so knowing we would be parting ways, at least until the next family dinner, the moms prepared a feast for us to gorge on.

It was as we cleaned the kitchen after dinner, the moms having gone to bed once dinner was done, while the rest of us dutifully cleared the table and did the dishes, that Sal's phone rang.

Not that it hadn't rung many times since we got home, but for some reason we all paused as he moved around the island, snatching it from where he had left it during dinner.

"It's Morelli," he said on an intake of breath, looking up at me from where I stood holding the tablecloth.

"Put it on speaker," Enzo said as Sal looked back down and answered the call.

"Sal."

"Hello, Mr. Lupo. I trust you're having a good time on your little vacation with family," Morelli said, his voice deep and dark as it seemed to fill the room from over the speaker.

"It's been very nice, but I'm ready to get back to work, sir," Sal said, bracing his hands on either side of the phone and leaning over the counter.

"That's good, because a lot of work has been created recently, but I'm sure you know all about that."

Sal's eyes snapped up to meet Adrian's this time.

"Yes, sir."

"I want to discuss some things with you. I hope all of you at the lake house are willing to take on another guest or two. I'm eager to see what you think your next steps might be and decided to come in person. I should be arriving in the next hour."

The tense silence was nearly palpable in the room. All of us seemed to be holding our breath.

"We'll see you soon, Mr. Morelli," Sal said, unconsciously reaching up to run his fingers through his hair.

"Good." The call ended, and we all just stood there for a moment, taking in the fact that the Big Boss, Manzo Morelli, would be in our lake house within the hour.

"I'll tell Liliana and get the room set up for him," Carmen said, dropping the dish she had been scrubbing back into the soapy water and walking directly through to the hallway that led to the primary suit.

There was no way Morelli planned to stay here with us, but none of us moved to stop her, all six pairs of eyes watching her disappear.

"Kia," I said, turning to my friend, who was like a statue on the barstool a few seats away from where Sal still leaned over the now silent phone. "Go to Daph and Rory." She looked up at me, brows scrunched in concern. "You don't have to be part of this. Go to their apartment tonight. Then head back to Washington. You did enough, and I will never be able to thank you for coming here. I'm not pulling you in deeper," I said, watching as her face seemed to recoil even more, like she wanted to argue.

"I'll go tonight, but don't think you're getting rid of me so easily," she said, her concern turning to a glare before she quickly moved to get her things from the room she had been staying in.

"I need to change," Sal said abruptly, pushing off the counter and strolling up the stairs a moment later, leaving me and the other three to make quick work of the remaining cleanup.

Manzo Morelli was going to be here, and we had no idea what to expect from the visit.

My mom moved to a room next to Maria, though neither was sleeping, not with the impending visit; they decided to stay out of sight. My mom, at least, had done her fair share of entertaining the Big Boss over the years. She didn't need to be involved this time, now that her role as a wife was over.

After cleaning up the kitchen and fetching Morelli's favorite drinks of choice, cognac and merlot, we all changed out of our casual clothes, donning nicer things to be in the company of the man who ruled over the underworld we had been born a part of. Carmen was finishing touching up her makeup when the sound of multiple cars pulling up to the house closed in.

Sal had changed into a suit and slicked back his hair. I could see the way his hand flexed at his side, eager to run through the strands again to relieve his stress but not wanting to muss his clean look. Adrian got to him before I did, placing a hand firmly on his shoulder and squeezing. They had to be a united front. Capo and his second.

There was no knock at the door, merely a moment after car doors slammed, the door opened, and several of Morelli's guards pushed through, encircling the entrance and looking menacing, before the man himself walked through.

Morelli was long-lived for a man in the Mafia. He was slightly older than our fathers had been, the age and stress of the job clearly shown in the lines of his face and the gray at his temples and peppered through his hair. His dark, shark-like eyes looked over each of us when he stopped in the middle of the living room.

Without a word, he moved to sit on one of the couches, leisurely spreading out his arms across the back. We all moved, waiting for Sal to choose the place directly across from him, with Carmen and Enzo beside him, and Adrian and I standing behind. My hand immediately went to Carmen's shoulder, the feel of her skin the only thing to keep me rooted while it seemed like everything was crumbling around us.

We all knew that doing what we did might result in our own deaths, but it was worth it. We weren't sacrificing Carmen for the rest of us to live. Still, the evidence of our consequences sitting across from us didn't make the anxiety of this meeting any less.

"My Capo is dead, it seems. Your father, Salvatore," Morelli started, his fingers drumming on the backrest of the couch, as one of his men moved to fill a glass of cognac for him.

"Yes. In Chicago," Sal said, keeping his voice rather robotic and neutral.

"I was quite surprised that he was there, given his relationship with his brother. But then it was more surprising when I heard the reason."

His eyes landed on Carmen, not even looking away as the glass was placed in his hand. After several days, she looked much better, but the bruising was still visible, especially the one at her hairline. His gaze was assessing, looking from each wound and into her face. I couldn't see her expression, but whatever he saw there, he seemed satisfied, since he looked up at me next.

"Carmen wasn't his to use," Sal said, bringing the attention back to himself.

"No, she wasn't." A quiet settled over the room for a few moments, Morelli seeming to be waiting for us to say something to him, or perhaps just wanting to see if we'd squirm.

"I have a problem now that my Capo is dead, Salvatore. What do you think I should do about this predicament?"

"There are many men that would be happy to take that position, I'm sure," Sal said, his shoulders going tense and rigid.

Morelli watched him for a moment, before pulling his hands from where they were splayed over the sofa back and leaning forward onto his thighs with his elbows, so the glass sat between his hands. He was so relaxed. He knew he was in charge here, and he was fully aware we also knew that.

"Romolo got in contact with me."

I wasn't sure what we were expecting. Of course, Romolo would go to Morelli. He was involved in his brother's death, quite intimately, since he not only provided the drugs we used, but the distraction, the location for his demise, and the disposal of the body. If he hadn't gone to Morelli, he would most likely be facing harsh punishment himself.

"He told me what your father was planning. Interesting how some men think they know better than me. Trust me, when I say, anyone who tries to make deals of that scale without my approval, would sooner see a nap in the dirt. I don't sell people. That's not something I want any part of, no matter how lucrative it is," Morelli said, his voice menacing as he watched my brother for a reaction.

"I don't want to be involved in that either," Sal said, nodding his agreement.

"But you didn't come to me, Sal. You chose to do this on your own, to kill your father for what?"

"For me," Carmen said.

"Ah yes. For the LaMartinas," Morelli said, a smile flickering over his lips for a moment as he looked at her. "Was she worth it, boys? There's a lot of fallout from something like this. My Capo dead, the two heirs to the O'Shea clan dead, Julian dead, and a war might be brewing for us now. If I choose to let you all live, the amount of work you'll have before you will be staggering. I'm not sure you thought that through when deciding to get her back."

"We thought it through, sir. She was worth it," Sal said, his voice unwavering as he said it. I couldn't help the swell of love I felt toward my brother at that moment, for all of them. They fought with me to get her back, sacrificed and jeopardized their whole lives, and regretted nothing.

"And what about you, Leo?" Morelli asked, turning his dark eyes on me.

"What about me?" I asked, not sure of where he was going with this question.

"You understand that Sal will not be granted the position of Capo unless he has a solid team at his back, one that he can trust implicitly."

"Of course."

"I would not grant him Capo unless you are in his circle. Without you, I'm not certain he has the strength to maintain this territory," Morelli said, watching me for a reaction with eager eyes.

I knew weeks ago that the only way to truly pull this off and have it stick, was getting involved. I may have run to the military to escape my father and his attempts to add me to his ranks, as my brothers were made to before me, but not only would I do anything to keep Carmen safe, I would lay down my life for any of the men in this room with me.

"I don't plan on leaving my brother with this mess. I'm with him," I told Morelli, watching as that flicker of a smile grew wide on his face.

"Good, good," Morelli said, lacing his fingers together. "Now, I cannot simply *give* you the title, Sal. You're going to need to earn it. Without my full support, I trust rivals will try to dominate this territory. We'll see how well you handle that, and we'll see if you are worthy of being my Caporegime. In the meantime," he stood, crossing the distance between the two couches to stand before Carmen, "I'm very pleased you made it out of the hands of the Irish, Carmen LaMartina. Your roots are too good to be sullied by the likes of O'Shea," he said, before taking her hand and bending to kiss her knuckles softly.

"You'll hear from me, Sal, Adrian." And then he and his men departed, leaving the house in a strange state of shock in his wake.

We all waited until we no longer heard the sound of his caravan of cars leaving the lake community before any of us moved. Sal leaned forward, taking in deep breaths while Carmen rubbed soothing circles over his back.

"We need to get to work," Adrian said, pulling out his phone. "Pull in our men, try and make connections with the smaller gangs in the territory before others do."

"We need to expect retaliation," Sal said, turning a mournful look toward Carmen. "Not just you. Anyone close to us could be targeted."

He was right, of course. Anyone not in the life connected to us could be seen as a vulnerability. That meant Daph and Rory, potentially Kia, but she had her own skills and resources to stay out of trouble. Our moms were, of course, at stake and who knew how far the potential went? Even Ash and Ingrid could be at risk simply for working for us.

Sal stood abruptly, turning to Adrian, who was already sending texts out with rapid fingers.

"We leave now, go back to the city, and stake our claim," Sal said.

"I'll come too," Enzo said, already scanning through any alerts he had received on his phone about finances and potential breaches. "The house has been kept secure."

"We'll take Paolo and Travis. You," Sal said, pointing at me and then Benny. "Stay with the moms and Carmen tonight. I'll send more guards, but we return to appearing normal, only increasing security. We'll have to figure out how to protect those closest to us a better way, but for now, stay together, go home. I'll call in the morning."

The authority in my older brother's voice wasn't new, but it somehow felt more than it had been before. He may not officially be the Capo, not until he proved his worth, but he was ready for it.

EPILOGUE
CARMEN

I was finishing wiping down the counters. The last customers had left for the day, leaving me alone for the last half hour, or at least I had the illusion of being alone. Paolo had switched between hanging out in the shop to sitting in the car he had parked in front, off and on today. Currently, he was smoking, leaning against the driver's-side of his car, and looking around the neighborhood.

Honestly, I wasn't sure how he hadn't scared some of our customers away. He certainly didn't look friendly as he scowled up and down the street. But I supposed I wouldn't have been too pleased either if I had been him and my guard detail for the week had been watching over a coffee shop and the three women who worked there. He was much more accustomed to following Sal around and doing his bidding, which had to be more exciting than espresso and pastries.

Leo had been in the city most of the week with Sal and Adrian. None of us were pleased that Leo had to be involved, but then again, there was no escaping it now. He made his choice. He chose me. And by doing that, he chose the life at his brothers' sides. If only Salvatore had known that his death would finally bring them all fully into the fold, he might have died sooner.

I chuckled to myself at that thought.

I was closing for the last time in quite a while. We had moved into a little apartment in the city last weekend, but I had stayed this week to help train our new hire, Sasha. I wasn't going to be gone from the shop forever, but once I started the pastry program, I would have had to be away from the shop a lot more anyway. Liliana would have been upset if she wasn't so happy that Leo and I were together. A lot of "I always knew" and talk of fate were thrown around in the past few weeks by the moms.

I moved to the kitchen, double checking I had finished putting everything away when I heard the chime of the front door opening.

"Just one more minute, Paolo! Then we can head to my house to grab the last few things," I called toward the front as I took off my apron, placing it on the hook in the office.

Before I turned around, two strong hands found their way to my waist, a familiar manly scent flooding my senses.

"You're back early," I said, my voice coming out more like a whisper.

"I wanted to take you back," Leo said, pressing his front to my back and fully encasing me in his arms. His lips found their home on the skin of my neck as his hands began caressing me like he was trying to memorize the feel of my curves.

"We won't be going back any time soon if you keep that up," I said, letting out a little whimper as he palmed my breasts through my shirt and bra.

"Do you know how much restraint it took to stay in the city when you sent me those texts?" he practically growled.

I let out a breathy chuckle, turning in his arms and looking up at his face. His expression was all hunger, love, and need. While he was gone, we had talked some on the phone and, of course, texted each other. We had tortured each other with all the things we wished we could do to one another, and fantasizing about all the things we would do in our new apartment.

"Can we wait 20 more minutes?" I asked, running my hands up his chest, over the back of his neck, and up into his hair.

Instead of responding, he just ducked down and kissed me, his lips meeting mine in a searing kiss. The heat that had already been building in my body at his touch was set ablaze. He pulled away after just a moment with a pained groan.

"Let's get home before I can't stop myself," he said gruffly, pulling away from me and leaving me breathless and burning for him. He smirked at the look on my face before grabbing my hand and pulling us from the shop.

Paolo had made himself scarce. I assumed since Leo had arrived, he no longer felt he needed to stick around. Leo had been using my car, which I now saw was loaded with the last bits of my belongings I had packed up over the last few days. He must have been eager if he stuffed the car and then came and got me. Didn't want anything getting in the way of us getting out of Lee's Summit, apparently.

Leo drove fast, not that he wasn't already a lead-footed driver like all of the boys, but he was especially motivated it seemed. The lust had died down some, and now there was a new sort of impatient excitement that seemed to come off him as we got closer.

"You know I've seen the apartment," I teased as he pulled up in front of the building.

"Not like it is now," he said before getting out of the car and rounding to my door. I wasn't sure what he meant. I had just seen the apartment days ago when I brought another load of things. It was covered in boxes and insanely messy. I was planning on spending the whole next week making it a livable space.

He led me up the stairs we had traveled together more than once now, and unlocked the door, before pausing to cup my face in his palms.

"You can change it however you want, but I tried," he said, bending to kiss my lips softly, before scooping me into his arms and opening the door. We weren't married, but something about him carrying me through the threshold of our new home together made me feel so many things as I looked at him and not the apartment we entered. This man was my forever. He had been for a long, long time.

"Do you like it?" he asked, looking down at me, concern lacing his face. I took that as a cue to look around. The boxes that had once nearly filled the living room were unpacked, a couch sitting in a defined space, with a rug and a television mounted on the opposing wall. There were a few things hanging on the walls, mostly art pieces of Rory's that I had kept in the hopes of having my own place someday, and a few pictures of our families.

"Did you—" I couldn't even complete that sentence, so taken aback by how nice it looked in the small space that we could call ours. How did he have time to do all of this in a few days?

"There are still a few boxes in the second room, but I thought you might want to choose where some things went."

He set me down, and I walked farther into the room, touching the couch we had talked about buying sometime before I started school.

"You did all this for me?" I asked, turning to watch as his face changed from worried to softened. He crossed the short space between us and smiled down at me.

"Do you like it?"

I didn't want to say anymore. Between this show of love and by him making this place more like a home, and the time apart, however hard it was, I couldn't wait any longer. I grasped at the hair at the back of his head roughly, bringing his lips to mine and immediately being awarded with a groan in response.

There was still a lot of work to do for us to be any semblance of safe, but for now, we could be happy wrapped in each other.

"You haven't even seen the bedroom yet," he murmured when we broke the kiss, only for him to press me against the wall.

"Later," I snapped, pulling roughly at his belt, which was met with a lust-filled chuckle.

Yes, he was my forever.

He was mine.

BOOK CLUB QUESTIONS

1. Why do you think Carmen thought she had ruined everything for their families when she sent the photo at the beginning?

2. Who are your favorite characters? Who would you like to see fleshed out more in future books? Why?

3. What do you think the O'Shea's plan was for Carmen once she and Freddy were married?

4. How did you feel about the relationships between the two sets of siblings?

5. What mysteries do you think are hidden in this family history? What sorts of things do you imagine being revealed later?

6. As the only girl amongst all these men, how would you best describe how Carmen has coped with that? Do you think she coped well?

AUTHOR BIO

Chelsea Burton Dunn is a Kansas City native—the Missouri side, not the Kansas side. That matters to locals. Where is that you might ask? Right, smack-dab in the middle of the country. She has two beautiful children and is married to a superb partner, but let's not forget their snuggly cat and eager-eater of a dog.

Having always been a little strange herself, she instantly fell in love with paranormal, supernatural, and fantasy books, movies, and TV shows as a child. Did everyone think it was a phase? Absolutely. Was it? Absolutely not. Being weird is a blessing, not a curse. She's always embraced that part of herself and those around her.

She started writing from a very early age, initially starting and completing one of the *Dead Man's Hand* books in high school. She is a lover of music, having her other love and talent be for singing. She performed on main stage operas in the children's chorus from grade school to high school.

Chelsea loves to delve into the difficulties of life, love, and loss while spicing it up with a little magic and monsters. As she liked to say when she was younger, "The monsters in my head need to come out to play every once in a while," so giving them life on the page seemed appropriate.

You can see more about Chelsea, her projects, and find her social medias by going to www.chelseaburtondunn.com

Discover more at
4HorsemenPublications.com

10% off using HORSEMEN10